MW01146709

BY LAURIE R. KING

MARY RUSSELL

The Beekeeper's Apprentice
A Monstrous Regiment of Women
A Letter of Mary
The Moor
O Jerusalem
Justice Hall
The Game
Locked Rooms
The Language of Bees
The God of the Hive
"Beekeeping for Beginners: A Short Story"
Pirate King
Garment of Shadows
Dreaming Spies
"The Marriage of Mary Russell: A Short Story"
The Murder of Mary Russell
Mary Russell's War and Other Stories of Suspense
Island of the Mad
Riviera Gold
Castle Shade
The Lantern's Dance
Knave of Diamonds

RAQUEL LAING

Back to the Garden

STUYVESANT & GREY

Touchstone
The Bones of Paris

KATE MARTINELLI

A Grave Talent
To Play the Fool
With Child
Night Work
The Art of Detection
Beginnings: A Short Story

STANDALONE NOVELS

A Darker Place
Folly
Keeping Watch
Califia's Daughters (as Leigh Richards)
Lockdown

KNAVE OF DIAMONDS

KNAVE OF DIAMONDS

A NOVEL OF SUSPENSE FEATURING
MARY RUSSELL AND SHERLOCK HOLMES

Laurie R. King

BANTAM
NEW YORK

Bantam Books
An imprint of Random House
A division of Penguin Random House LLC
1745 Broadway, New York, NY 10019
randomhousebooks.com
penguinrandomhouse.com

Hardback ISBN 978-0-593-87398-4
Ebook ISBN 978-0-593-87399-1

Printed in the United States of America on acid-free paper

2 4 6 8 9 7 5 3 1

First Edition

Title page frame and chapter opening ornaments: pingebat/Adobe Stock

BOOK TEAM: Production editor: Kelly Chian • Managing editor: Saige Francis • Production manager: Meghan O'Leary • Copy editor: Kathy Lord • Proofreaders: Barbara Jatkola, Jane Scarpantoni, Nancee Adams

Book design by Caroline Cunningham

The authorized representative in the EU for product safety and compliance is Penguin Random House Ireland, Morrison Chambers, 32 Nassau Street, Dublin D02 YH68, Ireland. https://eu-contact.penguin.ie

Now more than ever,

this family story

goes to those who build

their communities

KNAVE
OF
DIAMONDS

PROLOGUE

First of all, none of what happened was my fault. Not really.

Well, wait. I suppose this is only going to work if I'm honest (mostly honest) with my intended reader. And also with myself? So, okay, I'll come clean: *some* of it could be laid at my feet. But I swear, the business that had started as a prank and ended up rattling governments and destroying lives (*my* life most of all!) would have taken place whether I'd happened to be in London that long-ago summer or not. And I will say that if I'd been in charge, things would have gone a whole lot smoother, beginning to end, and a couple of men who ended up shot might not have been.

Because look, I take pride in my work. Too much, maybe, I suppose that's part of the problem, but honestly, I do know what I'm doing. (Usually.) My mistake here was instead of setting it up and making the decisions, I took my eyes off of who could be trusted and left a couple of key steps to others. And they of course made the most idiotic decisions possible.

Yes, I of all people trusted the wrong man. No surprise, then, that things flew out of control. Before I knew it, I'd lost my family and friends and had to scurry off to parts of the world that weren't quite so hot for me.

It could have been worse. (Not a whole lot worse.) At least I wasn't in prison. (Or dead.)

And the world is an entertaining place. A few years went by, then more. I lived most of it far away from old friends and actual family. But I kept busy, and I certainly had the means to be wherever (and whoever) I wanted. I made new friends. Some became almost a new family.

However, I'm not good with unfinished business (that pride thing, again). So when I got word that the situation concerning this dangling piece of an old job might have changed, I began to wonder if I couldn't combine it with some unfinished personal business as well, an absence that had nagged at me for a long, long time. One that had grown more troubling with the passing of each year, not less. I did keep track of her. A handful of times I arranged to catch sight of her from a distance, but it wasn't the same.

Surely, I began to think, after all these years, things might have cooled down, the tracks grown muddy?

I did my research, I laid out plans (and back-up plans), I spent a long time thinking about the dangers involved, and the possible benefits. The first steps went well, then the next, and I began to think . . .

Late September, in a village near Paris. An artist—a sort of relation-by-marriage with a dubious past who was big in the art scene—was marrying a lady doctor, this small, redheaded woman from the wilds of Scotland. Odd place to find a gathering of the most *avant* of the *garde,* but they'd somehow managed to weed out the troublemakers before the champagne corks popped, and a couple of nice muscular sculptors had been assigned the task of tossing out the more obstreperous drunks and poets, both of which meant that no children or old ladies were trampled.

The doctor made a stunning bride, dressed in a gown that

should have looked like something pieced together from a scrap-basket, but managed to be a glory rendered in fabric. She shone. So did the artist—Damian Adler is his name, you may know it, and if you're reading this, you may also know that he is the illegitimate son of the singer Irene Adler and the detective Sherlock Holmes. If you didn't know it, well, there you go.

Anyway, between the shining bride and her beaming husband and the cutest little bridesmaid in the world—the artist's daughter—to say nothing of the spectacle made by the guests, half of whom were experimental artists and the other half were either equally modern writers or their wealthy but bohemian patrons—well, it made for quite a picture. Newspaper reporters were lined up in the dusty little road across from the house where the party was taking place, nudging each other when someone important flitted by, nodding their heads to the tunes of the jazz band.

That's where I was, dressed like a reporter, waiting for a glimpse of a particular young woman, step-mother of the groom (funny thought, she being six years younger than him).

Before I go any further, it occurs to me that there's something I should maybe make clear, especially if you were expecting that Mary Russell herself might be telling you this. If you were, I can understand—she is usually the one behind these stories, so it's only natural to assume it would be her voice (her hand?) here. (Though truth to tell, the girl's always been more likely to be the one taking on the guilt for some misdeed rather than the one denying it. She even thought she was responsible for the death of her family—a crazy idea I didn't learn about until years later.)

Anyway, no, this isn't Mary you're hearing from now.

My name is Jake, Jake Russell. (One of my names, at any rate.) I'm Mary's uncle, her long-dead-father's kid brother. The closest living relative she has. A man she's probably thought dead for many a year.

You'd think I'd find it hard not to race across the road when I saw her standing in that garden, smiling and strong and shining out the joy of the day—race across the road and plant myself in front of her and wait for her to recognise me.

Instead, I stepped back a little among the men with the cameras.

It was grand to see her. Less so to see the tall, thin, grey-haired man at her side. (I'd spent too many years avoiding *him* to be really comfortable.) But in fact, my primary feeling was one of regret.

The best thing I could do for my beloved niece would be to disappear again, permanently.

But then, I've never been one for sensible.

CHAPTER ONE

RUSSELL

Damian's wedding was proving something of a contrast to my own.

Holmes and I had wed by night, slipping like thieves into his family's country-house chapel on a cold winter's eve, holding our festivities with a few cherished friends while the house's current master was away.* Appropriate, perhaps, considering the participants, but hardly boisterous.

This nuptial was halfway to riotous, a gay, tipsy crowd beneath the genial sun of a late-summer's afternoon, with half the artists of Paris and most of the village's residents merrily jostling elbows and glasses. Francis Picabia and Gerald Murphy had cornered the village blacksmith and seemed to be discussing anvils. Sara Murphy was writing down the recipe for one of the dishes in Mme LaRue's open-air banquet. Pablo Picasso's intense eyes were drilling into the unfortunately damaged face of the village postmistress, making her giggle nervously. At the far end of the garden, a

* See "The Marriage of Mary Russell," in *Mary Russell's War and Other Stories of Suspense.*

jazz band was setting up while two dark-skinned American women—one a Paris nightclub owner, the other a recently-arrived chorus girl—walked through some moves the dancer had brought with her from New York.

"Charming lass," said a voice at my side.

I looked down at one of the bride's brothers—Hugh, was it? No, this was the youngest, Gordon, his Scots accent barely discernible under the weight of English Public School. In a group, all four brothers tended to revert: last night, the sound from the sitting room had resembled a pack of badgers gargling.

"Gordon, I hope you're enjoying your first trip to Paris?"

"Thank you," he said. "Indeed."

I looked more closely, wondering if he was too terrified for conversation. Then I noticed that his eyes had not moved from the musical gathering at the end of the garden, and realised that he was not actually responding to my question, merely automatically flipping words in my direction.

"Would you like to meet them?" I asked. "The musicians and ladies?"

His face instantly turned the same colour as his hair, and badger-sounds came from his throat. I put down my glass and seized his wrist, steering him through the groups to where the two Americans were laughing with the jazz band.

I planted him there, made the key introductions, then faded away and went to claim another glass.

"Who is the girl?" asked a very different voice at my side, one whose Scots accent had become delightfully touched by French in recent months—tongue shifting forward in her mouth, her rolled R's gone soft. Every so often, her gerunds included the G sound.

"Josephine something," I replied. "A dancer just arrived from New York, came out to join a 'revue nègre' in the city. She seems very sweet."

And lest young Gordon's older sister feel that she should be protective, three more interested males had already drifted up the garden, including a couple of American writers: Scotty Fitzgerald (whom I had met that summer) and a friend of his named Hemingway. Under their barrage of masculinity, the boy's innocent charm hadn't a chance. I turned to her.

"You look magnificent, Aileen."

She glanced down at the dress. "Nice, isn't it? I couldn't imagine how it was going to look until it came together. Though my mother may never forgive me for not wearing the family lace."

The gown was, literally, a work of art, a collaboration by the new husband's colleagues and friends, panels of brocade and silks in a dozen varieties of cream embroidered over with flowered vines. I'd never seen anything like it, and even on a woman nearly a foot shorter than I, it was breath-taking.

"I'm sorry she couldn't make it over."

"It's a long voyage for her, and in any event, we'll be there in no time."

The three Adlers were headed over to Scotland for a grandmother's 90th birthday in early December. But not, apparently, for Christmas. A Henning family Christmas, the doctor had confided in us, was too much to demand of a new husband. It would be at least a year before she presented him with a kilt and inflicted him with a Henning familial assault by bagpipe.

"I'm glad all your brothers could come," I told her.

She laughed. "I'm grateful Damian gets on with them. It must be quite a shock, for a man with nothing but a father—and the father's wife, of course."

"Don't forget the uncle who never leaves London," I added. Holmes' brother, Mycroft, had predictably sent his regrets, and said that he looked forward to seeing the Adlers when they came to London for Boxing Day. His absence was probably just as well, considering the number of Topics Requiring Discussion that I was piling around his feet, like firewood at the base of a large stake.

"Do you have family, Mary? I mean to say, Damian told me that your parents and brother had died, but he didn't know beyond that."

"I am remarkably unburdened by relatives," I said, trying to sound matter-of-fact and probably failing. "A few on my mother's side, none of whom I get on with. My father's parents are still alive, but they never approved of my mother—or me, really. I cut those ties when I rather dramatically left them a note and sailed off to England on my own at the age of fifteen."

I'd walked away from my grandparents' mansion with little more than a valise of clothes and a couple of books that I'd purchased myself: no mementos, no reminders of the life I was leaving behind. In the following years, I had built myself a new family, beginning with Holmes and Mrs Hudson, and now including Damian and his wife and child—and, I supposed, that very old woman who had appeared at the edge of the wedding ceremony before vanishing again. I was happy . . . but I did occasionally wish I felt more of an ancestral foundation beneath my feet.

"Your father was an only child?"

"Pardon? Oh, no, he had a brother. Younger."

Aileen was studying my face. "You knew him."

"Not as well as I'd have liked. He was . . ." I smiled. "Jake was a rogue and a ne'er-do-well, who was disowned by my grandparents when I was seven or eight. He used to send my brother and me the most peculiar and inappropriate gifts from all corners of the globe—a kit of explosive chemicals, a Maasai spear, the throwing knife I often wear. Whenever he appeared, adventures were sure to follow. Sometimes he came to escape trouble. Other times, he'd leave for the same reason. My brother and I adored him. My mother called him 'The Knave,' and treated him like a beloved pet that kept chewing on the furniture. My father shook his head a lot. He was the responsible one in the family."

"What happened to your uncle?"

"He just . . . disappeared."

My last sight of Uncle Jake had been the Christmas when I was eleven, a visit that began with Mother opening the door to a familiar figure—then taking a sharp step back when he'd thumbed up his hat-brim to reveal a spectacular black eye—and ended with a clever bit of criminality that involved two innocent minors.

The last time I'd heard from him was a brief letter that reached me on November 10, 1914. The War in Europe was raw and new, as was my own loss—father, mother, brother, all gone in an instant. I was in hospital when Jake's well-travelled letter arrived, containing two playing cards that were a reference to our shared past. *My heart has been ripped from its chest,* his note said, and I did not doubt it. He loved my parents and my little brother. He said he would come, if I needed him. I did need him—I was all alone, in pain, wracked by guilt and desperate for a familiar face—but at fourteen, I was old enough to read between the lines: his hesitation most likely meant there was a warrant out for his arrest, for some crime or another. So, I did not ask him to come. I never had asked, though I'd thought about it scores of times over the years, mostly after glimpsing a familiar-looking head of hair across a crowd. He was sure to be dead, or in prison. But so long as I did not reach out to him—so long as I did not put a notice into the *Times* agony column and wait for him to see it in some distant corner of the globe—I could believe him alive, and happy, and getting up to the same criminal mischief that had seen him banished from family conversation.

"I'm sorry," Aileen said.

I pulled my thoughts away from darkness. *Don't spoil her day,* I told myself, and summoned a laugh. "Whatever my Uncle Jake did, and wherever he died, I have no doubt that he lived life to the hilt the entire time. That's nothing to be sorry about."

She smiled, and lifted her near-empty glass. "To all the black sheep we have known and loved."

Including, I thought but did not say, her newly-wedded husband. I raised my glass, and drank with her.

"Oh," she said, "did your friend find you?"

"Which friend was that?"

"I didn't get the name—he telephoned yesterday, when you and your husband were in town. Something about a reception in the city next week? I told him I thought you'd be leaving for England Monday, but he said he'd ring back tomorrow, for a chat."

I shrugged. Probably one of the stray members of the Academie Français who had attached themselves to Holmes recently.

The band started up soon after that, and Aileen was claimed for the first dance by the groom. Halfway through the song, the pair separated long enough for Damian to snatch up little Estelle, and the three of them circled the temporary dance floor together, faces alive with laughter.

Perhaps it was the sheer physicality of their affection that caused me to lean my shoulder against the man who had come to stand beside me. He was reassuringly solid, and no one was looking in our direction. There was such a close link, I reflected, between emotion and the body's memories: comfort received on my mother's lap—her arms, her warmth, her scent; comfort given the same way—my arms so tightly wrapped around that little dancing girl, as if arms alone could save her from an aeroplane falling to earth; reassurance and fear and rage battling for dominance, as I clung to an unconscious Holmes on horseback.

"It's good to see Damian so happy," I said to my husband.

"They are well matched," he agreed.

The song ended, the next one began, and other couples moved forward to join the Adler trio.

"What were you and Aileen talking about?" Holmes asked.

"Her dress. Amazing piece of tailoring."

"Something else. You looked . . . wistful."

"Oh, she asked about my family. I spotted your mother, by the way. I'm glad she came, even if she left before anyone could see her."

"Time enough for that revelation," he said—inaccurately, I thought, since the woman was a century old. "But why should my mother put you in a pensive state?"

"It wasn't her. I was telling Aileen about Uncle Jake."

"Were you?" He sounded surprised. I didn't talk about him much, it was true.

"I suppose I'd been thinking about him. Family weddings, and all. And I saw someone who looked like him, out on the road."

"That's happened before."

"Every so often. I suppose there are a lot of small, blond-headed men in the world. I'll catch a glimpse of one and think it might be him, until I get closer and find that, rather than a middle-aged man, it's a boy of fifteen, or a young woman in a suit. Or in this case, one of the photographers hoping for a shot of someone with a title."

"The local gendarme is enjoying the task of keeping them all under control."

"As much of a challenge as corralling cats, I'd have thought."

"Alcohol is being applied to the problem."

"And some of Mme LaRue's canapés—yes, I saw."

"I had a telegram this morning," he said abruptly. "From Mycroft."

I turned to look at him. He did not take his eyes away from the merriment.

"Of congratulations, I presume."

His mouth twitched, though it did not quite break into humour: my flat tone told him that I did not actually believe that the wire had contained his brother's congratulations on Damian's wedding. "An old case has come to life. He wishes to consult."

"Immediately?"

"I sent a reply giving him the date of our return."

"Good."

"Although we might wish to leave a day earlier."

"So, tomorrow, then?"

He took a sip from the glass in his hand.

After a moment, I did the same. "I'll finish my packing tonight. Let's not forget to send Patrick a telegram in the morning, so at least we'll have milk and a loaf of bread." Or, knowing my farm manager, milk, bread, and enough supplies for a platoon.

At last, Holmes' gaze slid down to mine. "I took the liberty to send that one, as well. Since the telegraph boy was already here."

"Of course," I said.

Well, I supposed that being taken for granted was better than arriving to a kitchen bereft of supplies.

CHAPTER TWO

RUSSELL

Guests were still snoring when we left in the morning—draped on the sitting room sofa, in Aileen's surgery offices, under the dining table, and around some trees in the garden—although the Adlers themselves were up, and looking remarkably chipper considering how late the festivities had ended.

Or not ended, evidently, merely broken off for the night.

Mme LaRue had already been, leaving coffee and a small mountain of breads and fruits for our breakfast. We gratefully swallowed coffee, helped M. LaRue carry things out to the motorcar, and took our leave.

Little Estelle clung hard, first to Holmes, then to me. I told her we'd see her in a few weeks, when they came to London for the holidays. She wanted my promise that I would give her lessons in knife-throwing. I told her that would depend on her parents.

I had little doubt that she would talk them around to the proposition.

. . .

It was some very dark hour after a very long day when the taxi's head-lamps illuminated our Sussex front door.

I had set off through that doorway in the first week of June, for a short trip to Venice that turned into a detour to the Riviera, followed by a case in Roumania, then the better part of a month in France. It was now the third week—no, the fourth—of September, but other than a fresh layer of gravel in the drive, the house had not changed. No weeds had sprouted from the steps, no uncollected envelopes mouldered in the little protected stone porch. And yet, as always after one of our long and inevitably eventful times away, it felt like a different world.

Particularly as France's beautiful autumnal warmth had succumbed to the English cloud-bank halfway across the Channel. It was cold and wet, the kind of dispiriting rain that clearly had no intention of pausing much before April, except for brief forays into snow.

I had taken care to dig out the house key before leaving France, and now trotted through the drizzle to thrust it into the lock. It turned easily, the hinges gave no creak—and then I raised my head, startled at the trace of mustiness in the air. Why had Mrs Hudson let things . . . ? But no, Mrs Hudson was no longer here. I suppressed the moment of bleakness and had the kettle on and fire lit by the time the driver had dropped the last of the bags on our tiles.

The bed that we finally climbed into—fresh sheets, smelling of sunlight—seemed to sway, as the land tends to after weeks at sea. I told myself not to be ridiculous, the crossing had only been a couple of hours, and curled on my side. I listened to the rain, and the familiar creaks of the old house, and eventually slept.

Holmes was gone when I woke, but he came in through the kitchen door before the coffee had finished brewing, shaking the wet from his old overcoat before dropping it onto a hook by the door.

"How are the bees?" I asked.

"Surprisingly well. Though there must have been a wind-storm recently, my friend Miranker has tied down the two more exposed hives."

"If you want to take a closer look, I'll come out and hold the umbrella while you lift off the tops."

"I'll do that when it's clear, tomorrow or the next day."

I thought that forecast wildly optimistic, but there was no point in arguing. "You're going up to London today?" *Snapping to heel at Mycroft's call,* I thought but did not say.

"After I bath and shave."

"Shall I telephone to Patrick and ask him to bring the motor around? Oh, and I found a note from him next to the coffee canister, to say that Tillie has some food for us and he'll bring it by later."

"Let him come with that, I'll ring down for a taxi."

In an hour, he was gone. The house was empty, as it had been before we left in June. Short of miracles, Mrs Hudson, our long-time housekeeper, would never again bustle around the kitchen, taking the coffee-pot from my hand, scolding me about some sin I had committed to her best knife or saucepan. I was going to have to hire some help—either that, or be reduced to Holmes' cooking and my own burnt offerings. Or put up with the girl Lulu's inane chatter.

I winced, and instead picked up the telephone to let Patrick know that I was home. It took some time, since the Exchange was simply *thrilled* to hear we were back, and wanted all the details as to where we had been and what we had done—and oh, did I know that while I'd been away. . . .

But in the end, she put me through to my farm manager, and I told him that he needn't hurry with Tillie's excellent food, since

Holmes was sure to be away until evening at best. More likely, I thought, a day or more. He hadn't taken a valise, but there was no need, not when he had a brother's flat and numerous bolt-holes in Town.

"You're sure?" Patrick's rural accent was stronger than I remembered. "He's not just gone around the corner for a time?"

"No, he went to London. At least, he dressed for London, took his good umbrella, and rang for a taxi to take him to the station."

"Ah. Good," he said, and rang off.

That was odd, I thought, returning the earpiece to the stand. *Did he think I was lying to him? Or—that Holmes might have been lying to me?*

I stared at the device for a moment, then shrugged, and set about the task of hauling trunks and emptying valises.

Two dusty hours later, I was interrupted by the crackle of tyres on gravel. I shoved the last empty valise onto its shelf, paused in the lavatory long enough to clean my hands, and trotted down the stairs.

The little viewing window was filled with the side of Patrick's greying head. I pulled the door open and greeted my old friend, an uncle in all but blood, with an affectionate hug. "It wasn't locked, you should have come in." A thing I'd said a score of times, but as far as Patrick Mason was concerned, this house belonged to Holmes, unlike my own farmhouse a few miles away. "Lovely to see you, come in, get out of the cold."

With his usual deliberation, he scraped his clean shoes on the coir mat, but said, "So, Mr Holmes is not here, then?"

"I told you he wasn't. Patrick, what is going on?"

Instead of stepping inside, he turned back towards the motor he'd parked directly in front of the door. "It's fine," he called, "you can come."

"Patrick, what on earth are you up to, I thought you—"

The figure who emerged must have been crouched down on the

backseat, out of view of the house. He emerged, shut the door, and turned.

A short, middle-aged man with cornflower-blue eyes and suntanned skin, wearing a crisp white shirt and a beautifully cut suit that was modern without being extreme, with a golden-brown overcoat that could only be vicuña. He planted a pair of gleaming shoes—as bespoke as the suit—on the gravel drive and raised his head, tipping back his hat with his thumb so as to see me unimpeded.

It was the gesture that strangled the words in my throat, that caused the house around me to shudder in reaction. Beneath the jaunty hat-brim was a small, blond man I'd seen in my imagination so many times over the years, yet not in fact. Not since the winter of 1911.

Uncle Jake.

CHAPTER THREE

RUSSELL

The boyish figure on my doorstep was showing his years. Fifty . . . four now, I realised, the nonchalant tilt of the head, the gleam of mischief in his blue eyes tamped down by the same burdens that had sketched wrinkles in his face and added half a stone to his waistline.

Fourteen years. *Where have you been?*

He waited. Patrick waited, too, for me to draw myself up in anger and accuse my uncle of abandonment. To charge him with betraying the profound affection my mother had had for him, of failing the responsibilities left behind by his brother.

Silence, other than the drip of rain and the complaint of a seabird.

Perhaps it wasn't only the burden of years that was stifling the mischief in his face. Perhaps uncertainty, apprehension. Fear, even.

Fourteen years.

Jake was not the only one to have had his heart ripped from his chest by the motorcar wreck that killed my family. He had abandoned a bereft and badly injured young girl, forcing her to piece herself together as best she could, all alone. To retreat across the sea in search of the only scraps of comfort she had, under the care of a woman who loved her not, in a house on the lonely Downs on the edge of a country wracked by War.

But in the end, I did the only thing I could do: I walked past Patrick to wrap my arms around my only uncle. Patrick nodded in relief and went to put on the kettle.

With his apprehension about how I would react set aside for the moment, something of Jake's perpetual youth returned. Oh, when he dropped his hat on the rack by the door I could see the silver glints among the gold of his hair, and when his overcoat joined the hat, I thought his shoulders had lost some of their confidence. Certainly the lines beside his eyes were not entirely due to laughter, but his attitude was as I remembered, the ease with which he faced the world coming to the fore.

"That *was* you I saw, in Ste Chapelle, wasn't it?" I asked. "Among the newsmen."

His face twisted in self-reproach. "Oh, I *knew* that was a bad idea. Not enough of a crowd, and me the only blondie. I saw you do a double-take on the doorstep and got out of there right quick. Hey, this is nice." He stood surveying the house's main room, where Holmes and I spent most of our hours together. A room of comfort, practicality, solidity.

"Come through to the kitchen, Patrick's making tea. But that couldn't have been the first time you found me, in Ste Chapelle?" Not if he'd been keeping close enough track to know that Holmes had a son, who the son was, and that he was marrying in a village outside of Paris. In fact—"Was that you who telephoned on Friday and talked to Aileen?"

"'Fraid so. I needed to know how long you'd be there, before I set off across the Channel."

"For years, I've been thinking I was imagining things—but I haven't been, have I?"

"No, you probably did spot me once or twice. Every so often I would sneak up from a distance, just to see how you were."

One could hear America in his voice, Boston modified by the West—though more in his words than in the accent itself, which had settled somewhere in the middle of the Atlantic. I'd met enough con men like my uncle to know that the accent itself would shift, according to his audience.

The thought made me sad. And the reminder of what Jake was made me realise why Patrick had been acting so oddly on the telephone. I turned my eyes to my farm manager, at the sink spooning tea leaves into the large ceramic pot.

"You didn't want Holmes to see Jake until he'd had the opportunity to explain himself to me," I said.

The kettle had just come to a boil. Patrick methodically poured it over the leaves, stirred it three times, replaced the top, and carried it to the wooden work-table, already laid with cups and accoutrements. "He asked me. And I thought . . . your mother would have given him the chance."

Since boyhood, Patrick had loved my mother, that exotic bird from the wilds of London whose Jewish family had, unlikely as it seemed, taken for themselves a farm as a summer cottage on the Sussex Downs. And he well knew the soft spot my mother had for her wayward brother-in-law. Some men might have harboured resentments for half a lifetime. Patrick was not such a man.

I shifted my gaze to my blood relation, seated on the other side of the table from me. He was watching Patrick pour the tea, but when he reached out to take the cup set before him, the fingers of his right hand gave a brief tremble before coming down to meet the porcelain. I wondered if something about this conversation was making him nervous—or if those shakes were another sign of ageing. And with that, I noticed that both Patrick and I had been speaking with slightly raised voices, an almost unconscious response to the small tip of the head and look of concentration from someone whose hearing was less than perfect.

It was a melancholy thought: my Peter Pan of an uncle succumbing to the years.

However, sadness and the regret of age notwithstanding, it was not hard to piece together the outlines of what was going on here.

When I was very young, I knew my uncle as a person who swept in on a wave of excitement and life, in a way my more stolid father did not. We all knew when Father would be coming home and when he would leave again for California, but none of us could ever guess when Jake might blow our way—literally, once, in a hot-air balloon across the Channel. Birthday presents from my father would be a heavily-hinted-at book in a shop's colourful and precisely folded paper; from Uncle Jake, an Ecuadorean shrunken head wrapped in butcher's paper thick with stamps from a previously-unheard-of part of the world. Treats from Father would be a visit to our favourite ice-cream shop; from Jake, it could be anything from a tin of candied insects to a box of exotic American breakfast cereal or a delicate basket of wild strawberries. My father taught me to throw a cricket ball; Uncle Jake, a knife.

I began to suspect the darker truth behind his light-hearted visits that final year, when he appeared at our farmhouse door in the winter of 1911, very much the worse for wear. Later, I would have recognised the signs of a beating, but even at the age of eleven, I could feel the currents of apprehension and disapproval in how my parents approached him. And it was during that visit that Jake had pulled my brother and me into one of his schemes—not exactly a criminal one, but one that could have had severe repercussions for two small Jewish children in a rural community.

A scheme that even Levi knew could never be told to our parents.

Then later yet, in the long years where thoughts of him were retrospective, a form of mourning, I would wonder about his history and personality. How much of his—to be frank—criminality was rooted in being younger and smaller than his brother? Did he, like his Biblical namesake, always feel that he was following, and that the only way to win their father's blessing was by cheating? Was his boundless energy, like that of T. E. Lawrence (whom he resembled in a number of ways), a compensation for his relative weakness? I was certain that my father and uncle had loved each other, but I was a child then. If there was rivalry, I might not have seen it.

All of which meant that if Jacob Russell had come to Patrick—his niece's farm manager, his sister-in-law's childhood friend—before making an approach, and if said childhood friend had taken great care to check on the absence of the house's other resident, there was a reason.

"Oh, Uncle Jake," I said. "What trouble are you in now?"

CHAPTER FOUR

JAKE

The last time I'd been face to face with Mary, she was a kid, all skinned knees and fraying braids and bent-out-of-shape spectacles. Since then, like I said, I'd only seen her at a distance, usually while I was hiding behind some post-box, wall, or false beard. Three times down here at the end of the world, five or six times around her Oxford college. Once, I'd snuck into the back of a lecture hall to hear her give a talk. (Not a clue what it was about—there was a lot of Latin, and half the old men in the audience walked out.) And once, I'd spent an afternoon watching her come and go from a dotty women's club in London. (The club was dotty, I mean—though come to think of it, some of the women were pretty odd.) Now, sitting across a table from her, with the leisure to look into her eyes, she was . . . well, I could only hope the old man she'd married appreciated her.

(He'd seemed to, the times I'd glimpsed them together.)

I could see her mother in her. Or maybe it was just the expression on her face, one that Judith had turned on me any number of times. More like a fond but long-suffering mother with a mischievous son than a woman and her husband's besotted brother. *Oh, you silly boy, what have you done now?*

What had I done? Nothing much. (Yet.) (Although, sure, I'd done a lot, to bring matters to where they were now.)

"It's kind of a long story," I told my niece.

As I'd hoped, Patrick Mason took that as a signal to leave. Mary saw him to the door, telling him to thank Tillie and that she'd return the dishes in a few days, while I looked with resignation at the cooling tea in my cup. Far too early in the day to go looking for a bottle of something to ease the aches. (And the coming conversation.)

I rose to put the kettle back over the flame. If I couldn't have a stiff drink, at least I could have something hot.

But when Mary came back in, she looked at the kettle and said, "Do you actually want more tea?"

I moved the kettle off the heat. "What else have you got?"

She pulled a bottle from one cupboard and two glasses from another, and although it wasn't the spirits I might have chosen, at least it didn't seem to be ginger ale or grape juice. (The Prohibition lunatics hadn't come to plague England, thank God.) "Let's sit in front of the fire," she suggested, and led me to the sitting room.

She settled into a worn basket chair that creaked and popped as she wrestled the cork from the bottle. I sat in a nice quiet armchair, having pulled it closer to the flames. (I'd been spending time in warm places.) (Warm in both senses, come to that.)

"Mead," she said as she put a glass of the pale liquid on the low table between us. "Honey wine. It's what Holmes gave me, the day we met."

And having thus firmly (and deliberately, I had no doubt) summoned her absent husband into the room, she took a swallow and sat back in the chair. I gave a wry toast to the missing brewer and tried a tentative sip. Not bad (for something that looked like baby's piss). I ventured a larger swallow.

"Very nice," I said. "Summery."

"What's happened to you?" she asked abruptly. "I can tell that your back hurts. Is it related to the shake in your hands?"

Damn, I thought, *the girl is both sharp-eyed and quick as hell. Take some care, Jake, my boy.* "Nothing serious. I got blown up, just a little."

"Blown—how do you get 'just a little' blown up?"

"By moving fast in the other direction when the thing went off, of course. It was months ago, I'm fine."

"Is that why you're having problems with your hearing?"

(Hell.) "It's not that bad. And the ringing's nearly gone."

"When Holmes had a bomb go off near him, it was months before his hearing cleared."

"You see? It'll be fine."

She didn't look convinced. She also looked like she was having to push herself not to be too sympathetic. "You were injured when you showed up at our door the last time I saw you, too. That was fourteen years ago."

There was an edge to that last phrase, although I couldn't tell if she was aware of it. (She probably was.)

"Seems like a lifetime," I said mildly.

"More than half of mine, in fact," she replied. This time, her voice had gone from edged to pointed.

"I was in Bolivia." (Why the hell had I told her that? Well, too late to take it back.) "Not then—later, when I heard about the accident. I couldn't leave—literally could not. I had to give a note to a friend who was headed for Southern California, and asked him to put two playing cards in it, so you could be sure it was from me. Did it reach you?"

"The eight of hearts and the jack of spades."

"That's right, the cards you helped me beat that innkeeper with." I smiled at the memory. "Did the bas—the slimy creature ever show up again?"

"I never saw him. But that food Patrick brought? It was cooked by the woman who bought the inn from you."

"Yeah, I heard you tell him to thank Tillie—wondered if it was the same woman. I'm glad she's still around. Though I've been here since Saturday, you'd think he might have mentioned her."

"He and Tillie are seeing each other. He probably would prefer that she keep her distance until he's sure what you're up to."

"Fair enough," I had to admit. "Fair enough." (I doubt *I'd* let me close to a nice lady like Tillie Whiteneck, either.)

"You said you had a lengthy story. I don't know how long Holmes plans to be away."

"Yes." I had somehow already emptied my glass, so I reached out for the bottle and poured a generous dose of the old man's distilled summer (the rattle of glass against glass made me curse under my breath—but then, the rattle of glass against glass illustrated why I was here in the first place). *Go slow with that wine,* I told myself. Parts of this story needed to be handled with, shall we say, delicacy?

"You're probably aware," I began, "that certain periods of your uncle's past have been a bit . . ."

"Criminal?" she supplied dryly.

"Chequered," I finished. "Even before your Granddad blew a fuse and flat-out disinherited me, I'd dabbled my fingers in a few, well, questionable dealings. More for the challenge of it than the actual money, though every time the dollars were cut off, money would become more of a consideration. A self-defeating kind of a circle, you'd have thought, but old Dad seemed to think that a young man needed to take on some of the family responsibilities. Poor judgement of character on his part."

"You stole from Granddad?"

I blinked at the speed at which she'd put those facts together (and set my glass to the side). "That's awfully blunt," I objected. "I'd rather think that I claimed a little of my inheritance while I was still young enough for it to do me some good. This was the year before the thing I'm trying to tell you about—and I swear,

God's honest truth, I wasn't going to steal his precious dollars, I was going to put them back—with interest, mind—and then show him what I'd done, with an offer to tighten up his system so none of his other employees could do the same thing. Benefitting the company in the long run, you see?

"Except I had a slight misadventure before I could set things tidy again, and he discovered it—not even him, it was your father who spotted it, damn his sharp eyes, and told Dad rather than coming to me. Not that, if he had, I'd have been able to . . .

"Anyway, water under the bridge. And once it was back in the coffers he forgave me, more or less. But to make a long story short, it felt like a good time to hit the road for a while and let things cool down. This wasn't long after the San Francisco quake and fire spooked your mother into going home to England with you and your brother. I saw her as she was leaving New York, and told her I'd go out to help your father for a few weeks, but when I got there, I found something going on that was making him short-tempered—something more than your mother's absence and a city in chaos, I mean. I never learned what it was, but we were getting on each other's nerves, so once the house was in some kind of order, I got on a boat and headed for Europe.

"I started in London and more or less worked my way south as the summer faded. London isn't at its best in late summer, so after a while I went over to Paris with a friend, poking around museums, hearing some new music, getting myself introduced to rich people. Who can sometimes be interesting, despite what you'd think. Anyway, my friend had business in London, so I went south, to Spain and then to Italy. Italy was great—there's nothing like a country run by a church to make it easy to pick up odd jobs on the side. And they had a brand-new casino up on the Riviera in San Remo, with a very comfortable hotel right on the water—lots of things to do, plenty of friends to make.

"But I don't tend to spend too much time in one place, not

when I'm working, so when my London friend wrote to say would I like to visit him in Dublin, I said sure. I got there in March, I think it was. Springtime anyway. You been to Dublin, Mary?"

"Once," she said.

"Nice town. Wide streets, pretty buildings, if you steer clear of the slums. This was well before the Easter Rising, of course, and the troubles in the north and the partition and all that. Dublin was England across the Irish Sea, that great castle squatting in the middle. You know the Russell family came from Ireland?"

"But not Dublin. Somewhere in the south, wasn't it?"

"Outside of Waterford, mostly. Grandpapa washed up in Boston with his sacks of gold a generation before the famine began, well before all the starving peasants showed up there. The Russells were loyal to the Crown, despite everything—until your father and I came along, that is. Charlie usually kept quiet about politics when the rest of the family was in earshot, but I wouldn't. Made for some lively family dinners."

"But that's not why you were banned, was it?"

"No, the slam of the family door happened the year after this thing I'm telling you about, and I hadn't been home for a while before that. Though I guess politics was always around the edges. And come to think of it, I suppose my Republican leanings did have something to do with—"

She slapped her glass down with a *crack* (my own drink nearly ended up all over my new suit—guess my nerves weren't in the best of shape). "Wait. You went to Dublin the spring after the earthquake: that makes it 1907. And it was the following year that Grandfather disowned you, after some act too dreadful to be told to the children—even Mother wouldn't talk to me about it.

"Uncle Jake, were you—did you have something to do with the theft of the Irish Crown Jewels?"

(*Damn,* but the girl was fast.) "Well, I . . . sort of. I was on the periphery, to start with. And then afterwards a little more, and then things got a bit out of hand, and it was kind of like walking next to a painter's ladder, you pick up splashes that are hard to get off."

"The *Irish Crown Jewels*? Uncle Jake, what were you *thinking*?"

"They weren't really Crown Jewels, you know, just Regalia that the King was going to wear for some idiotic—"

"Oh, Jake! How *could* you? I suppose you had them broken up and sold to keep you free to play?"

"Wait, now, I—"

"People were ruined over that. The insult of it damaged relations between Ireland and the Crown forever."

"Well, relations were pretty—"

"For God's sake, Jake—Holmes himself worked on that case!"

I waited, to make sure she wasn't about to go for my throat. She'd got to her feet at some point and was panting as if she'd just come running in, so I made my own voice nice and calm when I replied to that last and greatest of her accusations.

"Yes," I said. "I know he did."

CHAPTER FIVE

RUSSELL

I was appalled. My own uncle? A ne'er-do-well, sure; a rogue and the family's black sheep, I had no doubt—didn't every family have one such in the wings? But Jake, my father's brother, a small, funny man my mother had adored like the brother she'd never had? *Jake?*

The Jewels of the Order of St Patrick—romantically dubbed the Irish Crown Jewels—had vanished from an impregnable safe at Dublin Castle in the summer of 1907, a few days before King Edward and Queen Mary had arrived for a formal visit, during which the King was supposed to oversee the investiture of a local baron into the Order. The investigation that followed brought in Scotland Yard, but was then suppressed—according to Holmes, because it had uncovered a multitude of idiocies that ranged from the farcical to the humiliating and on to the frankly scandalous. The whole thing had left a trail of shame and ruination in its wake, and eighteen years later was still as tender as a bruise.

Holmes did not talk about it. I only knew he'd been involved because I'd directly asked him one time, in the course of a vaguely related conversation. His stormy expression and curt replies made it very clear that he had not so much failed as he had failed to convince the authorities to use his evidence to prosecute those he thought guilty. He'd been theoretically retired when the investigation began; he'd been more adamant about retirement afterwards. Especially because his literary agent, Arthur Conan Doyle—the "author" of Dr Watson's case histories about Holmes—had been somehow involved in dragging him into the matter. It was, in its way, worse than Doyle's gullibility when a young girl claimed to have taken some photographs of fairies in the family garden.

And here I sat—stood, rather—in the midst of a building catastrophe. My husband and partner on one side. My beloved and long-lost uncle on the other.

Which thought brought on the next bolt of revelation: I suddenly knew, with no doubt in my mind, that behind it all, working from the shadowy recesses of governmental manipulations, I was going to find that all-pervasive, massively clever, and questionably ethical representative of the Crown, one Mycroft Holmes.

CHAPTER SIX

SHERLOCK HOLMES

"Mycroft, I believe I made it abundantly clear at the time: I wish nothing more to do with the Dublin Castle theft." Holmes twirled the end of his cigarette against his brother's ornate marble ash-tray, using the gesture to underscore his disinterest. "I shall be vexed if you have brought me up from Sussex on that matter alone."

"Even if I were to tell you that we may have word on where the Jewels themselves are?"

"The whereabouts of a handful of shiny bits of crystalised carbon held together by rare metal are of considerably less interest to me than the welfare of the bees whose hives I had intended to examine today." Holmes abandoned the cigarette and picked up his coffee-cup, found it nearly empty, and filled it from the pot. "Just out of curiosity, when you say you 'have word,' that does not mean you actually know where they are, is that correct?"

"Ah, so you are interested," Mycroft purred.

"You have my attention for the length of time it takes my trouser-legs to dry before your fire."

"What do you remember about the investigation?"

Holmes raised an eyebrow at his brother.

He had wondered, when Mycroft had summoned him to discuss "an old case that had come to life," whether this was merely a pretext, to avoid openly referring to the discovery that Holmes had made—that Russell, to be honest, had uncovered—in France.

However, it would appear that was not the situation. Mycroft seemed genuinely unaware of his younger brother's startling—shocking, even—encounter with the old woman living on the outskirts of Paris. Granted, both Holmes brothers were skilled at concealing their hidden thoughts, but Holmes doubted that Mycroft's acting talents were good enough to hide the knowledge from him. In which case, Mycroft knew nothing about her. He actually did wish to speak about this eighteen-year-old burglary.

This in turn raised the question of whether Holmes wanted to go along with the topic under consideration, or derail it abruptly and decisively.

He rolled his half-smoked cigarette back and forth between finger and thumb, considering. To raise the matter of Louise Holmes, a woman who had committed suicide when her sons were eleven and eighteen, only to greet the younger one on her own doorstep in the Nanterre suburbs two weeks ago, would put paid to any discussion of missing diamond Regalia. And although his first impulse was to brush the Dublin case aside with any excuse available, he was curious to know why Mycroft was interested. Why revisit an investigation they had both long finished? Had the political situation in Ireland taken some unexpected turn, one that—Mycroft being Mycroft—might be manipulated by the retrieval of the long-missing St Patrick's Regalia?

As he contemplated the possibilities, Holmes discerned in himself a decided lift of spirits. Due, no doubt, to the rare foray into the little-explored territory of having knowledge that his brother lacked.

He stubbed out the cigarette and laced his fingers together over his waistcoat, stretching his legs to the warmth.

"The case of the so-called 'Irish Crown Jewels,'" he mused. "Where did you get this new information? And where do you think might they be?"

"You knew that Richard Gorges was released from prison in the spring?"

"I did not. They should have hanged him, killing a police officer."

"They might have, but for his War record."

"Not because someone placed a word in the Judge's ear that Gorges was threatening to implicate the wrong people if they brought out the hempen rope? Is that why he's been let out early—he's got the ear of some newspaperman? Or has he finally decided to give some details of the crime?"

"If he had, I would not have needed to call upon you. No, he hasn't talked—to us, at any rate. But when he settled down in Hampstead—his brother is supporting him, thanks to a wealthy wife—we arranged an informal watch to be kept. Neighbours and a newsagent, that sort of thing. But he hasn't sneaked away, shows no sign of returning to his old ways other than some boasts in the pub that turned out to be empty. But this summer, he began to have a regular visitor. A well-dressed man in his fifties with blond hair and an Australian accent. Sound familiar?"

"I finished with this case many years ago, Mycroft. I have no intention of reopening it."

"Not even for the opportunity of being restored to the Crown's good graces?"

"I have managed quite well ever since the previous King made it clear that he no longer required my services."

"His Majesty was livid."

"I did offer to send back the emerald tie-pin his grandmother had given me as thanks for that case of the submarine-boat plans."

"I think he'd have happily driven the thing into your chest."

"Mycroft, I did what I was asked: to identify the thief or thieves of the Dublin Jewels. That the culprits carried with them some unfortunate baggage was nothing to do with me."

"And you told His Majesty that to his face, instead of letting someone with a faint sense of diplomacy find a way to break the news."

"'Tigranes sat while war blazed up around him, giving ear only to those who flattered him.' If the King of England also prefers comfortable ignorance over a messenger with bad news, who am I to offer my neck for a second time?" As if the word "blazed" had served as a reminder, Holmes leaned forward to toss more coal onto the fire.

"I hardly think one can blame the theft of the St Patrick's Regalia for the Irish Rebellion," Mycroft objected.

"One spark among many."

"Surely you must remember something other than the dissatisfaction of your monarch," Mycroft said, firmly circling back to the beginning of the conversation.

"And that lunatic Doyle dragging me into it in the first place—I remember that."

"Sir Arthur Conan Doyle did recommend that you be consulted, that is true, but plans were already in the works."

"I was busy in 1907," Holmes said. "I had moved to Sussex little more than three years before, and was only starting to get things under control. I'd heard of the theft when it happened, in July. But since no one died, it did not much interest me. In September, Lestrade came down to ask for my help with the Camden Town murder. He found me trying to harvest honey, far too late in the season, but that was my first year with the bees, so what did I know? I was making a complete mess of the matter. Must have been stung a dozen or more times."

"Sherlock: the Jewels?"

"You asked me what I remembered," Holmes said sharply. "I am telling you."

Mycroft did not quite shake his head, but instead reached for his coffee.

"I rode back up to Town with Lestrade, and as we went, he told me of the Jewels case, on which one of his colleagues had assisted. 'Kane' was his name."

"Detective Chief Inspector John Kane," Mycroft murmured.

"Lestrade took me to meet the man, when we had finished in Camden. In fact, I could see that meeting with Kane was of near-equal importance in his mind as my advice on the Camden woman's murder."

"Kane struck me as capable enough, for a policeman."

"I thought him remarkably naïve for a Scotland Yard inspector, and rather too impressed by the King's interest in the matter. Anyone who paused to think would have seen that the only reason for Dublin to bring in Scotland Yard was to have an English scapegoat on whom to pile the burden when the inevitable truth came out. It could only have been an inside job, which meant that scandal of various flavours was about to erupt."

"The Regalia were stolen from a safe within the castle strongroom, isn't that right?"

Holmes all but snarled at his brother's attempted innocence. "Mycroft, this is not some schoolboy viva voce. You know full well what the situation was."

"Plans had gone awry."

"Vicars was a fool."

"Sir Arthur Vicars, Ulster King of Arms, Registrar of the Order of St Patrick, Knight Commander of the Royal Victorian Order—"

"Pompous prig, covert homosexual, abysmal judge of character, and ultimately victim of an Irish Republican Army gun, fourteen years later. It was the second of those attributes," Holmes noted, "that sent the case off its tracks."

"Sherlock, we could not have His Majesty in any way associated with—"

"So you said at the time. I received several lectures on the scandals that were then sweeping the government of Edward's German cousin—to say nothing of Ireland itself back in the Eighties, with the Jack Saul matter. Everyone was terrified at the risk of another huge uproar in press and Parliament over 'aberrant behaviour' at the centre of power, just when the entire Irish situation was beginning to bubble in threat. Whitehall must have seized upon Vicars' clear incompetence with cries of gratitude, since it gave them the chance to avoid contaminating the government."

"Sherlock, the loss of the Regalia shook the government, offended His Majesty, and weakened our authority in Ireland."

"Is that why you're suddenly interested in them again? Are you up to something in Ireland, and the Regalia would provide you a bit of leverage?"

"Sherlock, you can't think—"

"No, I know you wouldn't tell me. But losing the Jewels was hardly a pebble's drop in a pond compared to centuries of behaviour. Nor is it the highest price the Crown has paid for silence, is it? No arrests made, Inspector Kane's official report stifled, my recommendations shelved. And the Jewels never recovered."

"You needn't sound so pleased at that last," Mycroft complained.

"Why should I not be pleased? My name was tainted by being associated with an apparently failed investigation; it is only fair that those responsible should pay a price. Beyond their cheque, which I returned."

"The Viceregal Commission report remains public."

"The Viceregal Commission's sole purpose was stiflingly narrow: to state whether or not Sir Arthur Vicars, Ulster King of

Arms, etcetera, and chief genealogist for the country, had been sufficiently vigilant in his job. Since clearly, if he had been, the Badge and Star would still be in the castle safe, theirs was not a demanding assignment. Their only venture outside their specified remit was to note that since Vicars' friend Francis Shackleton had so generously travelled all the way up from his Italian sick-bed just to volunteer evidence, he could not possibly have been involved. This, of course, after Shackleton's actual testimony had dropped several high names and blatantly threatened to drop others. To say nothing of the fact that his brother, Ernest, was already a national hero and a favourite of the King."

"Did you see Inspector Kane's report?"

"Before it was suppressed? I did. I'm sure you must have, as well."

"He, too, put Vicars at the centre of it."

"The most dullard of constables would have seen that Vicars was startlingly irresponsible, and had been for quite some time—and that his friends had taken full advantage of his distractions. But unlike the Viceregal Commission, Kane did look at the evidence. He named which of Vicars' friends should be questioned, undermined a couple of claimed alibis, and even suggested where the Jewels might have gone.

"And then, to the surprise of no one but himself, Kane's report instantly disappeared from sight, and he was ordered to take no further action—and indeed, to say nothing about the matter to anyone at all."

"And yet," Mycroft mused, staring into his coffee, "neither the report nor your share of the investigation was complete."

Holmes glared at his brother. "You're talking about the missing man. The blond possibly-Australian visitor who may or may not be the small man visiting Gorges this summer."

"Shackleton's friend, yes. A regular visitor to the castle that spring, up until the week of the theft, when he then conveniently disappeared."

"Mycroft, either your mind is beginning to lose its hold on details, or you are deliberately making mistakes in order to provoke me. We both know that the blond man had not been seen for at least three weeks. Also, that Shackleton was well known to have short-lived friendships, in London certainly."

"And yet you chose to look no further into—"

Holmes sharply set down his cup. His eyes had gone icy, and he bit off his words with the precision that indicated absolute fury. "I was *ordered* to keep my hands off of the matter. I was threatened, for God's sake—with arrest. For *treason*! The King was very lucky I did not offer my services to the IRA then and there."

"You've gone against orders before. Perhaps not from as high as Buckingham Palace, but I'd be surprised if you didn't continue working on things behind the scenes."

Holmes put out his cigarette and got to his feet. "Then prepare to be astonished, brother mine. I was angry then, I remain angry now. My opinion was, if a client—*any* client—refuses to take my advice, they deserve to lose a few shiny baubles. I told you and I told Kane that there was a person missing from amongst their pool of suspects. Why was it my responsibility to find him? The fellow either had nothing to do with the matter, or else he was clever enough to win my admiration."

"Sherlock, I'd like you to—"

"No." He walked across the room to retrieve his damp overcoat.

"Sherlock, the King—"

"*No.* Not unless you can guarantee me that prosecutions will actually be made, in open court. And you and I both know that this King will not permit such a thing any more than the last one did. Let Vicars' friends keep the Jewels. May they bring them much happiness."

He paused, hat in hand, before the door, then bent over to write something on the note-pad Mycroft kept on the console table.

Hat on head, door open, he looked back at his brother before the fire. "There's an old woman in Nanterre, outside of Paris," he said. "I've written down her address. I strongly urge you to tear yourself out of London and go see her. You, yourself. Before it's too late."

He shut the door, and headed for the lift.

CHAPTER SEVEN

JAKE

I sat and waited for my brother's little girl to settle back into that creakety basket chair. None of this was going to be easy on her. (Or on me—but then, I deserved it.) Though this probably wasn't the only time she'd be tempted to rise up and bash me one. She loved that husband of hers, admired him, worked with him—and I'd just declared myself his enemy.

(Smart work, JR.)

But instead of settling down, she spun on her heel and stalked out of the room. I got a little tense around the sprinting muscles until I heard the sound of water going into the kettle, followed by the *clunk* of it going onto the hob. No slam of a back door, no sound of a telephone receiver being picked up. At least she wasn't calling the police on me. (Yet.) I made myself relax, and in a bit, she came back in with another tea tray, which she half-dropped onto the table, rattling the pretty cups.

"I forget how English you are," I told her.

"What do you mean?"

I nodded at the teapot—or rather, at the teapot's handle and spout, sticking out of some knit thing that was either supposed to hide its ugliness or keep the stuff warm—and said, "You had a cup just ten minutes ago, I'd have thought that would do you for the day."

"You prefer coffee?"

"Sorry, but tea tastes like hot mop-water to me."

She shrugged, and made no move towards the kitchen. If I wanted coffee, was the message, I could make it myself. (My status as honoured guest sure hadn't lasted long.) Instead, I helped myself to the last of the honey wine, and picked up where we had left off.

"I know that . . ." (What was I supposed to call the man, anyway? "Holmes" would be regarded as too personal here. I wasn't about to call him "Sherlock." "My nephew-in-law"? I know he is only ten years older than me, but maybe I should use "Mr Holmes"?) ". . . your husband worked on the Irish Crown Jewels case. Well, he wasn't your husband then, since you were still in pig-tails, but I'm not surprised he told you about it."

"He didn't tell me much, just that it was one of his failures. Although I did get the impression that his brother, Mycroft, was somehow to blame for that."

Luckily, she'd been reaching out to the teapot and didn't notice the jerk of my hands. I checked my trousers, then cleared my throat. "Mycroft Holmes—he's the older brother, right? Something big in the government?" (I knew all too well who Mycroft Holmes was.) "I didn't realise he was involved." (And if I had, I sure as hell wouldn't have come waltzing in here so openly.)

"I think he asked Holmes to look into it."

"Okay. Well, look, this is a long and complicated story."

"Then you'd best get on with it," she said. (Her tone was caustic enough to etch steel. And that was Charlie, not Judith.) She poured the tea, she added milk, she picked up a spoon. Waiting.

"I wonder . . . that is, if your husband didn't plan on being gone all that long, would you maybe like to carry on this conversation somewhere else? Like, your farmhouse rather than his?"

"No." She finished stirring and sat back with her cup, looking as if she didn't plan on moving for a week.

I gave her a shrug. "Okay, your choice. But if I hear tyres in the gravel, I'm out the back door. I have things to do before talking to the police about ancient history."

"Dublin Castle, 1907," she said.

"That's right."

I'd planned this. (I plan everything, so you can bet I'd worked on how to do this.) (Not, mind you, that I'd entirely decided just how much to tell her.) (And about whom.) But sitting four feet away from her, in the house where she lived happily with the man I'd been avoiding for a very long time now, the words seemed a little less clear. What to tell her—especially knowing that it would get back to him, and from him to that brother of his. Gorges, yes, I had to include him—but what about my day in Cator Road?

Even without that, I wasn't at all sure how she was going to look at me when I was finished.

While I was trying to find the correct words to get us going, she frowned at a thought. "That summer of the hot-air balloon, when you came sailing across the Channel and landed on the Padgetts' roses. Was that 1907, too?"

"No, that was the following year, 1908. The third week of a beautiful warm August." I found myself smiling at the memory, all those children in a gang around Mary and her brother. I'd have been far better to spend 1907 doing *that* rather than finding myself skulking through Dublin Castle.

"Like I said, I was in Italy, in early 1907. Mostly up in the north around San Remo, but popping over to Monaco sometimes for a change of scenery. One day I got a letter from that fellow I'd met in London. I . . . I'd liked him. Clever, funny. Handsome devil—and he knew it. Anyway, he said he was headed to Dublin and wanted to know if I'd like to go along. I thought, I haven't been to Ireland in years, why not?"

"His name?"

"Does it matter?" (It did matter.)

She turned and fixed me with her mother's same eye, that one that pinned a guy down and asked him if he wanted to still be sitting in his chair in five minutes. "Uncle Jake, I'm pretty certain that this is going to end with you asking me either to lie to Holmes, or at least try and convince him to help you with something. For that I require all the facts, not just the pretty ones."

I couldn't really argue with that, I decided. And at least she was leaving the door open to taking my side. "Shackleton," I told her.

"The explorer?" Her voice rose in astonishment.

"His younger brother. Frank—Francis."

"Ah. Yes, that makes more sense."

"You've heard of him."

"I'd say most people have, because of Sir Ernest, but the family lived a few miles from here, in Eastbourne. I never met him, but Holmes used to come across him from time to time, on the Downs. So yes, I know of Francis Shackleton's reputation."

The word "reputation" made me shoot her a glance, but it was clear that she only meant Frank's criminal side. (The crimes he'd been charged with anyway.) This was trickier than I'd thought.

"Frank Shackleton was a friend." (More than a friend—but in the end, less. Still, no reason to go into that with Mary.) "I hadn't known him long, but like I said, he was clever and good-looking, he knew everyone, had a way of bringing a room to life. I knew he had to be something of a fast one, but London's full of flash people who spend money like water. This was before it became obvious to everyone, of course."

"You mean before he went bankrupt, defrauded some friends and a bank of a fortune, and fled the country for West Africa."

"Er, yes, before that. When I knew him, he was still building up his big Mexico land-speculation scheme—the one that went belly-up and got him fifteen months at hard labour. That fifteen months broke him. But when I knew Frank, he was a golden boy. Everybody loved him.

"One of the people he'd charmed was the Ulster King of Arms, a weedy fellow named Arthur Vicars, whose great passion in life was working out genealogies. Which as you might know is a key job in a place where a person's family status counts for everything. Vicars was a self-important little man with a well-tended moustache, who'd made a sort of fiefdom for himself there in the offices of the castle. He had three men under him—honorary positions, not paid, but they got to rub shoulders with Dublin society. One of them was Frank Shackleton, who shared a house with Vicars in Dublin, paying half the rent even though he was only there a couple weeks a year. The other two were a nephew of Vicars named Pierce Gun Mahony—his half-brother's son—and a man named Francis Goldney, who didn't have much of a connexion with Ireland but was the mayor of Canterbury and curator of a museum there. I met Goldney a couple of times when I was there and found him a bit of a dry stick, but funnily enough, when he died a few years later, it came out that he'd made a habit of helping himself to things that passed through his hands, paintings and the like.

"Finally, there was an Army captain who worked around the castle by name of Richard Gorges: tall, smooth, handsome as the devil, decorated Boer War hero—someone told me they'd called him 'Daredevil Dick'—and a belligerent brute when he was drinking. Which was a lot of the time. Vicars wanted nothing to do with him, told Frank he couldn't bring him to their house anymore. Oh, and I suppose I should include Lord Haddo, the Viceroy's son, who was great friends with Vicars and Frank, although he wasn't in Dublin most of that year. And Pierce Mahony, who also wasn't around much, since he'd been sick most of the spring . . ." (Oh, for heaven's sake, JR, can't you put your points into a straight line for the girl?) "Look, how about I start with the basic story, the way it was reported in the newspapers and police reports and such. That okay with you?"

"You may start there, yes."

(Had to appreciate that sharp little thrust she got into the word "start.")

"Okay, so that gives you the main characters in this little farce. And the setting is a tower in Dublin Castle that Vicars had taken over for his genealogy department a few years before. When he was hired, he wrote up a bunch of regulations, one of which was how they had to store the treasures connected with various rituals that the Office of Arms was involved with, mostly investitures. They built a new strong-room, and the rules he'd drawn up said that the Jewels themselves were to be kept in a safe inside the strong-room—and by 'Jewels' they meant two great lumps of diamonds and gemstones that were the actual Regalia of the St Patrick's Order, a Badge and a Star, along with some of those massive gold ceremonial collars that also had gems on them. A safe was ordered, delivered—and it turned out they'd measured wrong and got one too big to get through the strong-room door. Vicars was mad, and probably embarrassed, but then, he regarded that whole side of his job as an irritation, compared to the joy of hunting down names in mouldy old records books. Rather than go to the expense of ordering another safe or tearing apart the strong-room to get the thing in, he had them stick it in the library. A room used by dozens of people, with a guard whose office was in the next room, out of sight from the safe itself.

"The strong-room had four or five keys—one of them was usually lying around in the guard's office—but the safe had only two. Vicars kept both of them. One he wore on his watch-chain. The other he left at home, in a drawer in his office under some papers."

Mary's eyebrows rose. "This is the home he shared with the charming fraudster Francis Shackleton."

"You see where this is going. The last time anyone saw the Jewels—anyone other than the thief, of course—was June the eleventh, when Vicars opened the safe to show all his shiny possessions to a visitor. He liked to do that, showed how important he was. Another visitor was supposed to come on the twenty-seventh, but they ran out of time that day before they got to the safe. After that, the next time Vicars planned to open the safe was when King Edward came in July, when he would be wearing them to invest Lord Castletown into the St Patrick's Order.

"One week before the King arrived, the cleaning lady got there and found the main office door unlocked. That had never happened before, so she reported it to the guard, who told Vicars, but with all the whoop-de-do of getting ready for the royal visit, he ignored it. Three days later—a Saturday—she was surprised to find the door to the strong-room itself standing open . . . but again, Vicars paid it no mind."

(Truly the man had been an idiot.)

"Then that afternoon, one of the collars that had been sent away for cleaning came back from the jewellers. Vicars handed the safe key to the guard and told him to lock it up with the other jewels—the first time anyone could remember that he'd let the key out of his possession.

"And when the man turned the key in the safe door, he found it was already unlocked. He ran for Vicars, and as you know, they found the Jewels missing from their cases. Including, by the way, a diamond necklace that had belonged to Vicars' mother. The guard himself couldn't have taken them, he didn't have the time, especially since it later turned out that the case that had held the Badge contained just the ribbon and clasp, and taking those off was a fiddly task that needed a good ten minutes."

I looked at my niece, trying to figure out how she was reacting to this, but she was very good at the old noncommittal expression.

"Shackleton's name came up early, both because he could have known about the second key and because there were already rumours he was having money problems. However, both Shackleton and Goldney had been off in England for weeks, prominently appearing in all sorts of social affairs. As for Vicars' third appointee, Pierce Gun Mahony, like I said, he'd been sick and off in his country house under the eyes of a load of servants.

"A locksmith was summoned. He found no evidence that the safe's lock had been tampered with, and said that it had to've been opened with a proper key. Everyone could see that either Vicars had stolen the Jewels himself, or it was someone with access to the key. In either case, an insider was involved.

"Oh, and one other thing that came to light. In addition to showing off his little realm to important guests, Vicars liked to entertain his closer friends within the walls of the Office of Arms. Sherry parties and the like. Unfortunately, he had no head at all for alcohol."

"Oh dear."

"Yes. There was a story going around that one night, he took the Jewels out of the safe to let his friends play with them, and woke up in the morning to find himself wearing one of the collars. And another time, this would have been the previous winter, two of the big pieces disappeared entirely, only to arrive in the post a couple days later."

"Good Lord."

"Pranks. At first, Vicars seems to've thought this was another one, and that whichever friend had lifted them would bring them back just as Vicars was going frantic about the King's visit."

"Amusing friendship."

"Well, he was the kind of guy who seemed to have a sign on his back saying, 'Kick me.'"

"But the Jewels did not arrive in the post."

"They did not."

"And as far as I know, no arrests were made."

"No one was ever charged," I agreed. "Not officially. And when the Viceroy appointed a commission to look into the matter, they weren't asked to point fingers, or even offer suggestions. They were told to answer a simple question: Was Arthur Vicars careless?"

"Not a difficult decision, I'd have thought," she said.

"No. They did talk to most of those involved, from the cleaning woman to Pierce Mahony. Everyone except Vicars. He, and his lawyer, and his half-brother—calls himself 'The O'Mahony,' he was Pierce Gun's father and is a famous character—when they learned the meeting would be closed to the public, they decided Vicars shouldn't have anything to do with it. Frank Shackleton, on the other hand, impressed the commission by having been so helpful as to travel all the way from Italy to speak to them, and they made clear that, despite the nasty rumours, old Frank couldn't possibly have been involved."

"So no proper investigation was ever done?"

"Oh, but it was. A detective inspector was sent over from Scotland Yard. He interviewed everyone in sight and wrote a report."

"Saying what?"

"Nobody knows. It was never published."

"What? Why on earth would— Ah." I could see that quick brain of hers click the information into place. "Scandal."

"You got it."

"The last thing any government wants is a scandal in high places, and I imagine that behind those closed doors, Shackleton threatened to raise one."

"Not in so many words, but it didn't take a strong pair of glasses to read between the lines, especially for those who knew Frank Shackleton's reputation. And there'd been a huge uproar centred around the castle just thirty years before, dragging in Majors and clergymen and MPs and even a handful of policemen. This time, the Viceroy's own son, Lord Haddo, was involved—not when the Jewels went, but he'd been smack in the middle of the parties. You can't get a lot higher than that."

"To be clear, we're talking about a homosexual uproar, right?" she said. "What the newspapers like to call a 'homosexual ring.'"

I looked at her carefully, and could see no indication of shock, or even judgement. Just a matter-of-fact recognition of political truths. (*Should* I tell her about Cator Road? No, not yet.)

"Yes." I needed something stronger than this pale wine, so I got up and opened cabinet doors until I found the spirits. I did return the decanter to the shelf when I was finished pouring, but the glass that I carried back across the room was pretty full.

I lowered the level of the glass an inch or so, and pressed on. "No one much minds if a man is quiet about his preferences, but after Frank finished dropping his not-so-gentle hints, they could see that this was going to be the very opposite of quiet. And none of them wanted the King anywhere near that. I mean, his nephew the Kaiser's friendship with Prince Eulenberg was just then blowing up. Suicides, courts-martial, and duels all over Europe."

"So, Vicars and Shackleton?"

"Probably." (Undoubtedly.) "Vicars did have a circle of friends who were, as they say, 'artistically minded.' Although he did marry, some years later—which I would say surprised his friends, except by that time, he didn't have many left. Frank Shackleton, however. His main pal was that drunken thug I mentioned, Gorges, who'd already been kicked out of the Army once because of his . . . indiscretions. He'd signed up again, and ended up in Dublin."

"The Army took him back after a dishonourable discharge?"

"South Africa is a long way from London, and a decorated war hero from a good family is allowed to resign a commission."

"I see. Well, it sounds as if the police had a wealth of possible suspects. Could they find no one to arrest who didn't risk shaking the government to its core?"

"Not really. I'd bet the Scotland Yard detective's missing report said pretty much what everyone in Dublin knew: that Shackleton and Gorges had put it together, but that since Shackleton took care to be far away in London during the actual theft, and Captain Gorges, who had all kinds of excuses to be around the castle on his duties, hadn't been out of anyone's sight long enough to have disposed of the Jewels afterwards—well, unless one of them gave the other away, there was no way to break it open."

"Except," she noted, "if there was another partner. Someone, say, that Shackleton had befriended in London the previous year."

My brother's clever daughter had dug down into the cold facts and found the heart of the story. I grinned at her—I couldn't help it—and said with a broad Australian accent, "Summan' loik a blond feller from Down Under, maybe a mole on his upper lip, that Frank met in London and invited to Dublin durin' the spring?"

CHAPTER EIGHT

SHERLOCK HOLMES

Coming out the door of his brother's block of flats, Holmes dodged taxis and a delivery lorry to the other side of Pall Mall, ducked into Marlborough Road, and crossed over into St James' Park.

He fully intended to walk the path alongside the lake and past the Palace to Victoria Station. He could be home by dinnertime. Patrick would have delivered Tillie's cooking, and if not, he and Russell could stroll down to the Tiger Inn.

And yet . . .

He had been walking in a controlled, even pace, but now he found his footsteps slowing, then pausing entirely near a bench overlooking the lake. Ducks, ever optimistic, drifted over. He studied them, then arranged his coattails over the damp wood and took out his pipe.

He'd had his investigations put to the side before, his recommendations ignored—generally, it was true, by clients who had lived to rue their decision. Or occasionally, not lived.

And Sherlock Holmes had made it a foundation stone of his practice that all the clients he accepted were given equal weight in his attentions. Queen or cleaning woman, industrialist or street-sweeper, all received the same attentions from the consulting detective.

Being spurned by a King should, therefore, hurt no more than failing to convince a spinster of her vulnerable position.

He also had a nagging feeling that it might be thought . . . immature, were he to automatically refuse the investigation simply because Mycroft was the one to ask. He hoped he might have outgrown childhood rivalries.

It also might be thought petty to base a decision purely on eighteen-year-old resentments.

He sighed, knocked the pipe out on the ground under the bench, and left the ducks to their search. When he reached Birdcage Walk, his hand came up to summon a taxi from the passing flow.

"Scotland Yard," he told the driver, and shut his ears to the man's reminiscences about passengers over the years whom he had delivered to that august address.

Perhaps inevitably, Lestrade was not in his office, but a bit of pushing gave the location of the murder that was requiring the inspector's current attentions. Holmes was soon stepping down from another taxicab and making his way through onlookers, uniforms, and irritated would-be passers-by.

"Lestrade," he called, pitching his voice to cut through the tumult.

The policeman's head came up and his eyes swept the crowd, to fasten on the tall, thin man at the back. His eyebrows went up, and after a moment, he tipped his head at the nearby doorway, clearly indicating a question: *You here for this?*

Holmes shook his head, then raised his chin in the direction of the Lyons shop across the road. Lestrade nodded, held up his hands, fingers deliberately spread, to indicate a brief wait, and turned back to his conversation with the uniformed constable.

It was closer to ten minutes before Lestrade came through the tea shop door, by which time the tea in the pot was nicely brewed. "You looked hungry," Holmes greeted him, "so I asked the Gladys for crumpets. They should be here—ah."

The girl darted up, swung a laden plate onto the table, arranged the butter and jam around it, gave them a perky near-wink, and whirled away.

Lestrade watched the uniformed figure retreat. "They say we're to call the Lyons girls 'Nippies' now, did you know that?"

"Nippy? Is that to suggest that they need to wear a cardigan, or to indicate they will take a bite out of an intrusive finger?"

"Apparently it's a reference to their quickness. Thanks for the tea."

"You've been on site since an early hour," Holmes noted, helping himself to one of the toasted rounds.

"Nearly finished. A pleasant old lady got fed up with her wastrel son slapping her around and conked him one in the head. She telephoned us herself, and only got upset when I told her I'd have to take the rolling pin as evidence. Wanted me to wait til she'd finished making all of us nice policemen a batch of scones. But if you're not here for the crime of the century, what can I do for you?"

"The Dublin Castle robbery, 1907. DCI John Kane."

"I remember."

"Is he still around?"

"He retired years ago, though as far as I know he's still alive. You need to talk with him?"

"I'd like to."

"I'll see what I can find." Lestrade took a bite of what, by the looks of it, was both breakfast and lunch, then realised that Holmes had not replied. His eyes went up to the older man. "You need him now, I take it."

"That would be helpful."

"I'll use the telephone when I've finished my tea."

Holmes nodded his acquiescence, and topped up his cup.

"Have you found them?" Lestrade asked. "The Jewels?"

"Mycroft thinks he has some new information."

"He thinks?"

"As you know, my brother prefers to have others do his work for him."

"What does he want you to do?"

"One of the peripheral characters, Gorges, has—"

Lestrade set down his cup with a bang. "*That* bastard!" He caught himself, glanced guiltily at the shocked faces nearby, and lowered his voice. "What has he done now?"

"Nothing, so far as I know."

"He should have hanged, for shooting DC Young. Instead of which his solicitor makes people sad about the bas—about the headaches he's had since getting sunstroke during the Boer War, and how his injuries make him drink to the point of insanity. Twelve years, my a—my foot. *And* they let him off early."

"Well, apparently he's been telling friends that he might have remembered something to do with where the Jewels went."

"He has friends? No, never mind. Is that why they've let him out?"

"I don't think so. If true, they'd have interviewed him and tossed him back into Broadmoor when he failed to come up with anything."

"So what's your interest in it? You want to talk to Kane about the report he wasn't permitted to file?"

"Will he talk to me?"

"Not on the record. But . . . hang on." Lestrade washed down the last of his muffin with the dregs of his tea, claimed the final round on the plate, and headed for the telephone in the back. Holmes signalled the waitress—the 'Nippy'—for a fresh pot, and settled in to wait.

The tea was well stewed by the time Lestrade returned with a piece of Lyons note-paper in one hand. He held it close to his chest. "I promised him that anything he tells you stays off the record. His wife has health problems, and he can't risk losing his pension."

"Agreed."

Lestrade nodded, and laid the piece of paper on the table in front of Holmes, saying pointedly, "And now that's two of us whose pensions are in your hands."

"Your future will be safe," Holmes said. Although as he slipped the page into his breast pocket, he wondered if losing one's police pension might be more, or less, problematic than being arrested for treason. Best not to mention that possibility to Lestrade.

CHAPTER NINE

Sherlock Holmes

Detective Chief Inspector (retired) John Kane did not look like a man who would take the suppression of a case lightly. Someone with that glint of intelligence in his eye and that amount of determination in his chin, Holmes reflected, might seriously have considered handing in his resignation back in 1907.

"I know you," Kane said, making no move to shift out of his half-open doorway.

"We've met," Holmes agreed.

"Lestrade didn't say who it was he was sending over, just that you knew how to keep your mouth shut. You're that Holmes fellow, aren't you?"

"One of them, yes."

"The 'consultant.'" He made it sound like something he'd found on the bottom of his shoe. "That writer foisted you on me. Doyle."

Holmes sighed, and shifted to redirect the drizzle of rain running off the edge of his hat. "He and Vicars were distant cousins. And Sir Arthur occasionally decides that a man who writes detective stories is himself a detective."

Kane just stood and looked at him for a while, and Holmes prepared for the door to shut in his face. Instead, to his surprise the glint turned into something closer to a twinkle. "Yes, I can see that might be somewhat trying. Come in."

The coal fire in the Kane sitting room was welcome. And it was late enough in the day that, when the girl brought in a tray with yet more tea, Kane felt free to offer a dose of spirits in it. Holmes was grateful to accept.

"What can I do for you, Mr Holmes?"

"The report you wrote, concerning the theft of the 'Crown Jewels' from Dublin Castle in 1907."

"There is no report."

"Oh, I imagine there is, somewhere, locked inside a safe considerably more effective than the Raley's in Dublin Castle's library."

"There could hardly be a safe less effective," the policeman commented.

"A safe is only as good as its keeper. As a report is only as useful as those who receive it. The suppression of yours was a miscarriage of justice."

Kane studied his cup. "I was upset, originally, I'll admit that. In the years since, I have begun to think that the decisions made were not completely without merit."

"Perhaps we should agree to disagree," Holmes growled. "However, I do not need the report itself at present, although I would appreciate your memory of the investigation. As I recall, the report was by way of a recommendation as to the path forward, be it to the Dublin force or Scotland Yard itself."

Kane's gaze had come up. "Sounds like you saw it."

"I did."

"How?"

"I threatened my . . . I put pressure on the man who had asked me to look into the matter. Independent of the official forces."

"Must have been some pressure."

"Oh, the menace went in both directions. Hence, my own silence in the intervening years."

Kane cocked his head to one side. "Did they wave the word 'treason' at you, too, or just say they'd take away your pay-cheque?"

Holmes looked at the other man's crooked smile, and nodded. "Something along those lines. And since there are reasons not to wake that particular sleeping bear, may I suggest that this visit to your house never happened. That you have not spoken to Sherlock Holmes since one brief conversation in the autumn of 1907."

"How can I help?"

"The drama's central characters were Arthur Vicars, who held the keys to the office, the strong-room, and the safe itself; Francis Shackleton, who had a growing ocean of debt and access to one of the safe keys, since he shared a house with Vicars; and the other two heralds, Francis Goldney and Pierce Gun Mahony. Mahony and Goldney were never really suspected, but Shackleton had both motive and, if one posited one or more assistants, opportunity. And since then has shown his true colours by defrauding any number of investors. He also had the wits to be away from Dublin at the key time, and friends who could perform several needed functions."

"The dreadful Richard Gorges," Kane supplied. "Who was well enough known around the castle that the guards didn't bother to note his comings and goings."

"Their laxity applied to a number of the personnel, as I recall," Holmes noted. "One of them, as you say, was Gorges. However, there was another man, seen on the edges of things that spring. A friend of Shackleton's."

"The fair-headed man."

"Small, blond, with a prominent mole on his upper lip, and an accent."

"Probably Australian. One of the guards was certain about that—he had a sister-in-law born and raised in Sydney."

"But you never found the man."

"No."

"Even though such a figure would be noticeable enough in Dublin."

"You'd have thought so. And that was why I particularly wanted to talk with him, and why, when he proved to have vanished so completely, I was pretty sure he'd been involved."

"Indeed. Could we perhaps review the chronology of events? As well as you remember them, that is."

Kane fixed him with a look. "Mr Holmes, the details of that investigation are carved into my brain."

The smile Holmes gave the retired inspector combined sympathy, understanding, and something with an edge to it. A promise, perhaps.

Kane rose and fetched two glasses, abandoning the tea for undiluted spirits. He sat back down, took a swallow, and settled his gaze on the glowing coals. "I knew from day one that Francis Shackleton had to be involved somehow. I'd come across him before, and found him a nasty piece of work with a pretty face and smooth manners. The old ladies loved him, even the ones he'd ruined. He twisted the government around his little finger, sucked his brother's reputation dry, and embarrassed the King—and all the time, he had an alibi as solid as the Tower of London.

"He had been Dublin Herald of Arms for a couple of years, and shared a house with Vicars, the man who appointed him. Since a herald's main duties were to show up for important ceremonial occasions, he, Goldney, and Mahony would have known the King's dates for months.

"Goldney lived in Canterbury—he was the mayor, in fact. Shackleton had a grand house in London, where he spent most of the year. Both men had been in Dublin earlier in the spring—Goldney was only appointed in February, and returned home in May. Shackleton left for London in early June, well before Vicars opened the safe for the last time before the theft, to show the Jewels to a visitor."

"Would Shackleton have known that the safe would be opened then?"

"He certainly knew that Vicars liked to show the things to important visitors. And he'd probably have known that the Duke of Northumberland's librarian was due to arrive. It would also have been a simple matter to plant the idea in Vicars' mind one morning over breakfast."

"That date?"

"June the eleventh."

"Three and a half weeks before they were found to be missing."

"With Shackleton in London the entire time. Nowadays, he might be able to commandeer an aeroplane, but in 1907? Even the fastest visit to Dublin would have left a gap in his social schedule. And you can believe we went over his calendar with a fine comb."

"But Shackleton had been in Dublin earlier in the spring, no doubt introducing his yellow-haired friend to Gorges and the castle staff. I imagine that, as with many such public places, the guards become so accustomed to people coming and going that when there is a familiar presence, they don't always make note of his entrance or exit."

"The castle paperwork left much to be desired. And Gorges was there the whole time."

Holmes nodded. "Shackleton then returned to London, although I believe the blond Australian remained behind for a few days."

"That certainly caught my eye—and you're right: when I got to Dublin, the Wednesday after the theft was discovered, nobody could remember seeing the man for at least ten days. But as you're suggesting, the Jewels could have gone anytime after the eleventh of June."

"Shackleton certainly delayed his return as long as he could, assuming he planned to attend the King's visit."

"His presence was required. But he knew he'd be a suspect, so he couldn't afford to have the Jewels disappear *after* he arrived. They had to be discovered gone while he was still attending to the Season's festivities in London. If you asked me to guess, the actual theft occurred between the eleventh and the twenty-seventh of June, when Vicars had another visitor to show around. But something came up that day, and the safe wasn't opened. After that, the press of the upcoming royal visit took over."

Holmes thought for a time, then said, "It does sound like a fairly convoluted plot, with Shackleton, and Gorges, and the stray Australian. If that was the case, then I imagine Shackleton would have been in an increasingly urgent situation. He had to be in Dublin by the tenth, but waiting to hear news of the theft can't have been an easy time."

"It certainly put the others in an awkward situation, since it all hinged on someone discovering the theft before Shackleton's boat docked in Kingstown Harbour—sorry, 'Dunleary,' it's called now."

"As I recall, your report cited a series of unlocked doors as an attempt to draw attention to the theft."

"That's right. The cleaning lady, Mrs Farrell, found the office's outer doors unlocked on the Wednesday before the King was to arrive. On the Saturday morning, she discovered the door to the strong-room, just off of the guard's room, standing open. Both times she informed the guard, who told Vicars. And both times, Vicars merely brushed away the news."

"Suspicious behaviour."

"Absolutely. Which was one reason he came in for some hard questioning in the days that followed. But either the man was the best actor I've ever encountered, or he was what he appeared: a vastly puffed-up lesser bureaucrat who believed the world would cease moving without his ability to create a detailed family tree, who regarded the Jewels under his care as a minor nuisance, apart from the times he could use them to display his importance."

"You looked at the guards and cleaner."

"Of course, but the timing and personalities were wrong. They weren't lying."

"You think Gorges opened the relevant doors?"

"Shackleton had access to the second safe key. The other doors had multiple keys, some left lying about the place. Gorges was around so regularly, he was like part of the wood-work. Who else?"

"Not the blond man?"

"I think he was the one who did the actual theft. I think Shackleton and Gorges made a habit of going in and out of the castle with him, to get the guard used to his presence. One day after Shackleton was gone, one of the two helped himself to the safe key in Vicars' house—probably the Australian—and hid himself inside the offices with it that night."

"They would not have had a copy made?"

"No locksmith in the country admitted to making one, and the experts who took the safe apart afterwards swore it couldn't have been opened by locksmithing tools, or even from a wax copy, since the fit would have been poor enough to leave marks."

"So: the blond Australian brings along a sandwich and flask, waits for a gap in the guard's rounds—which I imagine were regular?"

"As clockwork."

"—and then settles down in front of the safe."

"Wearing gloves, I believe, although by the time I arrived, half the people in Dublin had trekked through and pawed at the boxes. He took the Jewels out of their Morocco cases—one of the boxes held the keys to all the rest—and left the cloth wrappers, along with this blue ribbon he'd spent some time removing. The only case he took with him was the one that didn't have a key inside the safe, a necklace that had belonged to Vicars' mother."

"Interesting."

"I thought so. Either he didn't want to break the box, or he was concerned that it might be heard."

"When the thief finished, he closed the safe door—"

"But did not bother locking it," Kane added. "The office messenger who actually discovered the theft, after Vicars gave him the key to put something away, said the lock was unturned."

"Would it have been clear by looking at the safe door that it was not locked?"

"No, you couldn't tell by the position of the handle."

"And the messenger went to fetch Vicars, who finally realised he had a problem," Holmes said.

"Yes. And that was the end of the royal seating arrangements."

"And the actual thief was long gone, the second key returned to Vicars' home office."

"And Bob, as they say, is your uncle."

"Still," Holmes said, "that left behind one of the conspirators—"

"Richard Gorges."

"As you say. Left him to get through the nerve-wracking element of laying trails to make sure the safe was opened by someone."

"And Captain Gorges would have been the right man for that. He's one of those soldiers built for war, who fall apart in peacetime. Put him under fire, ice runs in his veins."

"Were Vicars and Shackleton lovers?"

If the blunt question made Kane uncomfortable, it did not show. "You know, I actually don't think Vicars gave the least consideration to sex. His interests were so rigidly narrow that nothing external to his genealogical duties had any importance at all. Later on, he was all but impervious to the threat of exposure as homosexual—but then, he was also more or less oblivious to the dangers in being suspected of the theft itself. All that mattered to the man was that the King's visit go smoothly. For him, trying to salvage the upcoming ceremony was vastly more urgent than figuring out who had robbed his department. That first day, when the Dublin police demanded he produce the second of the two keys to the safe, he flatly told them that the Jewels were sure to show up again. He wouldn't even go home to get the key and show them, until he had finished his day's work."

"That same blindness was what got him killed a few years later," Holmes noted.

"You're right about that—openly entertaining British officers in IRA country was suicidal. At least the rest of his household was allowed to leave before the Republicans set a torch to the place."

"Hadn't there been an earlier attempt?"

"The year before, yes. The local IRA militia showed up on his lawn and threatened to burn the place if he didn't open his strong-room—rumour had it his absent British neighbours had given him their guns to store. He flat out refused, and they were so taken aback, they left. This was when the campaign to burn down English-held estates was just getting started, although I suspect the thing that kept Vicars' house standing was his connexion to Pierce O'Mahony, his half-brother, the head of the Mahony clan and an ardent Nationalist. Styles himself as *The* O'Mahony, and by all accounts, he's something of an eccentric. But by the spring of 1921, the niceties of ownership had faded in importance. Vicars was taken out to the garden and shot, and the place set on fire."

"Hmm." Holmes had slouched back into his chair, his fingers resting together in front of his mouth. His mind was clearly miles away from the room.

"What?" Kane asked.

"Courage," Holmes mused.

"Sorry?"

After a bit, Holmes seemed to return to his body, and sat forward to retrieve his glass. "Courage," he repeated. "Mettle. Nerve." He looked over at the retired detective, and elaborated. "It takes considerable backbone to stand up to a group of armed men."

"Well, as I said, Vicars was nothing if not single-minded. I imagine they simply failed to convince him that he was in any danger. After all, it took months and the fury of everyone up to and including the King of England to convince the man that he was being pushed out of his office."

Holmes reflected, then shook his head. "Monomania does seem to carry with it a sense of invulnerability."

However, he couldn't help wondering if that was all it was.

CHAPTER TEN

RUSSELL

I sat for a time, studying my uncle. Yes, he would be very believable as a "blond feller from Down Under," an amiable Australian visitor to Dublin, befriending guards and grandees alike, adjusting his social status to the audience. I could also envision him curled up inside a cupboard or tucked under a desk, waiting for the slow tread of a bored castle guard to approach, then retreat, before he rose, padding silently across the floor to the waiting safe to slip a purloined key past its otherwise formidable lock. There is no defence against betrayal.

What then? With the guard safely off on his humdrum rounds, a cautious thief could count on a long, uninterrupted time to plunder. Would he have risked the potential brief dazzle of a torch? Or a dark-lantern—or perhaps there was a full moon and clear sky? Maybe the library remained dimly lit at all hours, from a lamp in the adjoining guard's room or entrance.

Where was the library, anyway? If the safe had been too large to fit through the strong-room door, it was unlikely that the delivery crew had wrestled it up a flight of stairs first. Which suggested that both strong-room and library were on the ground floor. And being a library, it would have windows—barred, perhaps, but large enough to brighten the pages of old, hand-written records books.

Outside the room, whether it opened onto the grounds around the castle or one of its courtyards, there would be a light burning all night for the sake of security. A man with a key might not require a torch until he tried to see into the safe's interior.

Then, however, unless he was lucky enough to have a convenient beam of exterior light spilling just so into its front, he would require a small source of light—either a cautiously shielded torchlight or a dark-lantern of some sort. Particularly if the moon was full enough to obscure any faint glow of the windows from the courtyard.

"When was the moon full in June?"

When he did not reply, I looked across, catching a most peculiar expression on his features. "What?"

"Nothing," he said. "Nothing at all. The moon was at its fullest on June twenty-fifth. A Tuesday."

Both facts would be odd things to have instantly to hand after all these years—except if they had been vital information at the time. "Which was two weeks after Arthur Vicars had opened the safe to show off the Regalia. How long was it before the next set of visitors was anticipated?"

The way Jake's eyes crinkled in an approving smile, the tilt of his head at an angle, were so like my father, it took my breath away. "Two days."

I needed to clear my throat, and my thoughts. "But . . . but you said that part of the visit was interrupted, so Vicars didn't open the safe until July the sixth. After," I added, "the cleaning woman had twice discovered doors standing open—different doors, on two different days. But before Francis Shackleton was due to return to Dublin."

"Another thing you should know. I told you about the sherry parties Vicars hosted, and how he'd become tipsy after a single glass of port. The winter before all this, he woke at his desk to find the St Patrick's Star around his neck, although he was never certain whether he had done the deed himself as a lark, or one of his guests had put it on him before they left. And then a few weeks later, he'd opened a package that arrived in the post and was appalled to find a piece of the Regalia inside. Haddo admitted to that particular prank."

"The Viceroy's son," I remembered.

"Yes. I think it was what gave Shackleton the idea in the first place. And it's also why Vicars was so convinced the things would show up again before the King needed them. Well, he was wrong there."

"Yes, because you'd already taken them. Were you still in Dublin?"

"Oh, no. The point was for me to do the job, leave the safe door closed but unlocked, hand the safe key over to Gorges, and let him figure a way to get it back into Vicars' desk the next day, when I was safely off to London. I'd be gone before Vicars' friend came to tour the castle on June twenty-seventh. Except that didn't happen. And by the first week of July, Gorges was running out of time. Up to then, whenever he had to be around the castle, he took care never to be out of sight of the guards. But with the King coming, he was forced to take some risks. On Tuesday night, he made a show of checking that the office door was shut, but left it open. Then when that didn't start up an alarm on Wednesday, he had to go into the guard's room on Friday night, just long enough to open the strong-room door and leave it open. He had to drink himself to sleep that night, and he got to the castle in the morning expecting to find it like an overturned ant's nest—but it was all business as usual. Anyone with a human nerve in his body would have cracked and given it all away.

"But finally that afternoon, Vicars dragged himself down to the safe and found it empty."

"And the safe was just standing open all that time?" I asked.

"Closed, but unlocked. You couldn't tell without trying the

handle, but anyone who fiddled with it would have got the surprise of their life."

Dozens of people, in and out of the library, and no one, not even one of the guards, attempted the handle.

"Anyway, I was gone, and the delay worked great for me. Who would remember much about a man who'd been there for a few weeks that spring but nobody had seen for a while?"

"So, what did you do with the Jewels? Take them to Amsterdam to be broken down?"

"Ah. Well, you see, my dear thing, that is where this tale starts to get complicated."

Starts? I thought.

CHAPTER ELEVEN

JAKE

The "complicated" part of the story was also going to be the most potentially uncomfortable. I picked up my glass, found it empty, but decided that a refill might not be the best idea. (Rule one of winning someone over: never show uncertainty.) Instead of a fortifying drink, I took a deep breath.

"A person might think," I told my niece, "that a fellow like Jake Russell, who makes his living by being just that much cleverer than the people with a load of dollars in their pockets, might be expected to stay clever. That someone who knows all the tricks, and is very aware of how helpful it is to have an amiable face, would know what to watch out for. Would automatically spot the tricks behind the appealing manner.

"Turns out, that's not always the case. Even people like me—and to be brutally honest, anyone who's got to my age, living as I do, without a spell in prison" (gaol, yes, but that doesn't count) "is both clever and careful—even people like me can have a blind spot. I liked Frank Shackleton. He was a cheat and a scoundrel, but he was *my* cheating scoundrel. He was a friend. I wasn't at all keen on Richard Gorges, but we needed him for that job, and I was pretty sure Frank planned to cut the knot as soon as we got safely away with the things and paid Gorges his share.

"So, I took everything over to London and gave them to Frank, who was—"

"Why?"

"Why what?"

"Why hand them over? Why not keep them for yourself?"

"Honour among thieves?" I offered. (Her face said, *Pull the other one.*) I gave her a sort of crooked smile. "Okay, you're right, I did *think* about it. But to be practical, I was new to Europe, and I just didn't have the contacts over here. Even if I pried out all the diamonds, dumped the fittings, and caught a steamer to New York, I'd never dealt with that quantity of raw gemstones before. I knew I'd lose a lot. On the other hand, Frank knew a guy in Amsterdam who could take care of them—I mean, the stuff was worth a King's ransom, and although his man would take an almighty chunk off the top, there'd still be enough to keep us all happy for a very long time.

"But I also . . . as I said, I liked the man. I'd been working on my own my whole life, and that spring I began to think, you know, this might be more fun if there were two of us. With his contacts and my experience, there'd be no limits."

"You trusted him," she said gently.

"I suppose. I'd rather say that I trusted my reading of the man. And that's what I got wrong.

"Anyway, I did hang onto this one piece that I knew couldn't have anything to do with the others. Not some massive slab of gems that would set off alarm bells as soon as it came into daylight, but a nice old-fashioned diamond necklace. I don't think Frank even knew it was in there, since he never mentioned it. It probably belonged to Vicars, from his mother or something—he was the sort of person who'd use a government safe as his own private storage.

"At any rate, I took the Badge, Star, and collars over to London, met up with Frank in a hotel that I'm pretty sure he wasn't staying in, and handed them over. I did check that he wasn't planning to leave them in his house in Mayfair when he went back to Dublin for the King's visit, since, alibi or no, it was very possible the police would want to have a snoop around. He said not to worry, he had a friend who was taking them to Amsterdam in a private car—the man was even having a larger gas tank put into the car so he and his driver wouldn't have to stop along the way.

"It sounded like he was on top of things, so we had dinner, and then I left. I had something cooking up in Milan that I needed to get back to, and we didn't want to have me anywhere nearby when Vicars opened the safe on the twenty-seventh and showed his friend a bunch of empty cases."

"The discovery that didn't happen," Mary noted. "So did Shackleton simply cut you out of things?"

"Well, like I said, it was a little more complicated than that. And it took me a very long time to get all the details.

"So, I got to London on the Thursday and gave Frank the Jewels. His plan was that, as soon as he heard they'd been stolen—either directly from Vicars or on the front page of the Friday newspaper—he'd take a day to put on a shocked act for his London friends, then take the mail train to Dunleary to do the same for Vicars and the police. Except Friday went by and he didn't hear anything, then Saturday. On Monday—that was July first—Gorges sent him a telegram to say that there'd been a problem with that outstanding business Frank asked him to see to, but that he—Gorges—would take care of it."

"That 'business' being setting off the discovery. Which he then tried to do on Tuesday night by leaving the outer door unlocked, and when that got no reaction, on Friday night leaving the door to the strong-room open."

"Everything short of painting an arrow on the wall of the library."

"Or blowing off the door entirely," she suggested.

"I think he'd have been happy to turn one of the castle's cannons on the place, by the time Saturday afternoon came around. But Vicars finally woke up, and his cable reached London on Sunday, which let Frank get to Dublin the day before the King's yacht arrived. Only problem was, the damned idiot took the Jewels with him."

Mary's jaw dropped open. (Like mine, when I'd heard.) "Shackleton took the stolen Irish Crown Jewels *back* to Dublin?"

"I know, sheer insanity. I guess his friend's car wasn't ready yet—or more likely, Frank didn't want to trust him on his own, and he decided the risk of walking around with them was less than leaving them in his sock-drawer in London."

"So he just carried them around with him?"

"Not quite that bad—even the local coppers might have noticed the great lump in his pocket. No, once he got to Dublin, he and Gorges buried it all in a nearby park."

"They buried the Regalia."

"Under a tree. In a city park. Less than half a mile from Dublin Castle."

"Good God."

"Shackleton was kept busy, first with Vicars, then with the Dublin police, who were desperately tramping all over and questioning everybody in sight, then finally with the man sent by Scotland Yard. But of course, all Frank had to do was put on an innocent face and tell them to ring up the Duke of Whatsis and the Earl of Wherever, who would say that their buddy Frank Shackleton had been firmly in London for weeks and weeks. They finally got tired of asking him, and after waiting a few days to make sure he didn't have someone on his tail, he took himself back to the park at night and dug around.

"And can you guess what he found?"

"He found them gone."

"Clever girl. You see, he and Gorges had a bit of a falling-out. All that sneaking around with keys in his pocket had sent even

Daredevil Dickie Gorges up to the very edge, nerve-wise. When Frank got back to Dublin and didn't seem to appreciate what Gorges had been through that week, our friend Dickie got huffy. I mean, he had a temper at the best of times, and the kind of headaches that leave a man blind. So when Frank just told him to stay calm and keep up the act, Gorges took offence. He picked up the bottle they'd been drinking from and threw it at Frank's head. He missed, but things escalated until Frank thought it might be for the best if he just left Gorges to cool down.

"Of course, when he went back to the park and found the stash missing, he knew Gorges had to've taken the lot, but Gorges just laughed in his face and kicked him out—literally, into the street. There wasn't much Frank could do then and there, not with all the spotlight on matters, but he figured there were only two things that could happen. One, Gorges would do something stupid and get caught red-handed. If that happened, well, it would be a blow to lose the Jewels, but even if Gorges swore up and down that Frank and I had been in on it, I was long gone and Frank had his London friends to vouch for him. The other possibility was that Gorges would sober up and realise that Frank's Amsterdam friend in the gem business was the only way forward, and he'd come back to Frank with the Jewels in his hand.

"Except," I said, "he never did."

Mary's chair let out a squawk. "What, had someone else seen them burying the Jewels?"

"That's what Frank came to think, when months went by and Gorges didn't get in touch. Gorges was drinking heavily by then, and resigned his commission the following summer, about the time when this article showed up in an American Irish magazine about the 'abominations' and 'nightly orgies' that had taken place under Vicars. Naming names, though funnily enough, the only name it got wrong was Gorges. And that, dear thing, is when your loving uncle was drummed out of the family. Dear old Dad had heard me mention Frank Shackleton, and though I swore up and down it wasn't anything to do with me, I found myself tarred with that brush. Anyway, Gorges ended up in London. Enlisted again when the War started, but he was too far gone by then so they let him go, and he crawled back into a bottle until the summer of 1915, when a policeman showed up at his door and Dickie panicked and shot him dead."

I had, I saw, managed to overcome even my niece's quick and subtle mind. All she could do was sit, open-mouthed and slightly unfocussed. (Maybe I should get *her* a drink?)

"Because of his Boer War record—he'd won medals, and after all, the headaches were from sunstroke during the war—they didn't hang him, just sent him to Broadmoor. And released him early, six months ago, in March."

Her eyes snapped back onto me. "Ah," she said.

"I heard about it in April, and came back from . . . well, you probably don't need to know that, but I got to London at the end of May, stuck the mole on my lip and the Australian accent back on my tongue, and went looking. It took me most of June to find him, and the rest of the summer to get him to talk to me. Broadmoor . . . changed him."

And here was where I got up at last to replenish my glass. I couldn't risk letting her watch my face while I told her my carefully constructed story. Hard enough to control my voice for her—let her think that emotion drove me to the drinks cabinet. Pity for an erstwhile colleague, my uncomfortable awareness that but for the grace of Luck, went I.

"Ten years of prison will do that to a man," she said.

"Richard Gorges was always a rough one. A bit of a savage, under his handsome face. I was amazed to find that his family was in *Burke's*—the *Landed Gentry* one, not the *Peerage*. But he's very subdued now. Living in a quiet little flat in Hampstead that his brother pays for, thanks to an American heiress wife. Not even drinking much, though when I knew him, I don't think he was ever completely sober. I took rooms nearby, to give me an excuse to happen across him. I even bought a dog to walk. There's nothing more disarming than a Jack Russell terrier.

"In August—hot day, it was, no rain in sight—I arranged to come across him. Surprise, astonishment, what are you doing here, all that. I put on a wary act, like I was about to back away, which took care of any suspicion he might have had. Though in truth, he didn't seem to have enough spirit left to mistrust me. We chatted, walked a bit, found a shady bench, and rolled up our shirt-sleeves. I bought us some ice-cream from the Italian vendor. I think it was the ice-cream that did it, 'cause that's when I finally found out what had happened."

CHAPTER TWELVE

RUSSELL

I was intrigued, and a bit distracted, to watch my long-lost uncle so effortlessly demonstrate the kinds of skills that had taken me years to learn. I'm not sure he was even aware that his words took on a trace of Australia as he spoke about the times he had worn that disguise. When he had settled again with his drink, his finger went to his upper lip a couple of times, as if rubbing at a mole that was not actually there.

"Gorges and Shackleton never did patch things together," he said. "Not really, although they did meet up a few times, in the years before Gorges went to prison. And though it took me most of August to prise it out of him, it turned out that as Frank thought, Gorges did go back to the park and dig up the box with the Jewels in it—but he'd then immediately reburied it, no more than twenty feet away. If Shackleton had gone during the daytime, he might've noticed. Instead, the investigation closed in, and before long Vicars fired him and threw him out of the house, then the police invited him to leave the country. Like I said, the next year Gorges ended up in London. He and Frank might have worked things out again, but soon Frank was up to his neck in an enormous bit of financial jiggery-pokery in Mexico that was about to come to pieces, and the last thing he needed was to have people reminded of his connexion to the Crown Jewels. The Mexico deal fell apart in 1910 and he left the country—to Portuguese West Africa, for some ungodly reason. He was arrested there in 1912, about the same time Vicars finally found a way to give his side of things in public—an article in one of the London papers accusing him of dalliance with a woman, of all absurd things. He sued the paper, which gave him the chance to stand up in court and say that Shackleton and Gorges had committed the crime that had ruined his name. As a plus, he won the verdict and had a neat £5,000 drop into his hands. Around that same time, Shackleton was being sentenced to a year at hard labour—but conveniently for him, the crime that convicted him was stealing a woman's £1,000 cheque. Nothing to do with bilking dozens of people including Cox's Bank of tens of thousands, but since that would have given him another chance at producing a huge scandal in high—"

"Wait," I said. "Stop." I could hardly believe I was about to say this, but . . . "Uncle Jake, I don't want to know any more about what happened in 1907."

"Well, not just '07. Shackleton didn't go into prison until 1913, and Vicars was shot by the IRA—"

"Vicars was—? No, enough of this tangle. We'll be sitting here picking over this story of yours when the sun goes down. Could we just—for the moment, at any rate—set all that aside. Uncle Jake, why are you here?"

"Brass tacks time, eh? But my dear girl, it's nothing but tangle."

"I can see that. However, I'm very much getting the feeling that there's an element of distraction about it. That you're hoping I look at the impossible mess and don't notice that you quietly have a pretty good idea where the main thread leads. So, essential data or no, let's start by straightening it out," I commanded.

"Well, any simplification of the whole mess will be wildly deceptive, but if you insist. The key points, I suppose, are: One, that Gorges was furious with Frank and so double-crossed him. That was in 1907. Two, it took a couple years, but Frank managed to soften Gorges up a little, and one night got him drunk enough to admit what he'd done with the Jewels. Three, Shackleton snuck over to Dublin and dug them up, but he didn't dare try to take them back out of the country, not when the Mexico project was threatening to fall apart and bring him a lot of very unwelcome attention. So he stashed them in the safest place he could think of. One that both appealed to his sense of humour and offered a chance at revenge."

"Not a third hole in the park, then?"

"No. In Arthur Vicars' desk in his home office."

"What?"

"I know. One of those fancy secretaire things with all the drawers, including some secret ones that, yes, Vicars had showed off to Frank. When Vicars had finally been pushed out the door of the castle, he went to London to work as a genealogist, but he kept the Dublin house, utterly certain that he'd soon be exonerated and could go back and resume his position. Delusions of grandeur, that man—although his half-brother, The O'Mahony, was just as bad, and paid for everything from lawyers to rent. Typically enough, Vicars never changed the lock on the front door, even though he knew Shackleton still had a key. And since the house was empty, and there weren't any servants around, Frank figured it was the last place anyone would go looking for the Jewels, including Gorges. If someone did come across them, well, bad luck and a big disappointment, but it was Vicars who'd take the blame, and who would believe him then when he accused Frank Shackleton? And if nobody found them, Frank could either go back himself or send some gullible fool to retrieve them."

There was a clear note of bitter anger in his voice, his humiliation at being used by someone he had considered a friend. "Someone like you?"

"Maybe not me, since he'd already made it clear where I stood, but there were always more idiots around."

"So what happened?"

"After his court case, Vicars finally had to admit that he wasn't going to be reinstated, so he took his £5,000 settlement and came home from London, closed up the Dublin house, and moved out into the countryside."

"And found the Jewels?"

"He must have at some point, wouldn't you think? Of course, by then he'd have been completely fed up with everyone who'd made him their scapegoat. Even the King sided against him. If he did find the things, he'd never have sold them, but it would have been just like him to not do anything at all. I mean, he couldn't very well just walk into the castle with them and say, 'Oh my, look what I found in my desk drawer' without stirring up the whole mess all over again."

"You're saying that Vicars kept the Irish Crown Jewels because he couldn't decide what to do with them?"

"It's been thirteen years since he moved out of Dublin, and none of them have come to light. Vicars sitting on them is the only thing that makes any sense. It's mildly surprising that he hasn't been showing them off to visitors, but perhaps he learned some lessons from—"

"And I suppose you plan to go and retrieve them from his desk in the country house?" I couldn't wait to hear why he needed me to help with the task. Because that had to be where this was going.

"Yes, although it's not—"

"—that simple. No, of course not. Because Vicars was shot. Unless he survived?"

"No, he's very dead. But it's more than he's dead. Kilmorna House, where he and his wife were living? When the IRA broke in and shot him, three years ago, they sort of . . . burned it down."

I let my head fall forward onto my crossed arms, and left it there.

CHAPTER THIRTEEN

SHERLOCK HOLMES

Night fell as London faded outside the train window. Holmes idly wondered if his brother had already left for Paris, or if he would find excuses to send some assistant in his place. Mycroft did not know the significance of the town of Nanterre, Holmes would have sworn that. Which in itself was worthy of note. Either Mycroft was losing his edge, or Louise Holmes was very, very good at covering her tracks.

He had seen no signs of softening in his brother, apart from this.

He hoped Mycroft would go—and that he would stay there for a good long time. If nothing else, it would put off the day when Russell marched up to Mycroft with an armful of long-accumulating disapprovals and resentments as to his personal manipulations of the British government and dumped them into his lap.

The confrontation was bound to get emotional, and Holmes himself would be asked to choose sides, between his wife's indignation and his brother's justification. Both had their virtue, but trying to straddle the divide would prove uncomfortable. And ultimately, impossible.

At least he did not have to announce to Russell that he was involving himself in Mycroft's long-cold investigation into the Crown Jewels theft. Having picked over the matter closely with Inspector Kane, he had to agree with the police on this one: the Jewels had long since quietly disappeared into the diamond marts of Amsterdam. He could see no reason to bestir himself to prove the actual culprit.

As he'd said to Mycroft, if the Crown doesn't care enough to risk a touch of embarrassment, why should Sherlock Holmes?

And he did have plenty to do at home. The bees, yes, and the experiment he'd been working on back in June concerning the possible grouping of human blood, but he'd also glanced through the accumulated mail and found a letter from August Vollmer, who had returned to the Berkeley, California, police after an unsuccessful stint in Los Angeles. Vollmer wanted his advice on the potential for the new polygraph machine, and Holmes had already been considering possible tests based on the Larson-Keeler design.

Yes, he had plenty to occupy himself in Sussex. He pulled out the day's newspaper and shook it open, speculating on what pleasant surprise he would find waiting for him in the pantry.

CHAPTER FOURTEEN

JAKE

I looked at Mary's bowed head and wondered what I had done to the poor child. "Have you had anything to eat today?" I asked.

Her head moved back and forth, either to indicate that she couldn't remember, or that she was completely overcome by the problem I was presenting her. Same answer either way, I thought.

"Food," I ordered, and got to my feet.

I clattered around in the kitchen for a while. Eventually, she appeared. "Sit," I told her when she moved towards the cupboard. "I can find everything."

And I did: plates, silver, glasses for beer, food from the hampers that Patrick Mason's lady friend had sent. Game pie, I saw with approval, and apple tart, local cheese, and fruit. Enough for ten, but Mary had a cooler for leftovers.

She was looking considerably more settled by the time her plate was clean. I put on the kettle and looked for the coffee-pot, finding it and a fresh packet of grounds in the cupboard.

"Do you not have any servants?" I asked. (Odd they hadn't showed up yet.)

"We did. Our housekeeper, Mrs Hudson."

I glanced at her in surprise. (How had I missed that?) "The same one your husband had in London?"

"The same. She was his landlady then, his and Dr Watson's, but she came with him when he retired. I met her the same day I met him, ten years ago. She left us in May, for . . . various reasons, and we set off for Venice before we could make any other arrangements. I'm actually not sure how we're going to find anyone to . . . replace her."

(Sounded like Mrs Hudson had been much more than a servant.) "Tillie Whiteneck might know someone."

"She has a niece, Lulu, who is all right, but . . ."

(But not someone who fit into this household, it seemed. Then again, who would?)

I packed the food away into the cooler while she was washing the plates, then made the coffee and set it on the old wooden work-table. When the plates were dried and back on their shelves—she took charge of the delicate things, after I'd fumbled a glass and nearly dropped it—we settled at the table.

"I need you to go with me to Ireland," I told her as I poured, managing not to spill any.

"You can't imagine you're going to find the Jewels in the wreckage of a burnt house?" she asked with scorn in her voice. "It's been, how many years?"

"Only three. Three and a half."

"Uncle Jake, I just came home. I don't even have any clean clothes."

"You won't need your summer things in Ireland." (Did one ever?)

"No, just a platoon of soldiers."

"You'll be loads safer without the redcoats—and things have settled down a whole lot since the Treaty."

"Jake. It's practically a civil war."

"In the North, yes, but we're not going there."

"I'm tired."

"Trains are great places to sleep."

"I have a million things to do here."

"Two days, three at most."

"No. I'm not going off to Ireland with you."

"Sure you are," I said.

Her eyes came up. "Why would I do that?"

"Because if you don't, you'll always wonder."

And there was Judith again, looking at me from her daughter's face with that familiar blend of disbelief, outrage, and a dash of humour. "Does that approach often work for you?" she asked.

"Depends," I said, stirring some sugar into my cup. "With you, maybe."

"Why do you want me?"

"Well, I want you because I'd like to spend some time with my niece. But if you're asking why I *need* you, that's another question entirely."

"All right, why do—"

"Because I can't do it alone. Because I need a partner with the sort of skills I think you may have." I could see her jaw clamp shut against the urge to ask, *What skills?*

I gave her another winning grin. "Oh, come on, Mary. Put on your American accent so you don't ruffle any Republican feathers, bring some galoshes so your stockings stay dry, have an adventure with your old Uncle Jake. It'll be fun."

I waited for her to give way, for her eyes to roll like Charlie's used to when we were kids and I managed to talk him into something he knew was a terrible idea. I waited, and she stared at me, and I realised—with no small amount of surprise and, yes, admiration—that I had absolutely no idea what she was thinking.

And absolutely no idea of what I was going to do if she turned me down.

CHAPTER FIFTEEN

RUSSELL

Whatever it was my uncle wanted of me, it was sure to be unethical, or illegal, or both. Probably both. And definitely something he didn't want Holmes to know about, either because of the ethics and/or illegality, or because it was going to put me in the path of danger.

I'd been fifteen when I literally stumbled across Holmes; a gawky, guilt-ridden, still-recuperating orphan living with an aunt who hated me. More than once over the years I had reflected on how that meeting had saved me, delivering me into the hands of a teacher who might have been neither gentle nor terribly patient, but for whom justice was everything.

What if I had never made it to the Sussex Downs in 1915, I thought now. What if Jake had not been trapped in Bolivia (behind bars, by the sound of it) when my family died, but had instead breezed into my hospital room to claim me before my grandparents could intervene, spiriting me away while I healed, and grew, and became an adult?

I had long been aware that, had Sherlock Holmes been a different man, I might happily have trained as a pickpocket or "cat" burglar, or learned the techniques of ageing paper and concocting a forger's inks. Not the brutal side of a criminal life—for that, a person has to be broken first, reduced to a state of regarding life as a disposable thing. But trickery? Living by one's wits and outsmarting the slow and wealthy? Why not?

The thought made me laugh aloud, and I realised that Jake had asked me something. "Sorry," I told him. "I was distracted, thinking about . . ."

I reached down to my boot and drew out my throwing knife. "Remember this?"

"Is that the one I gave you?" He reached across for it, running his thumb across the smooth wooden handle, worn with years of use.

"That last year, after I helped you cheat the Evil Publican out of his business."

"You were good."

"I was eleven."

"Yes, and I was *persona non grata* for a while after your father found out."

"He knew? I didn't think he did. He certainly didn't learn about it from me."

"No, I figured that." He lay the slim little weapon on the table and slid it towards me.

The publican had been a wicked man. He was a danger to small children—even those who were *not* Jewish—and had brought a criminal element to an innocent village. People for miles were relieved when he was gone, and celebrated the rôle it gave to Tillie Whiteneck. Consensus was that the man had deserved to be cheated out of the pub.

And although I knew few details about my uncle's larcenous history, my mother's long-suffering affection and a few overheard parental conversations left me with the impression that this was his pattern rather than an exception. What was it that she had said one time? *Theft is wrong, but one does find that it's the cheaters who get cheated.* In other words, people who think they deserve financial short-cuts open themselves to being conned by someone like Jake.

I flicked the knife with a finger-nail, spinning it round on the worn surface. Could I trust him? With my life, yes, absolutely: he would not put me at risk. With my last handful of coins? Again, yes: he was not a man to rob the impoverished widow and orphan. With that estate my father's will had left me in the South of France? Ah, well . . . Keeping in mind that larceny had fuelled what was no doubt an occasionally rocky voyage through life, and considering that he was nearing the age at which an office dweller would be looking to retirement, he might well regard those extras as being fruit ripe for the picking. A pension, as it were.

Frankly, I'm not sure I would disagree.

"I thought you were dead," I told him.

"I know," he said, "I'm sorry that—"

"No, what I mean is, when I turned twenty-one and inherited my father's estate, there was no one else to take into consideration. If I'd known you were out there, I'd have tried harder to find you. But really, it isn't right that it all came to me. You don't need to go after these Jewels. Let's go up to London tomorrow and I'll—"

My gaze snapped up abruptly at the noise from across the table.

He was laughing open-mouthed, eyes crinkled, clear signs of genuine humour. His blue eyes sparkled as he shook his head at me. "No, dear thing, I don't need your stocks and bonds. Funny thing is, the one lecture your father gave me that I actually took to heart was about looking to the future. Most people who . . . do what I do have a habit of turning around and throwing the money out the window. I mean, I do like a new suit, and I travel First Class, but I never took to gambling or investing in wild schemes."

"You won the Monk's Tun in a card game," I protested.

"There was no more gamble in that poker game than there is in a round of Three-Card Monte," he said. "You know that. I taught you myself."

He was right. When one person controlled the game, the risk was entirely one-sided.

"At any rate, with no expensive habits to speak of, a lifetime spent liberating generous sums from fools all over the globe has meant that I'm probably worth more now than your father ever was, maybe even your grandfather. So long as I keep my head down, I'm comfortable for life."

"So, why are you here—why do you want those Jewels?"

The amusement in his eyes faded, and he sat forward, studying his hands. I found I had bent my head, so as to see the expression his face wore. It was complex, serious and thoughtful. As if he was trying to decide how much to tell me.

"One thing I've always hated," he said eventually, "and that's unfinished business. But even more than that, I hate being taken for a ride. That's only happened twice, once with a woman, and once with Frank Shackleton. I settled with her, which leaves Frank. Unsettled business, in both ways."

I eyed him warily. "What does that mean, that you 'settled with her'?"

"I mean we came to an understanding. Heavens, child, you don't think I damaged the poor thing, do you? No, merely taught her that she got lucky once, but she's not clever enough to count on it again. She's retired now—at least, retired from that business."

"But Francis Shackleton is still around?"

"He is. Changed his name to Mellor, lives in south London. His brother got him a job with a friend, some investment company."

"A convicted fraudster handling other people's money?"

"Sounds like a bad idea, but the man he's working for at least knows what he's got. And serving a year at hard labour didn't agree with Frank Shackleton at all."

"You told me about your conversation with Captain Gorges, but you didn't mention what Frank Shackleton had to say."

"I very much hope I never have to talk to Frank again. In any event, whatever he had to say is bound not to help much. A person knows that Frank Shackleton is lying by the fact his mouth is moving."

I was coming to know the subtleties of Jake's face, and I thought that the open innocence it wore now was to some degree contrived. Some faint change of timbre in his voice also hinted at secrets—and that reply did not actually answer my question. Jake had spent weeks prising information out of Gorges. He had researched the Mahony house, followed up on Holmes, and discovered things about me and about Mycroft that were not common knowledge. Was there any way he'd have omitted visiting Frank Shackleton? And he'd told me that prison "broke" the man: how would he have known that without at least laying eyes on him?

Yes, there were things Jake was not telling me. On the other hand, his relationship with Francis Shackleton had clearly been more than a professional partnership. It had been personal, and it had ended with a brutal betrayal. That change of timbre in his voice could as easily be an echo of the humiliation I had seen earlier, rather than an attempt at deception. Particularly if he imagined me the naïve young girl I was not. Perhaps I would set aside the quest for details, just for the moment.

"But you think Gorges told you the truth about the Jewels?" I asked.

"I think he told me what he knew about them. I won't know if that's enough until I go to Ireland."

I studied his features, trying hard to look past the resemblance to my father and see the man beneath. The man who had merrily cheated and lied his way through life. The man who had used his wits, his boyish good looks, and his charm to get himself into, and out of, an unguessable number of nefarious enterprises.

"What skills?" I asked.

CHAPTER SIXTEEN

SHERLOCK HOLMES

The house was dark.

Holmes had the taxi driver wait with his head-lamps shining into the portico until the door was open, but one step inside and he knew the house was empty.

As always when this sort of thing happened, he had to stifle the thought of catastrophe. Instead, he dropped his umbrella into the stand and methodically hung his overcoat up to dry.

The fire had long since burned down to coals, which he topped with a handful of Patrick Mason's distinctively uniform kindling and two lengths of split wood from the apple tree that had come down in a storm the previous winter: Russell had used perhaps ten hours' worth of wood, which agreed with the state of the coals. She'd not left until afternoon—although the curtains were pulled shut, which suggested either she'd stayed until dark, or she'd felt an uncharacteristic desire for privacy.

He went into the kitchen, flicked on the light, and saw the note on the table:

> Holmes, an old friend unexpectedly showed up and asked for some help with a project. I may be a day or two, sorry I couldn't

wait for you, we needed to catch a mail packet. There's food in the cooler, Tillie's game pie is very nice—grouse, I think.

R.

One eyebrow rose. He read the message again, noting the lack of any of their agreed-to code words that might suggest her absence was anything but voluntary. He went into the pantry to open the cool-box, examined the contents, then walked back to the kitchen to take in the tiny details of the room. One friend, unless she'd been truly ravenous, with whom she'd shared a bottle of last spring's honey wine. Also, coffee, since the device had been used since the morning. And one of them had used a glass from the drinks cupboard where the spirits were kept. He took the strong torch from its shelf and went out of the front door, going to his knees to examine the floor of the roofed-in porch and the ground outside. Back in the sitting room, he played the beam over the back of his backet chair. He picked out a hair—light in colour, the length of Russell's: she had been sitting in his customary seat. He moved over to the one across from it, and found two hairs: also light in colour, but considerably shorter than hers. And—was that a trace of oil he felt on them?

A glance under the microscope in his laboratory confirmed the evidence of the glass, the shoe-print on the porch, and the length of the two hairs: Russell's guest had been male.

Holmes changed his jacket and tie for an old dressing gown, then settled with pipe and drink before the flames, dedicating his mind to meditation. Mycroft, and Inspector Kane. A note that took care to reassure, yet also betrayed almost no information apart from a steamer crossing. A male visitor: an old friend, one she was willing to accompany with little notice. But not an emergency: they had sat eating and drinking for some time.

The man did not smoke, and was not a particularly heavy drinker.

An hour later, rather than fill his pipe a third time and his glass a second, Holmes stood and crossed the room to the telephone. Inevitably, the young woman working the Exchange wanted to chat, and it took a firm voice to convince her that, yes, even though it was late at night, he did indeed wish to be put through to Mr Mason, now please. And when the number of rings in his ear reached eight and she came back on to say that Mr Mason seemed to be asleep and perhaps he might like to try in the—

He cut her off. "No, let it ring. I shall wait."

She made the sort of noise that was generally accompanied by a toss of the head, and Holmes stood, listening to the telephone ringing in the room below which Russell's farm manager slept.

After twenty-seven rings, the buzzing sound cut abruptly off. The scrape of chair-legs on tile, the sound of a weight thumping down. A throat being cleared, an unshaven face being rubbed into wakefulness, and finally a syllable that might have been, "Yes?"

"Patrick, this is Sherlock Holmes. Has Jacob Russell returned to Sussex?"

CHAPTER SEVENTEEN

RUSSELL

"I don't care for sea travel," I told my companion.

Army rucksack over one shoulder, hat clamped firmly onto his head, he looked out across the Channel. We had stayed the previous night in Holyhead, and were tossing our way towards Dublin's port of Dunleary. "I don't know that I'd call this a sea," he remarked.

"My eyes agree with you. My stomach does not."

"Ah. Gotcha. I thought maybe your coming up on deck was one of those modern fads, fresh air and clean living."

I squinted at the morning through my rain-splattered glasses, hoping for a glimpse of terra firma ahead. "The fresher, the better."

"You want some distraction?"

"So long as it doesn't involve taking my eyes off of the horizon."

"Did your father ever talk to you about the Russell family in Ireland?"

"Just mentions of it, here and there. He thought they came over in 1066 with the Normans, and some of them ended up in Ireland. I did ask him once about them, and he said I should talk to my grandfather."

I could feel him looking at me. "It doesn't sound like you did."

"It was about then I realised that they disapproved of my mother, probably because she was Jewish. They were very polite about it, but I could tell. And neither of my parents really denied it. So I was polite, too. But it did mean that I never instigated a conversation with them unless I had to."

"I do understand," he said. "Although if it wasn't her faith they disliked, it would have been something else."

"I'm not sure that helps."

"No. Though it is too bad, the old man would have enjoyed telling you about the family."

For a moment, I felt a pulse of longing. At the age of fifteen, I had cut myself off from the Russells for anything more intimate than my semi-annual letters: perhaps it was time—and then I shook off the melancholy regret. "Jake, the last time I was there, they wanted to take me to church."

He laughed. "Yeah, that sounds like them—if there's something inconvenient, just ignore it and it'll go away."

"And that is precisely what I did."

"Well, I'll do my best as an uncle to fill in the gaps. Like the name itself: French, meaning red-haired. Though I don't remember any real red-heads in the family for a couple of generations. Yours is about the closest."

I was grateful to leave behind the inner confidences. "If there were, the colour would probably be due more to the Irish blood than the original Norman."

"The Russells had land scattered across the southern counties, but like I said, their main estate was down near Waterford."

"I wonder if the house is still standing."

"As far as I know the IRA hasn't burned it yet, but last time I was here, the house itself was abandoned."

I took my eyes off the waves long enough to glance at him. "You've seen it?"

"I spent a day poking around it, a few years ago. You should go.

The house itself isn't much, but the countryside is beautiful—green, of course, with woodland and a small river. There's a hill about five miles from the house that some keen amateur archaeologists dug up, and decided it had been a Viking village. And in the other direction, you can see the remnants of a stone circle, mostly overgrown by trees. Then when I was in the local pub, one of the regulars told me there was an Ogham stone up in the woods, though no one else there had ever seen it. You know what those are?"

"Ancient Celtic writing carved into an upright stone. Oh, I'd love to see it."

"And—do you remember a painting in your grandparents' house, woman in a kind of greeny dress? It used to hang in the hallway next to the door to the dining room."

I took my eyes off the comforting distance again to look at his face. His expression hadn't changed, but his voice had, in a way that indicated this question mattered.

"I do. One of the few family portraits that looked like an actual person."

"She had a sort of gleam in her eyes, didn't she? Like she understood why a kid might want to get into mischief. Anyway, it was a little hard to see, but if you looked at it on an afternoon when the sun was coming in the windows, you could make out that same standing stone circle, off in the distance. Years and years of cigar smoke didn't help any, but the background was hazy to begin with, like the artist hadn't wanted to clutter his portrait with a bunch of rocks. Ladies ought to have lap-dogs or musical instruments around them, not stone-age monuments."

I laughed. "Interesting choice."

"Interesting woman. Her name was Maria, your—let's see . . . great-great-great-great-grandmother? Born about 1720. She was the amateur archaeologist—the early one. I think there were Victorians who went poking around, a century or so later. Would that make her an antiquarian? Either way, it just meant a person went out with some muscular servants and mucked around in the dirt looking for Roman mosaics or old coins. And in fact, Maria did find a sort of hoard."

"Really? Coins?" This part of the world had a long tradition of treasure hoards overturned by a plough or wrenched to light when a storm toppled an ancient tree.

"A few coins and a couple pieces of jewellery in the smashed remains of a little clay pot. In fact, if you've seen the painting of Maria, you've seen the brooch she found."

I frowned in thought. "I thought she was wearing pearls?" Three loops, against the expanse of pale chest that fashion demanded at the time.

"Good memory. The brooch is at her waist, half-hidden under a fold of fabric." He smiled. "I'd probably have missed it, but Father gave Charlie and me a lecture about it one time. He called it the 'Russell brooch,' and when Charlie asked what happened to it, he said that Maria's father had presented it to some royal society in Dublin. I was a kid at the time, but I remember thinking it was unfair that the family hadn't let Maria keep it."

"It's probably in a museum somewhere. Was it Viking?"

"How would I know? I do remember he used the word 'filigree' about it—I'd never heard that word before and it sounded so romantic, it stuck with me."

"Sounds more Celtic than Viking. I'll write to the museum in Dublin and see if they know what's become of it. I'd like to see Maria's find. Celtic jewellery can be lovely."

He stood beside me for a minute, looking across the choppy water, then shivered. "I think if you don't mind . . ."

"Go below, get yourself warm. And thanks for the distraction."

He touched my arm and left. I stood, battered by wind and thinking about my ancestress with the gleam in her eyes and a piece of exquisite jewellery given away by her family. Celts were settled here when the early Christians arrived, some four centuries after their Messiah died. Viking raiders showed up some four hundred years after that, and in the twelfth century, the Anglo-Normans swept in, invited by an Irish King desperate to regain his lost crown—and once the English were here, they stayed. There were others, of course, over the millennia—Picts venturing down from their northern kingdom, the odd Roman who decided that England wasn't rainy enough for him, Spaniards who escaped the slaughter of an armada, other sailors left behind by ship-wreck or trading venture.

It was odd, I realised, that I had never made the effort to visit Ireland. Granted, the island was still fighting its way out of a brutal and acrimonious period of civil war, but so was Palestine, and I had not hesitated to go there, to seize the chance to walk in the footsteps of my mother's people. It had simply never occurred to me that I might do the same for my father's.

Perhaps I should spend some time here. If for nothing else than to see the small piece of jewellery that tied together the Celtic peoples and the Vikings with a family of eighteenth-century Norman-turned-English landholders.

However, I didn't imagine this trip was going to offer much opportunity for museum-going and sight-seeing.

I was cold to the bone by the time Jake came up to claim me, unable to object as he steered me like an old woman along the terminal docks towards the Royal Marine Hotel, where the restaurant felt positively tropical. The teacup slowly drove the ice from my fingers and the quease from my innards.

When we came out again, pink of cheek and freshly combed of hair, I was surprised to find it a pleasant autumnal day, with the gales calmed and the storm clouds turned to wisps of cotton wool.

The train into Dublin waited directly across from the hotel. However, as we stood before the vast Victorian pile, Jake was looking around for something.

"The train station is over there," I said, wondering if now his eyes were going.

"It is, but—let's try this way. And let your accent go more American, it'll make people happier."

"What are we after?" I asked, taking care to harden my T's and bite into my R's.

"And don't forget, we're Catholics here."

"I'm not going to wear a cross or a wimple."

He glanced down at what I had put on that morning: a perfectly ordinary skirt and a pair of walking boots that had been polished in the not-too-distant past. "We'll stand out too much here," he said. When I looked pointedly at a passing group that would have been unremarkable in London itself, he added, "In the countryside, I mean. Women wear long skirts, aprons, and a shawl. Men wear cloth caps and sagging tweed. And, I'm afraid, brogues."

"So we need a men's wear store."

"I think—"

"Uncle Jake, I am not going to trudge across Ireland in an apron and shawl. My hair's short enough to tuck under a cap. Men's wear," I repeated firmly.

He raised a hand in surrender. "Men's wear it is."

We had to go well away from the docks to find the kind of shop that catered to individuals who would be required to enter the Royal Marine Hotel through its service doors. On the other hand, it cost us a pittance to outfit ourselves. And the suits we ended up with, while a considerable step up from those of manual labourers and farmers, were drab enough not to declare us as foreign until we got up close, and justified the additional bulk in my valise and Jake's rucksack.

They were warm, too, the kind of wool that took the rain a long time to permeate.

Back at the station, we bought tickets for Dublin, then south, to a line that meandered through some admittedly lovely countryside for what seemed a very long time. At some point during Jake's lengthy discourse on the family whose house we were going to investigate—yes, the "Mahony" family, headed by The O'Mahony, half-brother of Arthur Vicars, under whose supervision the Irish Crown Jewels had disappeared—my body decided that this was as good a time as any to catch up on my sleep.

And when I woke, we were in another world.

CHAPTER EIGHTEEN

RUSSELL

Dunleary had stunk of fish and industry, and Dublin itself had smelt like any other city, a blanket of coal, diesel, and petrol, with notes of wet wool and horse dung.

County Kerry was on the other side of Ireland, and we were now less than twenty miles from the Atlantic. Here, once the locomotive had whistled and chuffed away, I stood and drew in a deep breath. The air smelt of greenery and sheep droppings, of the ham in someone's smokehouse and a long, long memory of blood in the ground. Sweat and freshly turned soil from the man digging potatoes on the other side of the low wall. Bread baking from the house, offset by the miasma of boiling cabbage. And . . . "Is that peat smoke?" I asked.

"It is," Jake said, "though they call it 'turf' here." He handed me the valise that he'd carried from the train, and I followed him through a low wall and into what seemed to be a little village. A cow lay chewing in a velvety green field. A rook scolded from somewhere. Everything was very green and very quiet.

It was not quite raining, although the air was wet and soft.

"I see nothing resembling a hotel," I said to my relative.

"The public house will have rooms," he said. "But we're only a mile from Kilmorna House itself."

That sounded more hopeful.

The road was a road, not a mere muddy track, which pleased the ankle I had twisted a few weeks earlier. There were no motorcars. Houses were small, whitewashed stone, and mostly thatched, with tiny windows and half-doors at the front, the tops open for ventilation, the bottoms shut to keep out the livestock. We passed various residents—an old man perched on a donkey-cart, two women in long skirts carrying a cage of chickens between them, a barefoot urchin hurrying a goat along the road. One tiny woman led a large donkey, its two panniers heavily laden with blocks of cut peat—*turf*, I reminded myself. All the men wore cloth caps, baggy trousers with mended knees, and shoes that might have been forged by a blacksmith. The women, as Jake had said, wore headscarves, long-sleeved blouses, and calf-length skirts, with woollen shawls crossed over the chest and tucked into their coarsely woven aprons. Only the men smoked—pipes, not cigarettes. I saw no gloves, and little bright colour. All paused to stare as we came into view. We nodded, touched our hats to the ladies, and trudged past.

Jake had said it was a mile from the train stop, but if so, it was an Irish mile, and a long one at that. Another time, I would have enjoyed the stroll, but as the road grew rougher, my ankle began to protest, and around us the soft Irish mist began to consider turning to actual rain. We left the road and followed a drive that really was not.

No more than the house at its end was a house.

"It's a ruin!" I exclaimed.

"'Fraid so," he agreed.

There once had been a handsome terraced garden easing down to the curve of a small river, but its shrubs and wide granite steps were now half-buried by exuberant bramble and ivy, the stone of its terraces home to sprouting weeds. As we approached through the mist, I realised that the walls were an empty façade, that the decorative chimneys rose up through no roof, that only the outer-facing branches of the mature shade trees had any life in them.

He'd told me the place had burned three years ago, but he had not said it had been consumed down to its merest shell.

"Jake, there's nothing here," I protested.

"Oh, there's plenty," he said.

"Yes—charred timbers and broken glass." Broken everything, it looked like.

"Come, around the back."

Kilmorna House had been a grand manor, one of several either bought or inherited by Pierce Charles de Lacy O'Mahony. Arthur Vicars' half-brother was an ardent Nationalist who had, according to Jake, more or less invented the rôle of clan chieftain to style himself "The O'Mahony of Kerry." There were no indications that a rebuilding was under way, or even under consideration. Although if I owned a country house in Ireland, I might also wait until the IRA had abandoned its sport of setting alight houses with any faint link to England.

As I picked my way after my uncle, I began to see signs of activity. Call it "scavenging" or "looting," three years of small-scale retrieval operations had resulted in paths cleared through the rubble. Hazardous timbers had been dragged to less life-threatening positions, and heaps of smashed or melted kitchenware, scorched paintings, clothing too damaged to repair, and general débris awaited further attentions. Dozens of twisted lamps and candlesticks indicated that the house had not been converted to electricity.

"Here we go." Jake's voice came from around the house, so I threaded my way through several lead-frame windows in the process of being prised apart and over a half-dismembered suit of armour to what, judging by the massive slab of iron cook-stove glimpsed within, had been the kitchen.

The rubbish here consisted of misshapen pans and shattered

crockery rather than gilded frames and porcelain dogs. I looked around, but there was no sign of my uncle.

"Jake?"

"In here," he called.

Eyeing the looming walls, which looked as if a good sneeze would bring them down, I thought about going back for the helmet from the suit of armour. Instead, I tip-toed closer and saw Jake disappearing around an inside wall. "Is that really a good idea?" I said, keeping my voice low. He didn't hear me—at any rate, he did not reply. I repeated the query in slightly louder tones, and winced at the sound of scraping and a thud from within. "Are you all right?"

"Oh, yes. It's a bit of a mess but the walls look sound enough. You coming?"

I could just imagine what Holmes would say at the news that his wife's feet had been discovered sticking out from under several tons of derelict Irish manor house. However, the looters' pathway here was clear, more so than at the front door, so I found a dry spot to leave my valise and edged inside, trying to watch the littered floor and the crumbling walls simultaneously.

I cringed at another slithering thump. "Must you do that?" I demanded.

Here he was at last, peering into the space beneath a timber as wide around as my waist, which the fire had turned into thirty feet of black, alligator-skin char. "Leaning on that will probably snap it," I said.

"Do you think so?" He sounded interested, and to my horror put his hands on the upper surface and jumped against it experimentally.

"Stop that!"

He stopped, but only because the lack of a collapse indicated that the deep crackling was entirely on the surface, leaving plenty of ancient oak at the core. He rummaged around in his rucksack and pulled out a powerful little torch, ducking blithely under the massive timber and disappearing into the hole. His torch came on, giving glimpses of a room within.

I peered around the fallen beam, trying to avoid touching it. On the other side lay a self-contained little room: no windows, no other door, and wooden shelves that showed not the slightest touch of fire. Beneath my feet I could make out the shape of a door, but it was no ordinary wooden door. Iron, judging by the rust around its flaking paint and the shattered edge where its hinges had been. Someone had been very determined to get at what was inside this space. "Was this the butler's pantry?" An iron door seemed excessive, but in any such house, the silver would have been kept behind lock and key, and if the house had no dedicated safe, the odd necklace or jewelled stick-pin might have been kept here, as well.

But Jake was shaking his head. "Better than that. This was the strong-room."

That would explain the iron door and the unburnt shelves. "A bit elaborate, I'd have thought, for a country house."

"It's a long way to the nearest bank, and Kilmorna would have had a lot of pay-packets to cover every month."

"Looks like whoever broke in blew the door right off its hinges. That seems very determined." To say nothing of suicidal: one assumes they'd used a very slow fuse and stood well back.

"That would have been the police, looking for the guns."

"Guns?"

"There was a rumour that Vicars was storing guns for the other landlords, those who had taken their families off to the safety of England. But . . ." His face appeared in the gap, a black smear across his forehead. "There was an earlier IRA raid here, a year before the one when they killed him. The police assumed they were after the guns, but there were also rumours that he had the Crown Jewels in here."

"Hardly surprising," I said. "The things had never turned up, and suspicion would have lingered. Why didn't that earlier IRA gang force him to open the door?"

"They tried. He refused."

"Really?" I drew back, looking around at the devastation. What he'd told me of Arthur Vicars did not make him sound like someone who would stand up to a group of armed rebel soldiers.

"Personally, I think he would have opened it, if all it held was the neighbours' shotguns and deer rifles. But the Jewels? I can see that he might rather die than have them come to light. Speaking of which, aren't you coming in?"

"You want me in there?" My innards twisted at the idea.

"It's probably safer than where you're standing," he pointed out. "And I was hoping your sharp eyes might be able to spot his hiding place within the hiding place."

Oh, right—those "skills" that he'd brought me for. I took a steadying breath and dropped to a squat, threading myself inside without so much as brushing my coat against the beam.

Too small for a butler's pantry, the room was an eight-foot cube, its ceiling a bit lower than the rooms outside appeared to have been. Whatever had once been stored on those shelves was long gone. Marks on the floor suggested that someone had even swept the leavings in search of small valuables, although a faint whiff of stale urine equally suggested their displeasure at having found nothing.

"Vicars had some work done in here, not long after the first IRA visit," Jake said, his torch-light probing the room's corners. "He must have known that they'd be back, yet he was more concerned with keeping things hidden than he was with the safety of himself and his wife."

"How do you know? That he had work done?" I could see no obvious signs that the original walls had been amended.

"I have a . . . an informant. Who worked in the house before it burned. Here, take the light—I want to move some of these shelves."

I automatically accepted the torch as he began to rip the wooden shelves from their mounts and stack them in a bare corner. He had brought, I noted, not only a strong light, but a stout jemmy for prising things apart. How much else was he keeping from me?

"Tell me about this informant," I asked.

"A housemaid. Woman named Kathleen Walsh. In her early forties now, she worked for Lady Vicars before the marriage—can you grab that end? Thanks. Lady Vicars—Gertrude Wright as was, Yorkshire girl whose sister was married to Vicars' nephew, Pierce Mahony, and lived with the Mahonys in Kilmurry House, which isn't far from here. She was eight or ten years older than Sir Arthur, and more or less came with the house, you might say. Any rate, Mrs Walsh had been with Lady Vicars for a couple of years at Kilmurry, then came here with two or three other servants after the marriage."

"Is Lady Vicars still alive?"

"Oh, yes, in her seventies but going strong. The Mahonys kept her on after Vicars died, though she's now moved to a seaside town near Bristol."

"And Mrs Walsh?"

"Her, too. Although I'd say she's finding life in what you'd call a 'watering-place' a bit dull."

"Hence her willingness to provide you with information."

"About a wreck of a house? Sure. I doubt she'd tell me what her ladyship had for breakfast, but Kilmorna might as well be ancient history. And I'm not sure she ever had much loyalty to Sir Arthur."

"How much did you pay her?"

"Not much, if you're thinking of hard cash. Though if you mean how much in time and effort, the price was a bit high. I also—can you catch that?" I intercepted a sliding board and helped ease it to the floor. He held out a hand for the torch, then stepped back, playing the strong beam over the newly uncovered walls. "What do you think?"

The lines where the shelves had rested did resemble seams in the wall, but all fell away to a brushing hand. The floor was more difficult, being still thick with dust, so we ended up feeling our way along it, tapping for a hint to what lay beneath, poking with a knife-blade and pressing to search for something that was loose. To our growing puzzlement, we found nothing but undisturbed tiles.

Gingerly working two now-filthy fingers into a pocket, I took out my own, smaller torch and shone it to the ceiling. Other than ancient cobwebs, there were even fewer marks on that surface than on the walls.

Which left only one feature in the entire room: a sturdy decorative bracket with a hook at the end for hanging up a lamp. Its round base, stamped with petals like a daisy, was nearly ten inches across.

"How large were the St Patrick's Regalia?" I asked.

"Big," he said.

"Big" as a descriptor for diamonds was not exactly an objective term. "How big?"

"Larger than my palm. It was the collars that were bulky."

I pocketed my torch and dragged some of the shelf boards over to make a step, climbing up on them to see if the hook might be detachable. The decorative base had four screw-holes—or appeared to. The heads of screws filled the top and bottom holes. The right-hand hole had nothing in it, as far as I could tell. The one on the left had what looked like a tiny, inset button. I poked at it, but three years of dampness had rusted it immobile.

"Does your pen-knife have a screw-driver in it?" I asked. My hands were already so grubby, I didn't want to dig into my own pocket.

I felt it hit my outstretched palm, and applied it to the nearest screw, the one at the bottom. It was frozen, so locked up I could hear the knife's blade creak. I tried the topmost one instead. It resisted, then gave a little, and after that it was mine, although the screw proved surprisingly long. When it came free at last, I pulled the entire hook around, using the bottom screw as a swivel, until the hook dangled from the one remaining fastener. I leaned back so Jake could see.

The decorative base had concealed a circle of efficient-looking steel with a combination dial. A small, very sturdy, and eminently fireproof safe. Fortunately, it didn't appear to have rusted too badly.

I looked down at the torch Jake was shining onto the safe, noting the faint but perceptible motion of the hand that held it. And I thought about his slightly too-loud voice, both of which were a result of his being "just a little blown up." By comparison, my own absolutely motionless hand on the torch, my ears that could pick up the whisper of moisture dripping outside of the strong-room door.

My skills, indeed.

CHAPTER NINETEEN

SHERLOCK HOLMES

As always, Holmes' first impulse upon learning that Russell had done something potentially hazardous was to go after her. And as usual, his internal response—reminding himself that she was not a child, that she had proved her competence numerous times over the years, and that she would be furious at being judged less than able—eventually muscled itself to the fore.

He did, however, spend another pipe's worth of tobacco in front of the fire, considering the nature of family loyalty.

She had not seen her uncle—correction: she had not knowingly seen her uncle—since December 1911. Holmes himself had been away at the time, on a case in Munich that some years later led to the investigation of a German spy ring—one of Mycroft's requests, speaking of family loyalty—and came home to find that a local pub had changed hands in a mysterious fashion.

The publican himself had been both new and universally disliked, since he had been running a regular, highly illegal poker game that brought in undesirable elements from all over Sussex, Kent, and even London. But oddly, the man had then lost the pub itself in a game of cards—only to have the winner sell it for a fraction of its worth to Tillie Whiteneck, a local woman with more kitchen skills than monetary resources.

Both men had then disappeared.

The unlikeliness of the thing, and a certain degree of responsibility for crimes that took place practically in his back garden, led Holmes to look into the matter.

First, the publican himself: he turned out to have other options, and indeed he had already begun to suspect that his venture into a Downs village might prove less lucrative than he had imagined. Satisfied that the man did not seem likely to be bent on revenge against the local residents, Holmes sent the information he had gathered to the official forces, which would keep the man busy for some time.

Second, the woman who had benefitted: it took less than a morning to eliminate Tillie Whiteneck from suspicion. No woman who had deliberately helped to steal a pub could possibly have acted with such innocent, disbelieving delight in her good fortune.

Which left the card-player himself: a man named Jacob Russell, related to a London family who spent the occasional school holiday on the Downs. It seemed a most unlikely source of criminality—the husband was a wealthy American, the wife the daughter of a London rabbi, of all things—until he'd tracked down one or two participants in the night's poker game, and discovered an oddity: that Jacob Russell had been accompanied that night by the family's two children.

He dug further, and eventually came to the conclusion that Jacob Russell had actually employed his niece and nephew to help con the publican out of his establishment. That the pub-owner was both criminal and unpopular did not change the fact that Jake had used two children to commit a crime.

Had used them, one might almost say, as his Irregulars.

And yet, nothing about the matter proved simple. Jacob Russell had profited little from the sale of his winnings. And so far as

Holmes could find out, the children were not hardened criminals themselves. In any event, the Russell family moved away to America not long after, without Uncle Jacob.

Holmes had eventually concluded that the matter was of no further interest to the Downs neighbourhood, and thought little more about the matter until Russell herself had entertained him with her own memories of the affair, one evening a year or two ago.

At that reminder, Holmes had been curious enough to make a further series of enquiries, and though the results had proved thought-provoking, they did not alarm him any more than what he had learned ten years earlier. Russell's uncle was a thief and a scoundrel, whose career was marked by a certain degree of versatility. Card games were a regular part of his oeuvre, but also straight-out confidence tricks. Earlier in his career, he had been a highly successful second-storey man, who would ingratiate himself into the life of a victim, deeply enough to learn where valuables were kept, and when the victim was away, asleep, or occupied in a distant room, he would climb a ladder or a convenient trellis and help himself.

Both cards and burglary were pursuits that required smooth acting skills and steady nerves. However, so far as Holmes could determine, the man had never committed an act of violence. Nor, apparently, had he used children again.

Holmes had not told Russell the results of his wide-ranging enquiry. Had she ever decided to go looking for her uncle, rather than merely assuming that he was dead, he would have given her everything he knew. Until she made that move, he would allow her uncle's memory to remain in the shadows.

Nor had Holmes made any move to interfere with Jacob Russell himself. Someone who had taken care to hide the involvement of two children fourteen years ago was unlikely to be a threat to an adult niece.

Had matters changed now?

Russell's note used the words "friend" and "nice," both of which were deliberate signifiers of her lack of alarm. She had gone off with the man by choice (no blood on the floorboards—his eyes had immediately gone to the space under the window, when he found her missing).

Patrick admitted that he knew Jacob Russell was in Sussex, but did not know what the man had wanted, or where he and Russell might have gone.

To go any further might force an appeal to Mycroft, a step he would prefer to avoid even without the complication of the old woman in Nanterre.

Still, Holmes did not believe in coincidences. It was not mere happenstance that Russell's small, blond, criminal uncle had stepped back into her life at the very moment that a small, blond man was being debated in the context of the Irish Crown Jewels theft.

He would give them two days.

And then he would go looking.

CHAPTER TWENTY

JAKE

I knew, even without seeing, that what had caused Mary to go silent could only be one thing, but I didn't say a word. I figured that starting out with, "So, can you open it?" might earn me a kick in the teeth. (And the girl wore very sturdy boots.)

"Did you know this was going to be here?" she asked. (Her voice was a touch icy.)

"I told you Vicars'd had work done."

"I thought you meant he'd pulled up the floorboards or something. Jake, combination locks are a bear to crack."

"I know," I said. She turned to glare down at me; I turned to look down at the torch in my hand. I may have exaggerated the shakes a little—I know, the *poor me* routine—but I'd never been much for safe-cracking (even before those idiots that I was working with last April set off the explosion early and threw me top over tea-kettle) and now, well, I'd tried working a combination dial before starting all this, and I doubted I could do it. I did actually need a partner. Someone who both knew what they were doing and had steady hands and first-rate hearing.

I raised my head and gave her my most winning smile.

She gave me an expression exactly like Charlie's: exasperated and not fooled for a moment. "How could you possibly guess that I knew anything about breaking into a safe?"

"With a husband like yours, how could you not?"

She stared, then shrugged her admission of defeat. "I don't suppose you brought a stethoscope?"

My smile went wider, and I bent down to dig it out of my knapsack.

CHAPTER TWENTY-ONE

RUSSELL

I looked at the little wooden ear-trumpet Jake was holding, and shook my head. If I'd known from the beginning what this trip would involve, I would have come better prepared. As in, proper tools, a change of clothing, and a flask of hot tea.

"We need to come back in the morning," I said. "This is going to be hard enough with warm hands, and the sun will be down in a couple of hours." Did he intend to sleep here amongst the ruins? Did he have spare torch batteries in that bottomless rucksack? Did I really want to do this? In my years with Holmes, I had been dragged into any number of mad events, but nothing quite as daft as looting the burnt shell of a derelict Irish manor house.

"Let's at least try," he wheedled.

I snatched the primitive medical device from his hand. "This will take at least an hour, and longer if I'm distracted. Why don't you walk back to the village and locate some rooms and a meal? And if the place collapses around my ears, you can bring people to dig me out."

"You sure?"

"Go."

He went, taking his torch and rucksack with him. I listened to his footsteps fade, and got to work.

Safe-cracking, as I had told him, required absolute focus—not easy to attain while standing in a black hole surrounded by teetering stones. I switched off my torch, slid it into a pocket, and waited for my pulse to slow.

The house creaked with every faint breeze, but it did not collapse. The darkness pressed in, but if I kept my eyes shut, it was somehow less threatening. *Listen to your breath, Russell.* In, out. Slow, steady. I had no need of sight, or scent, or taste. The only sense impressions I required were hearing and touch: listening for the tiny variations in the clicks of the mechanism, and feeling for the faint differences in the dial's movements. I had done this before. No one was going to disturb me. A safe this small was unlikely to be particularly complex. All I needed to do was focus.

I raised my hand in the darkness, and paused at a memory.

I'd learned from an expert, in the company of an aristocrat, who had remarked, "You'll feel like a bloomin' fool if the thing was open when you found it, and spinnin' the dial only locks 'er up."

Obediently, I tugged at the handle on this one, but no, it had not been left unlocked.

I spun the dial to reset the mechanism, nestled the wooden trumpet into my ear, set it against the metal, and got to work.

CHAPTER TWENTY-TWO

Russell

And of course, the damned thing was empty.

CHAPTER TWENTY-THREE

JAKE

I have to say, I wasn't really surprised that we didn't find the Jewels at Kilmorna House, but I'd had to be sure before we could move on. However, my niece was in no condition to be told what would come next, since she was both short-tempered and exhausted (and no doubt needing to be fed) as she came out from the remains of the one-time kitchen and found me huddled on the terrace under my umbrella.

Yes, it was raining.

And despite the umbrella, she was also soaked through, limping (though I don't think the limp was my fault), and smelling of the flock of sheep that we had followed up the road by the time we reached what passed for a village inn. I sat her before the fire (my nephew, I told the man in charge of the Guinness—the poor boy'd been so ill over in New York) and brought her a hot whiskey followed by a vast plate of mutton stew, but I knew full well that if I'd tried to suggest our next steps, chances were good she'd overturn the stew on my head and walk out into the night.

Instead, I sent her up to a bed that, though lumpy and laid with musty blankets, was at least warm and free of wildlife. I spent the evening gossiping in my best American accent with the locals.

There may also have been a great deal of boisterous music.

In the morning, I paid for my pints of Guinness with a grim headache, while Mary beamed with the good cheer of her youth. She may even have been exaggerating her wholesome state, to rub it in. (God, she looked so like Charlie.)

"I expect you have some plan for the day?" she said, helping herself to a cup of powerful tea from a chipped and stained stoneware pot, then adding a generous dose of creamy milk from an elegant porcelain jug. I topped up my own cup (the tea was so dark, it nearly counted as coffee) and took care to tuck the Kilmorna House jug behind the larger pot when I finished. Perhaps she would not notice.

"I do." I sliced into my plate of what the Irish call "bacon," more like boiled ham than the crisp American stuff I had grown up with.

"Kathleen Walsh?" she asked.

I nearly choked on the bite, and had to wash it down with a swig of the peat-stream tea. "You a mind-reader, girl?"

She gave me a complacent smile. "I once accused Holmes of that. But no, I merely pay attention to detail. Such as, your lack of surprise when I told you the safe was empty, or the way that milk jug is from a rather better quality of table-ware than the teapot. Anything of value in that house has long since been carried away."

"We needed to check."

"You don't imagine that, if someone had found those Jewels, everyone in Ireland wouldn't know?"

"That'd depend on who found them, wouldn't you say?"

She thought about it, and nodded. "Fair enough. But if you weren't actually expecting them to be hidden in the strong-room, where do you propose to find them?"

I liked the "propose." (Way better than "hope.") (Unless she was being snarky? I don't think she was being snarky.) I arranged another dollop of jam on my toast.

"Like I said, the cops blasted off the strong-room door looking for firearms, as soon as the house cooled down. The safe itself had only gone in, like I said, the previous year after the first IRA visit. The servants had to've known it was there. And after the door was down, someone either knew the combination, or had the skills to open it."

"Closing it neatly behind them?" Mary asked. "It's more likely that Vicars himself changed his mind and moved the Jewels. The first attack must have made him nervous. Hidden safe or no, common sense would have told him that the IRA would be back, and they would find a way into the strong-room sooner or later."

"Common sense wasn't one of Vicars' chief characteristics," I told her. "But you're right. Any number of people could have got into the safe. But who of those would've just hung onto the Jewels and not tried to sell them? Say one of the servants—or the men who'd installed the safe—suddenly came into money. Wouldn't their friends and family start to talk? Or the IRA—they'd have been shouting it aloud before the sun went down."

"That leaves Vicars or his wife. Even if it wasn't a love match, he would have trusted her."

"*Might* have trusted her," I corrected her. "But I agree. There weren't a lot of people left to him." Though his brother, The O'Mahony . . . No, that would have required Vicars to admit his stupidity, at the very least, to the head of the family, the man who'd supported and fought for him all those years.

Mary buttered her slab of soda bread, corner to corner, lost in thought. "Lady Vicars was, what, in her middle sixties when Sir Arthur was killed?"

"Somewhere in there."

"Would she have been capable of climbing in through that wreckage to retrieve the things?"

I had to think about it. I'd known a lot of women in their seventh decade who would not hesitate to skip around among the fallen beams—some of them with titles and big houses—but Lady Vicars? I'd only seen her at a distance, and though she looked fit enough, I had to shake my head. "She'd have had to feel truly desperate. And even so, she'd have taken along someone she trusted."

"Someone like a housemaid she'd known for years."

"Someone like Kathleen Walsh," I agreed. I'd zeroed in on Mrs Walsh as someone who might remember Vicars' comings and goings during those key times, and found that she not only remembered, she was willing to gossip—up to a point. But she'd definitely been keeping things back from me. And I suspected there were brains behind the dither. Mary could be right: Mrs Walsh might have been actively involved.

"If Lady Vicars knew that her husband had the Jewels," I wondered aloud, "and she and Mrs Walsh retrieved them after he died, what do you suppose she'd do with them?"

"Was she in need of money?"

"Does anyone not need money? But no, she doesn't seem eager to live beyond her means."

"Then I'd say that, as with her husband, the risk of shame might have been a greater consideration than converting diamonds into cash."

"You think she'd just keep them hidden away?"

"It's possible." Mary thought, then shook her head. "However, in my experience, the more servants in a house, the harder it is to keep secrets. Some industrious maid out to do the spring-cleaning might easily come across them."

I busied myself with the ends of my bacon, and said, "Unless Lady Vicars followed her husband's example and had a private safe installed in her new house."

Mary's knife clattered onto the plate. I gave her my most encouraging expression. She glared.

"No," she said. "Oh no."

"It'll probably be an identical one," I reassured her. "And there's a good chance she had it set up with the same combination. And it definitely won't be in a ruin that's about to fall down on you."

I let the daggers she was looking just bounce right off me, and in the end (it was by no means a sure thing) I won. She picked up her toast and bit off a corner, chewing away as if she were ripping into my ear.

When she had swallowed it down, she growled, "I am not breaking into another safe without the proper equipment."

CHAPTER TWENTY-FOUR

RUSSELL

The more Jake told me about the housemaid, Mrs Walsh, the more complicated she sounded. She was not the housekeeper, that position of high authority in any country house, yet she was more than a mere domestic. She seemed to function somewhere between a lady's maid and a secretary—what was known as a companion, although Jake's description sounded more like a troublesome younger sister.

In any event, she'd been with Lady Vicars for several years.

And she had retreated to England with her employer, following the trauma of Vicars' execution and the destruction of Kilmorna House.

"You said that this house Lady Vicars moved into, the one that may or may not have a safe, is near Bristol."

"Town called 'Clevedon.' Seaside resort—well, it's the Severn's estuary, but close."

"Why move there?"

"She likes to take the waters, maybe? The town has hydropathics and what-not. Anyway, Mrs Walsh seemed to think that Lady Vicars wanted a complete break."

"Knocking the dust from her sandals? A seaside watering-place is fine for a bit of rejuvenation, but I'd have thought she would move back home. Did she no longer have family there—Yorkshire, you said?"

"All I know is that her sister, the reason Lady Vicars was in Ireland to begin with, died suddenly two days after the Vicarses' wedding. It wouldn't be too surprising if Lady Vicars wanted a place that didn't remind her of anything at all."

"And," I mused, "Somerset is a nice distance from the IRA."

"Plus that nobody'd think to connect Somerset with the Irish Crown Jewels."

"In your nice gossip sessions with Mrs Walsh, I don't suppose she happened to admit that Lady Vicars had a safe installed when she moved to Clevedon?"

"They did have renovations done. However, the two were in a London hotel during much of the work, and Lady Vicars dealt with some of the negotiations herself. Which sounded to me as if she was up to something she didn't want even Mrs Walsh to know about."

"Possible," I agreed. "But she'd only spent, what, five years of her life married? Spinsters and widows do get accustomed to overseeing things themselves. It could have been practicality rather than secrecy."

"But you'd agree that if she found the Jewels after Vicars died, she'd hang onto them, and take them with her when she moved?" he asked.

I plucked at a few crumbs on my plate, thinking about diamonds. I'd never liked the things, finding their dazzle harsh, more about power than beauty. Men bought their wives diamonds to declare that they could afford to splash money on sparkle. Governments seized them from colonies, displaying them on their chests and heads for ceremonies. Give me an emerald or ruby anytime.

But that was not the point, was it? Lady Vicars wasn't about to wear the Irish Crown Jewels around her neck. And she could hardly have them remounted into a spectacular necklace and tiara without attracting questions.

I had to shrug. "Unless she had some other place where she thought they'd be safe, like here in Ireland."

"Well," he reflected, "I did hear a theory that they were buried in Kilmurry Castle."

"Kilmurry—her sister's house?"

"The house and the castle are next to each other, and yes, it was where Lady Vicars lived before marrying Sir Arthur. Rumour has it there's a tunnel between the house and the castle ruins."

"Oh God—not more ruins?"

"These are older. Cromwell's work, I think."

Who had finished defeating Ireland by 1653. "I would guess there's even less of the castle standing than there was of Kilmorna House."

"A few partial walls. Possibly a tunnel."

"No," I said in a flat voice. "You're not getting me into a tunnel that's been collapsing for three hundred years."

"We should at least look."

"You look. I'll stay here by the fire." It was an inviting fire, glowing blocks of turf that had probably not gone out for the last century or so. Perhaps Cromwell's men had sat around it, resting up from a day spent crushing Ireland underfoot.

"Oh, come on, it's just down the road, the train goes right to it. You can sit under my umbrella and go for the police if the place comes down on my head."

Well, he *was* my uncle. I suppose I owed my father's brother at least that much . . .

He saw my face change and reached over to slap my shoulder. "That's my girl, finish up your tea."

The train tracks did lead more or less directly to Kilmurry—or at least to a town not more than five miles away.

A town where, after we'd hired a passing donkey-cart to jolt and splash us out to the castle ruins and back, and after we failed completely to penetrate the rumoured tunnel, we spent a second night in Ireland.

This time, I sent Holmes a cable so he wouldn't start summoning the troops.

CHAPTER TWENTY-FIVE

SHERLOCK HOLMES

Holmes reread the telegram, as if its message might have changed since he'd ripped open the flimsy envelope.

> APOLOGIES FOR ABSENCE UNCLE JAKE REAPPEARED NEEDING HELP MORE COMPLICATED THAN FIRST THOUGHT BUT HOPE TO BE HOME TOMORROW DEPENDING ON WEATHER OFF ROSSLARE THOUGH MAY BE LATE.

He frowned at the superfluity: three of the final four words could have been omitted, by saying "HOPE TO BE HOME LATE TOMORROW" rather than pay extra for the afterthought. Was there any significance in that?

He glanced up at the electrical wall-clock, and dropped the telegram onto the kitchen table.

CHAPTER TWENTY-SIX

RUSSELL

The large passenger-and-goods steamer crossing the Irish Sea to Fishguard bucked and plunged like a fractious plough-horse. We were sailing from Rosslare this time, rather than Dunleary, a route that Jake had promised was a bit shorter. Ten minutes out, any sense of reassurance had been blown overboard, along with half the hats on the deck.

I was not the only passenger clinging to a bit of railing in the all-too-fresh air. Jake, I think, found a card game in the smoking lounge—a phrase that had driven me up the stairs in the first place.

A lifetime in purgatory later, the green Welsh hills began to gather us in. Jake came up to find me, thoughtfully tossing the stub of his cigar overboard before he got too near. He leaned beside me on the railing, watching the slow process of approach.

"You okay?"

"I will be when we're tied up," I said.

"Cup of tea, right?"

"That will help. When does the train leave?"

He consulted the watch on his wrist. "We've missed one, there should be another in twenty minutes."

"And after that?"

"From here, not for a while, but the next station is only a mile or so. Lots from there."

The first ropes sailed out to the men on the quay, and I straightened. "I'll wash my face while you get us tickets, and I'll meet you in First Class."

We joined the crowd of off-loading passengers, the air filled with a mix of accents and the smell of wet wool and the steam from the waiting train. I peeled off to visit the Ladies while Jake made for the ticket office. Face splashed, hair combed, inner parts pleased at the lack of buck and sway, I took up my valise and made to follow my uncle.

Only to come to an abrupt halt halfway across the platform.

Jake stood, feet braced as mine had been on board the *St Patrick,* face wearing an expression that suggested he wasn't far from breaking into a run. He didn't—quite. Instead, he did make his giveaway gesture of uncertainty and determination: shoving up his hat-brim with a thumb.

He was facing a figure around whom the tide of departing passengers washed, an older, greyer, and definitely wiser man, his expression suggesting that his patience was nearing an end.

A man to whom I now owed quite a bit of explanation.

Holmes.

CHAPTER TWENTY-SEVEN

JAKE

I saw him as I was pocketing my change from two tickets to Bristol.

We'd never been face to face, but I'd have known who he was even if I hadn't glimpsed him at Mary's side. A man whose nose could've doubled as a paper knife, whose hands looked just the right size to fit around a throat. Whose icy grey eyes said he'd as soon pin you to a board with a dagger as shake your hand.

My first impulse was to leap the gate and disappear into the wilds of Fishguard, headed for Berlin or South America.

My second impulse was to hide behind my niece.

I managed, with difficulty, to stifle both and stand firm while Mary walked past me and up to her terrifying husband.

"Holmes," she said, "I didn't expect to see you here."

(Her voice sounded tight. Had she, too, felt a momentary urge to run for it? I'm not sure if that thought made me feel better, or made me feel protective. In either case, it straightened my spine and made me paste a less-panicked expression on my face.)

"Then why mention the Irish mail-boat terminal in your cable?" he asked.

"I knew that you'd—oh, sorry, Holmes, this is my Uncle Jake. Jacob Russell. Jake, this is my husband. I don't believe you two have ever met?"

There was actually a question in her voice, which confirmed my suspicions about the occasional secrets these two kept from each other. (Thank God for that tiny flaw in the otherwise impenetrable façade.) The thought firmed my spine up a bit more, and made it possible to step forward, hand outstretched.

"No, we haven't, though I feel as if I know you. Good to meet you, Mr Holmes."

"I have long looked forward to meeting you, Mr Russell."

I tried to ignore the feeling that he was about to pull out a pair of handcuffs, and shook his hand firmly. "Please, we're family, call me 'Jake.'"

A faint lift of one eyebrow told me how likely that was, and he prolonged the normal English hand-shake time by just a moment, to make it clear who was in charge. (And yes, I'd definitely be calling him "Mr Holmes.") When he let me go, his eyes flicked briefly across the tickets I was holding before they settled on Mary.

"I see you are not intending to return to Sussex," he said.

She glanced at the tickets, too, but to my astonishment—and admiration—she no longer showed the faintest trace of guilt or even surprise. "Not just yet, though if I'd realised that you were coming, I'd have asked you to bring me some dry clothes. Do you want to buy a ticket? We only have a few minutes until the train leaves."

"I shall come with you and pay the conductor, rather than risk the queue."

I suspected that the risk of a slow queue was less of a consideration here than his suspicion that at least one of us might take to our heels the moment he turned his back, but Mary simply nodded and moved in the direction of the waiting train.

"I hope you got us a First Class compartment," she called to me over her shoulder. "We need some privacy for this conversation."

Unfortunately for that plan, two of the seats in our compartment were filled. And unfortunately for the young married couple already in occupation, Mr Holmes proceeded to jump their claim. He transformed as he stepped through the doorway, twisting his body and features to look like someone two decades older, while addressing me in a voice that was both querulous and blaring.

"Put that bag up there—no, not that bag, the other. It isn't here. Where did you put it?"

The pretty young woman recoiled; her partner looked alarmed; Mary caught on before I did.

"Dear Uncle Holmes, you only had the one valise," she shouted into his ear. "Could you have left the other in the Gentleman's? You did visit it three times—do you want Jake to run back and look?"

But the offended couple were already on their feet and collecting their bags, fleeing for the next compartment. Mary shut the door behind them and lowered the blind to the corridor. Mr Holmes dropped his act and settled into the middle of one seat. Mary and I sat down on the seat facing him. (Don't know about her, but I felt a little like a boy confronting Authority.)

Mary spoke first. "Do you bring any urgent news?"

Mr Holmes shook his head. "Nothing that cannot wait."

"Fine," she said. "Me first, then."

She dove straight in, starting with Patrick's knock at her door and my climbing out of his car. She gave him what seemed to me an extraordinary wealth of details, everything from the times of the trains to what we ate, where we slept, and how she got into the safe in Kilmorna House. She did leave out most of the discomfort—and made the briefest mention of rain, the cold, her sore ankle, her shipboard seasickness, and the risks of a house falling on her head—but omitted little else of what we had done and seen. (Including, to be honest, a few details I myself had failed to notice.) It took her a long time to get us onto the boat in Rosslare.

Mr Holmes listened intently all the while, those brooding eyes of his half-shut. As she was scrupulously underplaying the state of Kilmorna House, while admitting the uneasiness its ruins caused her, he rose to push down the window, then took out a pipe, filling it with a pleasant-smelling tobacco. He sat, puffing in contemplation, and interrupted occasionally to ask minor questions—the make of the safe, the location of the inn. Somewhere along the line, the door to the corridor opened, and Mr Holmes fished out his coin-purse to pay the disapproving conductor for his "lost" ticket.

He looked directly at me only twice, but I had no doubt that those grey eyes were tracking my every move and reaction. (They probably would even if he had his back to me.)

Mary finished the story—her story, but including quite a few things I'd told her over the past four days (more than I'd realised)—just as the train took a sharp turn north. We were due to stop for ten minutes before returning to the main track and continuing to Swansea and then Bristol beyond. When we pulled into the station, I picked up my hat and told my niece and her husband that I was going to stretch my legs.

I expected Mr Holmes to follow me, but was surprised when I looked back from the Gent's entrance and did not find him on my heels. However, when I came out, there he was at the far end of the platform, standing with his back to the station, smoking a cigarette. When I came up beside him, he held out his silver case. I do not have the tobacco habit, but I took one, by way of a peace declaration, and used his matches to get it going.

He spun the ash off his cigarette, and spoke. "You seem an intelligent person, so I do not expect that I need to tell you that bringing any harm to Russell would be . . . unwise."

Unwise. Pronounced in the tone of voice that went with a cocked revolver. I beamed at him. "Oh, you Brits and your love of the understatement. Yes, Mr Holmes, I am very aware that if I dump any trouble on my niece's head, you'll have my guts for garters."

He turned, eyebrow up, and gave me a fairly thorough inspection, from the little feather in my hat down to the laces in my shoes. (God knows what it told him about my person and habits.) He then pinched out his cigarette and flicked it into the wastebin.

"Trouble is permitted," he told me. "Even, in my experience, inevitable. Premeditated harm, however, is not."

And with that he walked back to the train, leaving me to wonder: Could that faint twitch at the corner of his mouth possibly have been a smile?

CHAPTER TWENTY-EIGHT

SHERLOCK HOLMES

"Charm," Holmes reminded himself, came from a Latin word for a song or incantation, the semi-hypnotic casting of a magic spell. Disarming, attractive, amusing . . . in some charming folk, a cautious man could feel the deliberation at work. In others, the spell-casting was so innate and effortless as to seem innocent. No doubt many of those gifted with a spontaneous ability to enchant started out as innocents, but just as a woman born beautiful might grow tempted to use her beauty, so did those innocent charmers often find themselves depending on their magic to ease the way in their social and professional lives. Charm and beauty were two qualities he had learned to mistrust.

Jacob Russell was charming. And as a young man, he would have possessed beauty.

Holmes decided, while listening to the man give his version of why they were here, that Jacob Russell was not deliberately emphasising his natural charisma for his present audience. There was no air of manipulation in his vivacity, his cleverness, his humour. Which only meant that the man was intelligent enough to see the risk of alienating his clever niece and her vastly experienced husband.

He was, however, relieved to see that Russell, too, was managing to maintain a degree of distance from her charming uncle.

And he was amused to see that his own lack of response to Jacob Russell's narrative was beginning to make the man nervous. The American had, no doubt, anticipated challenges to his story, but instead, Holmes deliberately failed to question the glossed-over elements of his tale, and let gaps in the sequence of events go unremarked. Twice, Russell glanced over as if to check that he wasn't asleep, but she knew his methods well enough not to step in with questions of her own.

He listened to Jacob Russell's retreat into embroidery, the attempt to obscure thin patches in the story with mildly extraneous detail, and took careful note of each thin place, omission, and burst of rapid forward motion—but he said nothing.

When the tale came to an end at last, Holmes continued to say nothing for a long minute. He then cleared his throat and, rather than pick up his noted queries, set the past twenty-five minutes aside entirely, to say instead, "Russell, as you know, I received word while we were in France that Mycroft wished to speak to me upon our return." He turned his gaze to the blond man across from him, asking politely, "I believe you know who my brother is?"

"I've heard of him."

"My brother's rôle in the government is what one might call 'multifaceted.' He spends much of his time in international affairs, but is essentially the man one calls upon with any complex problem. One of those was the 1907 theft of the Irish Crown Jewels."

Curious, Holmes thought. *I cannot tell by the man's face if he knew this.*

He smiled to himself. This might prove to be a more stimulating business than he had anticipated.

Holmes' recounting of his day in London, first with Mycroft, then Lestrade, and finally Inspector Kane, took them as far as Swansea, where Russell greeted with enthusiasm the news that a dining car had been opened up. He pointed out that they had not finished with the conversation. She in turn pointed out that she had not eaten—or rather, had not retained—a meal in nearly twenty-four hours, and that they would be getting into Bristol late enough to make an actual dinner there a gamble.

"And," she added, "considering that the last time you and I got off a train in Cardiff, you were promptly arrested for beating me up, I'd have thought you might want to hesitate before having to explain that it's actually hunger that has caused your wife to collapse this time."

She then set off for the dining car, leaving the two men to trail after her, Holmes aware of Jacob Russell's disapproving gaze drilling a hole between his shoulder-blades the entire way.

At the table, with menus before them and a bottle of claret ordered, the gaze had not dropped. "You beat Mary up?"

Holmes met his eyes. There was no reason to explain. On the other hand . . .

"It was part of an investigation. We needed to be taken to the police station rapidly. That proved the fastest way."

After a bit, the man looked at his niece, who shrugged. "He didn't actually hit me."

The avuncular outrage subsided, the conversation turned general as they ate within easy earshot of their fellow diners and the attentive waiters, the darkening Welsh countryside going past the windows. Holmes was mildly amused to catch Jacob Russell glancing at him several times, clearly wondering when the heavy questions would fall upon him.

He could actually feel the younger man brace himself, once they had returned to their compartment after coffee, and saw the faint strain of wariness around the blue eyes.

So Holmes merely asked, "I take it you propose to wait until morning to present ourselves to Lady Vicars in Clevedon?"

The flicker of confusion on Jacob Russell's face was well worth a minor delay in the receipt of data. He had, Holmes saw, even managed to surprise Russell with his persistent lack of interrogation. And perhaps the trace of dismay there was no bad thing either.

Having thus established who was in control of the situation, Holmes took out his tobacco and prepared to listen.

CHAPTER TWENTY-NINE

RUSSELL

I have never been a mother, and having ended my formal schooling at the age of fourteen, I have limited experience with adolescents, but the jostling for position between the two men struck me as similar to the bristling competitions of schoolboys. I felt the urge to clear my throat pointedly. Instead, I sat back and let Holmes pursue his oddly circuitous questioning of my uncle.

"I don't know that there'd be much benefit in pounding on Lady Vicars' door at this time of night, no," Jake said.

"But you are certain she is here."

"She was here a week ago, before I set off for France. Mary's given you pretty much everything I told her about the theft," Jake said. "And you seem to have picked up a lot about Shackleton and Gorges in London. Have you spoken with either of them? Do you know what brought Mrs Walsh to my attention?"

"I have not spoken with them, no."

"Well, I did—Gorges, anyway, at the end of August."

"When you and your dog happened across him in the park," Holmes supplied.

"Buying him an ice-cream, that's right. Well, he told me—not right away, I had to spend a lot of time with the bas—with the man. But he did eventually let on that he'd heard Lady Vicars was living near Bristol. I'm not sure how he'd heard that, though he did mention being in touch with Dublin friends from time to time, who would pass on the odd bit of news they thought he'd like to know. More likely, things they knew would rub him the wrong way. Anyway, I tracked her down to this little town called 'Clevedon,' twelve or thirteen miles outside Bristol. Resort town, pretty pier, long rocky beach, salt-water bathing pool, that sort of thing. Lady Vicars' house—'Fairview,' she calls it, and you'll be astonished to hear that it does, in fact, have something of a view—is on one of the hills north of the town, looking out over the Severn Estuary. No doubt it's damn—er, *dashed* cold in the winter, with the wind coming off the water, but then, it is a summer resort.

"I started asking around about Lady Vicars, and after some false starts, someone pointed out her . . . I'm not sure what you'd call the woman's job. I thought she was a maid or housekeeper, but Mary thinks she's more of a companion to the old lady. She does seem to run the house, and act as secretary, and I suppose is a kind of paid friend. 'Walsh' is her name. Turns out that Lady Vicars, who's in her seventies, likes to take a nap after lunch, and gives Mrs Walsh most afternoons off. There's other servants, of course, but none of them live in, so everyone's away in the afternoons. Mrs Walsh is a lively thing, in her forties but acts younger, and very out-doorsy—likes to take long hikes up into the hills, then circles around and ends up at one of the sea-front tea-houses. That's where I found her, after I'd been in the town a couple days. We got to chatting, discovered we had some things in common, I told her stories about my days working for a grand family in Scotland, got her telling me about her days in Ireland."

I interrupted. "Did you ever work for a grand family in Scotland?"

"Of course not," he said, sounding a touch offended. "Well, working, but not *for* them."

I decided not to ask for details; he went on.

"I spent about a week here, and four or five conversations in, we had some laughs about the obsessions of the families we'd worked for. I told her how one of my employers was so convinced the servants were stealing from him—that the butler was substituting cheap silver plate for the family sterling—he had a safe installed and had to give over the key before every formal dinner. And that's when I heard about Vicars installing a safe inside the strong-room at Kilmorna."

"But she didn't go on to tell you that she'd wormed her way through the ruins for Lady Vicars to retrieve the contents?"

"That she did not. In fact, she specifically said that, although she'd spent many days at the house overseeing the rescue of what goods could be salvaged, she didn't much relish the idea of setting foot inside. I asked her who'd been sent in, but she just said that there were a lot of people working there, including some servants from The O'Mahony's house that she didn't know."

"But she and Lady Vicars did remain in Ireland long enough to oversee the clearance of the house? They then came here, bought a house—'Fairview'—and spent some time in London while it was being renovated."

"That's right. And," Jake said, this time to Holmes, "sometimes Lady Vicars met with the builders on her own, without Mrs Walsh at hand. So it occurred to me that she could have followed her husband's example and had a safe put in, maybe like the one we found in the strong-room at Kilmorna."

"I see," Holmes said.

And yes, I reflected, wouldn't it be nice if she'd told the safe installers to use the same combination? Since we all seemed to be assuming that we were going to break into Fairview.

Even, I realised, Holmes.

I looked at him with curiosity. "You seem to have no objection to the idea of committing burglary to look for the Jewels."

"Russell, in the course of our partnership you have supported any number of my, shall we say, less-than-legal exploits. I believe I owe you one or two ventures into criminality of your choosing."

I looked at his mild expression, then glanced at Jake, finding an oddly similar expression there. Husband and uncle; close partner and unknown quantity; a man who'd spent his life opposing criminals and a man who'd spent his life . . . well.

I could not envision an ultimate point of agreement between these two, not when it came to the fate of a mass of precious metal and gemstones that could buy a fair-sized village. Easy for Jake to say he had plenty of money and was only interested in tying off the unfinished threads of his career. And easy for Holmes to say he was happy to lend a hand.

Should I force the matter, here and now? Should I ask Holmes if he intended to return the Jewels to the Crown—or, to Mycroft? And what about Jake? Should I flatly accuse him of planning to pocket the Jewels and vanish again?

Would either man admit the truth in front of the other?

And, worse, would I be able to hear their lies?

Behind those friendly expressions they wore, I knew that the two men had to be manoeuvring for a quick pounce at the end, whether that be sleight-of-hand theft or a telephone call to the police. They would be acutely aware of every motion and word of their opponent, ready to make the faster move.

Which meant that, expert though they both were, they might not keep their full attention on the third person in the room: me. These two men, vastly my superiors in matters criminal, might so occupy each other that the ultimate decision could be mine for the seizing.

Not that I had any idea how I would decide—but it would be better than letting one or the other of them have his way entirely.

The thought made me ridiculously happy, and I relaxed for the first time since realising why Jake had waited until Holmes was away before he came to the house. This was a game of the Three-Card Monte he'd taught me, long ago. Another name for which was "Find-the-Lady." Why not have a lady step in and run it?

"So, gentlemen," I said, "when do we propose that I break in?"

CHAPTER THIRTY

JAKE

It was hard not to laugh, watching the two of them argue with such daggerly politeness. (Mary really had embraced her English side.) But my niece was right, although it took Mr Holmes some time to admit it. I couldn't do the break-in, even if my hands settled down and he decided to trust me: I had to be the one keeping Mrs Walsh occupied over her afternoon tea (and whistling up a warning if she returned to the house early). And someone would have to keep watch from the garden. Yes, Mr Holmes was no doubt spry enough to climb in an upper-storey window, but Mary was spryer, and though both agreed that he was the better safe-cracker, even he had to admit she was pretty good at it. (Besides, I thought, waking up to a strange old man in her house would terrify Lady Vicars into neighbourhood-rousing shrieks.)

Mary finally managed to convince him that, if she couldn't get the thing open, we'd find a way to sneak him into Fairview for the task.

She didn't even wheedle, which impressed me. Husbands tend

not to be altogether rational when it comes to their wives, and this one had already seen fit to growl a warning at me.

Perhaps, if this all turned out well . . .

(No, don't dwell on the future, Jake my boy. One project at a time.)

CHAPTER THIRTY-ONE

SHERLOCK HOLMES

As Sherlock Holmes sat back and watched his wife and her uncle plot out a felony, he reflected on the many unexpected turns in a life such as Jake's.

The two Russells were surprisingly well matched—or perhaps not entirely surprising, so long as one set aside the consideration of which end of the law each stood on. He had always assumed that the true brains in Russell's parentage had been from her mother, but Jacob Russell's obvious quick wit was making him rethink that judgement.

Holmes wondered if he needed to sit his wife down for a reminder of the salient characteristics of the confidence trickster. That air of comfortable familiarity mixed with a flattering attentiveness, a story designed to appeal, and a clear mutual goal: Here is this worthy project that only *you* can help me with. A blithe disregard for money—or at least, placing money lower in importance than a worthy objective and a dose of adventure. Until the goal began to shift, then shift again.

On the other hand, he had no firm evidence that Jake Russell was currently acting as a confidence man—at least, not one out to swindle his apparent partners. And although one could hardly claim that money was of no importance, it was true that in recent years there had been more complex motivations for his crimes than simple cash. There were lies in his tale, Holmes could feel them beneath the surface, but none so far that was cause for alarm.

Yes, he thought, this promised to be entertaining.

By the time the train pulled into Bristol, the plan was set.

They would go by taxi tonight to Clevedon—preferably two separate taxis, or if they needed to share, they would present themselves as a recently-met trio who happened to discover a common destination. It being both mid-week and the end of the season, hotels would not be full, and they would take three separate rooms.

In the morning, he and Russell would stroll past Fairview, to confirm Jake's description of Lady Vicars' house and its vulnerabilities, and to locate a place from which they might watch the entrance unobserved. Jake himself, well known to Mrs Walsh, would keep clear.

In the afternoon, he and Russell would take up a position in view of the house, and wait for Mrs Walsh to leave for her afternoon walk. Both maid and cook were habitually gone, and it was not one of the gardener's days. When Mrs Walsh set off, he, Holmes, would follow at a distance to be sure of her intent, then return to Fairview to watch Russell's back. Jake would wait at the hotel and if he heard nothing from his co-conspirators, would know that Lady Vicars was asleep and his niece was breaking and entering—less breaking and more entering, they would hope.

Jake would then arrange to happen across Mrs Walsh during her outing, and keep her in rapt conversation as long as reasonably possible. When she had torn herself away from his company, he would hurry to reach the house before her and give a sharp warning whistle, to alert any lingering burglars of the need to briskly vacate the premises. The trio would then reconvene at the hotel, and either admire their haul or rethink their strategy.

At no point, Holmes vowed, would Mr Jacob Russell be left on his own with the Irish Crown Jewels.

CHAPTER THIRTY-TWO

RUSSELL

The hotel we checked into—three separate individuals who had politely shared a late-night taxicab from the Bristol station, and shook hands with meaningless pleasantries as we parted—was a grand, cliff-top late-Victorian place that probably held more guests mid-summer than the entire winter population of Clevedon. My upper-storey room had a terrace overlooking the grounds and the water beyond, which from here looked and sounded more like the sea than a river's estuary.

My two gentlemen co-conspirators arrived within minutes of each other, tapping lightly at my door. Holmes made for the drinks cabinet and searched for an adequate brandy. Jake slipped in and stood admiring the suite.

"They've got me in a room the size of this one's bath-room," he commented.

As on his previous visit to Clevedon, Jake presented himself as a slightly up-scale salesman travelling in portraits, with a portfolio of photographs that fit into a slim note-case.

Holmes would occupy the rôle of a grandfather visiting family, but unwilling to sleep under the same roof as his daughter's seven noisy children.

I was merely that odd duck, the wealthy solitary woman. Probably an artist or poet, hints dropped to the desk man had indicated.

It was midnight, so after one drink, Jake left. Holmes stayed, attempting to deliver a lecture on the nefarious possibilities of my uncle's actions, but I was already tired, and thought I should be rested for the morrow, so I told him that I was not a fool, that I knew quite well the dangers of trust, and sent him back to his room on the floor below.

"Oh, and Holmes? I'd like an actual stethoscope for tomorrow, rather than a device reminiscent of the Medieval midwife." And having delivered that interesting task, I shut the door on him.

I took my time scrubbing away the grime of travel with a long, hot bath. When I was clean, I upturned all the contents of my valise save a single outfit into the laundry bag; crawled into the wide, soft bed; and spent a few very comfortable minutes listening to the sounds of the night.

Then slipped into the first deep sleep I'd had since leaving Paris.

In the morning, Holmes and I met up in the hotel lobby, exchanged the greetings that one might expect of two people whose sole acquaintance was the sharing of a late-night taxi, and set off in the direction of the little town's centre. Up and down we went, back and forth, before climbing the hills to the north of town for a look at Fairview, the house to which Lady Vicars had retreated after the loss of her husband and home.

Jake had described the place as a trim, 1890s, two-storey house with mature gardens around three sides, its front open to the view of the Severn. He had done a rough sketch of the outside, and sworn that the back of the house had no overlooking neighbours. Still, we purchased an Ordnance Survey map as we passed through the town, and were pleased to find that it agreed with him: the houses at the back all faced the next street over, a cul de sac poking into a section of golf course. All had long gardens, although immediately behind Fairview, the houses gave way to a churchyard.

Jake's drawing showed that he had done his own reconnaissance, and he had taken care to indicate that the conservatory where Lady Vicars habitually settled for her daily nap was far enough from his suggested bedroom window entrance that any sound I made getting in would not attract her attention.

Holmes and I strolled slowly past the house front, paused at the top of the hill to admire the Severn, then strolled back. We then turned into the cul de sac street, finding it filled with family homes of a similar vintage, all of them with trees showing around the roof-lines. We strolled to the end of the little street, pausing before a discreet notice indicating that the house at the end was for let, and went back again, nodding at three gardeners, a woman setting off for the shops, and a pair of pram-pushing nannies.

The churchyard was deserted and somewhat overgrown, with a dead branch of ivy betraying where Jake had pushed a way through a hedge to get at the back of Fairview. We went through, finding a large garden with plenty of shrubbery in which to stand. I looked up at my target.

"The last time I broke in through an upper window," I murmured, "we were in Wales."

"I hope I won't need to rescue you by raising a men's choir of carols this time," he replied. "I would say that downspout looks the best means of entry."

"I agree, it's the least visible route. It looks plenty sturdy, and the brackets are well placed. I find myself unexpectedly grateful for the Victorian love of bay windows." This one could not have been better situated for burglary had the architect's drawings specified CLIMB HERE.

"I saw an ironmonger's in the main street, if you didn't pack a jemmy."

"Probably best not to count on the window being unlatched," I agreed. "I'll also need that stethoscope."

"In the works, Russell. That singularly hideous rhododendron at the corner looks a good place from which to watch the front walk," he noted. We worked our way through the trees and shrubs, and found that, with a bit of a shove into the branches, the vast bush would offer concealment to half a dozen Sherlock Holmeses.

Back through the hedge we went, pausing to replace the brown ivy branch with a fresh one, and took some lunch in the town. We then parted, me to my room to prepare for my felony, Holmes to the ironmonger's shop.

"It feels odd to be committing a burglary in broad daylight," I said to my two partners in crime.

"Much safer," Jake insisted. "Mrs Walsh has good ears, and it sounds like she's rarely out of the house after dark. The maid should be gone, and the cook doesn't come in until four."

"So you said."

"Do you travel prepared like this all the time?"

"A person never knows what life is going to toss in her direction," I told him.

Instead of dark garments suitable for disappearing into the night, I wore ordinary daytime clothing—or at any rate, ordinary had I been a young man. Tweed suit, overcoat, and a light brown hat—all of which could be transformed by stepping into the gossamer skirt rolled into a pocket, reversing the overcoat to its bright lining, and turning the neck-tie into a hat ribbon. In thirty seconds, the young man was a girl (albeit one with an idiosyncratic taste in footwear) making her innocent way down the road.

My necessarily capacious pockets also held the jemmy, a piece of paper with a lot of numbers in Holmes' writing, a pencil stub, a face-flannel to keep from tracking leaves into the house, a length of light silk rope, a pen-knife, and a large, sheer handkerchief to use as a face mask, decorative scarf, or cloth to wipe away fingerprints. And yes, a proper stethoscope, stolen from a nurse's cupboard in the hotel offices.

Holmes gave my appearance a grudging nod of approval.

Jake was openly admiring. "Very clever. And if the old lady does happen to spot you, your shiny face will be a load less threatening in her bedroom than your husband's."

"If you need my assistance," Holmes said firmly, "you need only come to the window. I am not so decrepit that I cannot climb a rain-spout."

"I'm hoping that it's the same kind of safe we found at Kilmorna. Even if the combination has changed, at least I'll know how the mechanism feels."

"You have the page of numbers I put together for you?" Holmes asked.

"Holmes: you're not decrepit, I'm not imbecilic."

He nodded, picked up his hat, and left.

But I did check to make sure his page was securely in my pocket.

Jake peered around the door to see if the hallway was empty, then nodded and said, "Good luck, Mary."

"You're quite certain she doesn't have a dog?"

"No dog. I checked. Don't fret, Mary—it'll be a piece of cake."

Then I was alone.

I looked at myself in the mirror. Broad daylight, in a town too small for a nice, convenient crowd to disappear into, in the house of a woman who might not be asleep, during a brief window of time where another woman could return at any moment. Especially, I noted with a glance out of the window, considering that the morning sunshine had clouded over and threatened a drizzle.

What could possibly go wrong?

I shrugged into the overcoat, placed my hat on my head at a manly angle, and left the hotel through one of the side exits.

CHAPTER THIRTY-THREE

RUSSELL

Holmes was waiting for me in the garden beyond the churchyard. The leaves were glossy with what felt like a low-lying cloud. Not rain, but a penetrating dampness.

"Mrs Walsh may not go out in this," I said.

"She walked past the sitting room window a few minutes ago with a coat over her arm. I'll keep an eye on the front."

He slipped away to take up the spot behind the rhododendron, and I prepared to wait. Drops gathered and fell. For twenty minutes, nothing at all happened. And then, two near-simultaneous points of movement: upstairs, a sturdy, middle-aged woman with short brownish hair and wearing a square-necked yellow blouse walked up to my target window, pushed on the frame to make sure it was shut, leaned down to pick up what appeared to be a blue throw, and walked away. Downstairs, the door to the conservatory opened and a white-haired woman with a cane stepped in from the house. She made her way along the healthy-looking plants growing inside, turning over a leaf here, bending to sniff a flower there, ending up at a divan covered in brightly patterned cushions. She arranged them to her satisfaction, then sat down and bent over. Removing her shoes, I thought—and yes, now she was shifting back against the pillows and raising her stockinged feet to stretch out.

The other woman came briskly in. In the brighter light, I saw that her hair was as much red as brown, and she had the tanned skin of someone for whom a long walk outdoors was a daily affair. I could now see that she was wearing a pleated skirt in some dark tweed and a pair of sturdy-looking brogues. She held up a book with a bright cover, laying it onto a low table beside the divan, then arranged the blue throw over the older woman's legs. The two chatted for a minute, then the younger woman left. The older one pulled the throw up to her shoulders, settled herself into the pillows, and went still.

I waited, but heard no sound of a front door closing. My heart was just sinking into the acceptance that nothing would happen today when footsteps approached through the fallen leaves.

"She's left," Holmes murmured.

"Oh good, I couldn't hear. And Lady Vicars hasn't moved in seven minutes. Wish me luck, Holmes."

"I shall wish you silence," he said, and took up my position with the view of the window.

Behind the garden shrubs I went, around the little shed and along the back wall of the house to the vastly convenient bay window, which not only offered a place to stand on, but would obscure the view from the conservatory.

My boots slipped a few times on the painted downspout, but never lost their grip entirely, and I soon had one foot on the slates of the bay window roof. I took out my length of silk rope—never set out to commit burglary, or even a break-in, without a rope—and looped it over an upper bracket to await my descent. The bracket was not as sturdy as I might have wished, but at least it wasn't rusted enough to cut the rope, and if I took care to ease my weight onto it, the bracket should hold.

After all, if I did come away with the Crown Jewels, they would not add much to the silk's burden.

I set my hands on the lower portion of the sash window and pushed. Nothing happened. I retrieved the jemmy and set it under the bottom edge, but it only creaked. Mrs Walsh had not been testing that the window was closed against the rain, she had been ensuring that it was locked.

Feeling Holmes' eyes on me, I traded the bar for my knife, and got to work on the latch.

I winced at the *snick* sound of it coming open, and hoped it had been inaudible from any distance. This time, the jemmy lifted the window, and in moments I was inside and closing it after me, lest it create a draft.

I looked around as I tidied the soles of my boots. The room was surprisingly modern, for the boudoir of an old woman, with none of the heavy Victorian fittings I would have expected. The wallpaper was cheerful, the furniture made of some blond wood in simple, elegant lines, with curtains, bed linen, and carpet that would not have looked out of place in the house of a young woman. All new—Lady Vicars had, after all, lost everything to the Kilmorna fire three years before—but she seemed to have shed her past on moving here.

Curious.

The air smelt faintly of polish, as if the maid had run her cloth over the surfaces some hours earlier. Still, I thought I should check that the upstairs at least was as unoccupied as Jake promised. I poked my head through the open doorway, finding a dressing room and bath-room, both empty. I gently turned the knob of the closed door, which scraped a little as it came open. I froze, but when no peremptory voice from below demanded that I show myself, I eased into the hallway. Carpeted—and the slow tick of a clock from downstairs had covered the little noise. Nonetheless, I stood listening for a minute before moving to open the remaining doors. Storage room, linens, and cleaning equipment. A guest-room that looked as if it had never been used. Next to it was a bath, its tiles clean, but not as virginal as the room.

The following door was locked. I fingered the pick-locks in my pocket, but decided to first check the final door, at the end of the hallway. What I found rendered the pick-locks unnecessary, and also surprised me enough to draw me in.

It was a self-contained suite of two rooms and a lavatory—Mrs Walsh's quarters, no doubt, private but near enough to Lady Vicars to hear a call in the night. This first room was the smaller of the two, an ordinary bedroom that at first glance could have belonged to any middle-range hotel, although a closer look determined that the carpet on the floor was antique and magnificent, more like the treasured purchase of a Regency Grand Tour than something given to a servant/companion, and there were several lovely paintings of butterflies and birds on its rather ordinary wallpaper. Through a doorway lay the other room, which was not the servant's sitting room I expected—a place of second-hand chairs, third-hand carpet, and a gas ring for tea—but instead explained the paintings on the bedroom's walls.

This was an artist's studio, only instead of large easels and paint-splattered floorboards, this one had another handsome carpet (not as magnificent as the first) and a long table pushed up against the windows, covered with paints, cups of brushes and pencils, and delicate, detailed illustrations: leaves and flowers, trees and insects. And a few larger creatures—a cat, a tawny squirrel, birds in flight. Nature studies, accurate enough for a textbook, yet capturing the essential vitality of the subject as well. Half a dozen dry teasel heads lay on a sheet of clean paper, next to a page with multiple pencil studies showing the precise shape of the curve on the end of each bract.

A free-standing bookcase stood against the wall, explaining why the door behind it was left locked. Nearly all the titles had to do with natural history: *Trees of the West; The Book of Nature; The Natural History of the Garden; British Birds.* One shelf had entirely to do with Irish trees, flowers, birds, or wildlife. The next shelf was dedicated to Somerset. The oldest books, worn and sprung-spined and one or two of them written for the juvenile reader, had to do with Yorkshire. Jake had said Mrs Vicars came from Yorkshire, but it would appear that Mrs Walsh had spent time there, too.

On the work-table, propped against the window, was a watercolour study of fungal cups growing on a branch, tipped to show their smooth internal side of a brilliant, glossy red. I picked it up. If I had seen this framed in a gallery, I'd have bought it in an instant. I put it back reluctantly, and reached out for the stack of finished projects, then stopped: time was passing, and there were no diamonds here—at least, not of the carbonaceous sort.

Back in Lady Vicars' bedroom I closed the door, lifting it against the hinges to avoid the scrape, then began to circle the room, gently lifting each hanging picture—mostly watercolours, several by Mrs Walsh. One I recognised as the small river below Kilmorna House (although on a sunny day, rather than obscured by mizzle). Others included a multicoloured mass of flowers that showed the terraced garden before the devastating fire, a whimsical sketch of several small brown dogs racing across a field, and a group of three minuscule paintings of mushrooms, dancing above the leaf mould. I found no hidden safes, only wallpaper too new to have faded, furniture showing scarcely a dent in the cushions, and a small antique silver pot containing hand cream, which looked out of place amidst the modernity.

And in the drawer of her bedside table, a wicked little ivory-handled pistol.

I blinked at the last. I also pulled it out and checked: yes, it was loaded. I put it back and closed the drawer. Perhaps if the IRA had murdered my husband, I too might be tempted to go to sleep armed.

Next, the dressing room.

Here, elements of the late Queen's reign lingered, in the old-fashioned silver hair-brush set, the framed pictures on the mirrored dressing table, and the wash-stand with its flowered jug and basin in the corner. Even then, both the dressing table and its padded bench were modern cherrywood, and instead of free-standing mahogany wardrobes, her clothes were in built-in, floor-to-ceiling cupboards. Similarly, the adjoining bath-room had both a claw-foot bath-tub and a glassed-in shower-bath. Although, on closer inspection, the tiles of the latter did not look as if it had been used since it was installed: perhaps Lady Vicars had not gone entirely modern.

Three suit-cases and a travelling trunk stood in one corner of the room, which, when I investigated, all proved empty. Had Lady Vicars just returned from a trip, or did she intend to leave soon?

I started with the pictures on the walls again, although I did pause to open the lid of the jewellery box on her dressing table, just in case the woman was insane enough to have adopted the Regalia openly. It held some nice pieces, including an old-fashioned pearl necklace and another one of jet and pearl, but no diamonds. And no safes hiding behind the paintings on the walls. I turned my attention to the cupboard doors, pulling aside the garments and hat-boxes in search of a safe-sized interruption in the painted wood.

I nearly searched right past it. I had, in fact, closed the second-to-last door and was reaching for the final one when it occurred to me that while each of the cupboards had some kind of large hook, for airing and brushing off a garment, the hook in this one had been particularly oversized, its base a rosette some nine inches across.

Remarkably similar to the lamp-hook on the wall of the Kilmorna strong-room.

Like the other, it had four screw-holes: the top and bottom holes showed screw-heads, the left-hand one a small button. Here, however, there was no trace of rust, and when I pressed down on the little button, something clicked, and the entire face shifted away from its backing. I took hold of the hook, and the face of it swung down. Behind it was a shiny steel safe with a combination dial and a handle.

Again, I tried the handle in case it had been left unlocked, but it stood firm. I then spun the dial to reset it and entered the combination from Kilmorna House, but no, that was too optimistic.

So I shrugged off my overcoat and hat, pushed the hanging garments to one side, and leaned in, making myself as comfortable as possible, that I might bend all my attention to the dial.

Either because it was newer, or because it was a superior model, this safe did not make it easy to distinguish the minuscule differences in the clicks and motions. Without the stethoscope, I might have still been standing there with my lower half sticking out of the closet when Lady Vicars came up to bed.

Breaking into a safe without brute force requires several stages. First, one has to know how many numbers there will be—one for each wheel or tumbler behind its face. This one, as at Kilmorna, proved to have three. Next, one searches out the numbers on the dial, feeling for the faint differences that betray the notch where the lever arm fits into each wheel. Finally, one has to figure out the order for those three numbers.

Even with the assistance of the stolen stethoscope, it took me a good half hour to narrow the numbers down: 20 or 21; a 4 or 5; and a 14 or 15.

I pulled out the earpieces gratefully and draped the device around my neck, then picked up the scrap of paper on which I had been making notes and backed out of the closet to ease my spine.

People tend to choose safe combinations that they will remember, which most often are key dates. On one side of my paper were numbers Holmes had written down after two hours in the town library, including such information as "Jewel theft: 6 July 1907" and "Marriage: 4 July 1917." Depending on the number of wheels in any particular lock, the latter could translate as 4-7-17 (if three wheels) or 4-7-19-17 (four wheels), and so on.

I ran my eye down the list, searching for numbers similar to those I'd come up with, and saw three. Including, rather grimly, the date Vicars was shot by the IRA and his house burned to the ground. I eased my back again, reached out for the dial—and fell forward with a muffled crash into the garments when a voice behind me said, "May I help you with something?"

CHAPTER THIRTY-FOUR

RUSSELL

I fought my way out of the garments and whirled around. The woman I had seen in the window was sitting on the dressing table's bench, watching me with a pair of calm, dark brown eyes. Her pleated skirt had dried mud over the right knee, with a tear in the stocking beneath. Her brogues had been discarded, which explained how she had crept up so quietly. Her left foot swung back and forth above the carpeting. Her stockings did not quite match, and both toes had been poorly mended.

Damn it, Jake, where were you?

"If you're hoping for valuables, you won't find much there," she said. Her head tipped to one side. "You are a girl, right?"

I seldom find myself speechless. But then, I seldom find myself confronted with a person quite so composed in the face of a potential threat. Perhaps she was less mentally stable than she appeared.

I brushed my clothing and adjusted the glasses that I'd knocked askew coming out of the cupboard. "I am, yes."

"I've often considered dressing in trousers," she confessed, studying the pair on my legs. "Are they comfortable?"

"What? I . . . well, yes. For certain purposes."

"Such as climbing up a downspout." Her eyes rose again. Was it humour I saw in that composed gaze? I reassessed the brain beneath that somewhat dishevelled hair, and set aside the possibility of any mental deficiency. Odd she might be, but not stupid.

"Or walking in the countryside," I said, striving for a voice as even as hers. "One does save on the cost of stockings."

She looked down at her right knee, pulling up the skirt to frown at the results of her fall. "I was trying to reach a nice example of speedwell in a shade I hadn't seen before, and it was in an awkward spot. Clumsy, I know. You didn't fall climbing in?"

The conversation was rapidly moving from the peculiar to the surreal. I lowered myself onto the raised section of the cupboard, where Lady Vicars stored her shoes, and looked across the room at this unusual woman. "You're Mrs Walsh, is that right?"

"Sure."

The response struck me as a touch incongruous. Easy agreement, rather than a confirmation of identity. I decided to see what she would do with silence.

She swung her foot, raised it to examine the lumpy patch on her left toe, then said, "That is what Lady Vicars calls me, and I really don't mind."

"Why does she call you that if it's not your name?"

She looked up in surprise. "Oh, they do that, people like her. People who aren't quite as high in the social order as they think they ought to be—they give their servants a name and then pass it on to the next one. As if they can't be bothered to learn a new name."

I had indeed met women whose maids were always called "Molly" and their footmen "James." Although I'd have sworn that at the base of this woman's accent was a considerably higher social status than that of most servants. "Isn't a 'Mrs' usually the cook or housekeeper?" I asked.

"Mine is a compromise. I told her she could call me what she wanted, but only if I got the honorific." And with that, she gave me a grin that made her look about sixteen.

"How long have you been with her?"

"Eight years? Nine, maybe. When Lady Vicars surprised everyone by announcing she was going to get married, the previous Walsh—just Walsh, in her case, not Mrs—decided it was time to retire. I was looking for a position, Ireland sounded attractive, so I applied and she hired me. I was just thinking of moving on when the IRA showed up. They murdered her husband and burned the house. Did you know that? Lady Vicars didn't want to stay there, so I kept on with her when she came here. I'd lived around here for a time, so I already knew all the plants and animals. Not as interesting as I'd hoped."

"You're an artist, aren't you? I'm sorry," I admitted, "I had to poke my head into your rooms, to make sure they were empty, and saw your paintings. They're very good."

"I know," she said simply. "But the Irish ones were better. Fresher, I suppose? Ireland was new. Are you going to tell me what you were looking for in the cupboard safe? You don't look like a professional burglar."

I thought of asking her how many of those she had met but quailed at the thought of what meandering side-paths that might open up. Instead, perhaps I, too, could slap a blunt non sequitur onto the table. "How long before Lady Vicars wakes?"

"I imagine she's awake now, and reading. She has the new Ethel M. Dell. She won't hear us from the conservatory. Does this have to do with the Crown Jewels?"

I gaped at her, as much at the matter-of-fact tone of her voice as at the question itself. "How . . . why would you imagine that?"

"Oh, you're not the first to think she has them stashed away somewhere. Some children pulled apart the wainscotting in the house in Listowel where we stayed for a time after the fire. Then the groundsmen ran off intruders a few times in Kilmurry House, where we went next. That was when she decided to come over to

England, and things seemed to be better. But then she had a garden party last spring and I found one of the guests going through her jewellery case." She nodded towards the pretty inlaid box, and added, "She thought the fellow was just a burglar, but I'm pretty sure he worked for a newspaper."

"But you don't think there's much in the safe?"

"Nothing worth stealing—at least, there wasn't the last time I saw inside. Do you have the combination there?" She looked down at the paper on the floor, which I had dropped without noticing.

I bent down to retrieve it, and studied the side with Holmes' writing on it. "I might. I was just going to see."

"Go ahead," she said.

I looked at her in surprise.

She shrugged. "If there's nothing there, you might as well see for yourself. Of course, if she has managed to sneak a load of diamonds in since the last time I saw it, we're going to have a problem." This was more of a statement of fact than a threat, but it left me in no doubt that if the Crown Jewels were inside her employer's safe, this woman did not intend to permit me to remove them.

Well, I thought, *one step at a time.*

I rose and turned to the lock, to try the likely combinations. I began with the numbers 14-4-21—or as Holmes had written, 14 April 1921. The day Arthur Vicars had died in his garden of an IRA bullet.

And the lock opened under my hand.

CHAPTER THIRTY-FIVE

Sherlock Holmes

Holmes was weighing the risk of lighting a cigarette when the shrubbery between the garden and churchyard erupted into a mad rattle of branches and breaking twigs, from which burst Russell's uncle, red of face and short of breath. He looked around in a panic, spotted Holmes, and hurried over, scarcely bothering to conceal himself from the house.

"Did she—"

"Quiet!" Holmes snapped, yanking the man back out of view.

"Sorry. Did Mrs Walsh come back here?"

Holmes' hand, on the man's shoulder, dug in. He hadn't much assurance of Jacob Russell's ethics or intent, but he'd thought he could at least count on some basic skills. "You were supposed to be watching her."

"I was! We had tea, which she cut short because she had an appointment for a hair-cut. I watched her go into the salon, and when she hadn't come out after an hour, I went inside. They had a back door."

Holmes' head came up to stare at the house.

"What did you say to her?"

"To Mrs Walsh? Nothing."

"Tell me."

"There was nothing out of the ordinary, I swear. We talked about the weather, some mushroom that she'd seen on her walk, the shops in Bristol. I told her I'd arranged a commission for a family portrait—the idea here is, I know half a dozen artists and get a percentage of what they earn when I arrange a job for them. Mrs Walsh paints, though not portraits, so it gives us a point of common ground. What else? I asked her how her employer was, whether or not she'd got the dog she was thinking of—Lady Vicars, that is, not Mrs Walsh. I asked her what kind of tea she—"

"Did you say 'her employer,' or did you use the lady's name?"

"I probably said . . . hmm." Holmes, watching his face, saw doubt arrive. "I remember saying 'Lady Vicars.' But she didn't react at all. No, I'm sure she must've told me at some point, the woman talks all over the place."

In Holmes' experience, the phrase "I'm sure" invariably meant that the speaker was not.

They both turned to look at the house. It was silent, the windows without motion. After a few minutes, the sleeping woman on the divan stirred and sat up, but instead of rising, she merely adjusted her pillows and reached for the book her attendant had left for her.

The stillness was more disconcerting than a flinging-open of windows and a mad descent of a would-be lady burglar. Had the Walsh woman returned home? If so, would Russell hear her come in? Perhaps Russell was hiding in a cupboard or under a bed while the woman tidied. Or perhaps Lady Vicars' companion had found her and was holding her hostage until the police arrived. Houses that held only older ladies and their companions should not contain guns, but women these days did the most unexpected things.

Especially, come to think of it, women whose husbands had been shot dead in front of them.

Jake stirred. “Would you like me to—”

“I do not want you to do a thing except keep silent.”

So he did.

CHAPTER THIRTY-SIX

RUSSELL

Unlike its brother at Kilmorna House, this safe was filled to the brim. However, the contents were almost entirely paper: bundled letters, the deed to the house, communications with her lawyer and an accounting firm. Not so much as a safe-deposit box key. There was a long, slim jeweller's case pressed into the front, but the mixed gems of the necklace, while pretty, were not large, and even its diamond pendant was not of the first water.

Lady Vicars had not installed the safe to hide a fortune in stolen gemstones. She had merely wished to preserve her documents against another catastrophic house-fire.

Mrs Walsh had watched over my shoulder as I examined the contents, and watched as I worked them—with some difficulty—back into place. I closed the safe door, spun the dial, rearranged the clothes in front of it, and quietly shut the cupboard door.

She walked back to the bench and sat down, foot swinging. "What will you do now?"

"That rather depends on whether you plan on turning me in to the police."

"Surely you would run away?"

"I . . . yes. I would at least try. Mrs Walsh, or whatever your name is, why are you not worried about any of this?"

"Why should I be worried? Nothing you've done causes any harm to Lady Vicars—you didn't even meddle in her papers. And as I said, it's best to leave you satisfied there's nothing here to steal. And at any rate, I was curious, too. Where are you staying?"

"I imagine I'll be leaving town before sunset."

"Oh, don't do that. I'd like to talk to you and your colleague."

I felt a chill. "Which colleague is that?"

"The small blond man who befriended me in the tea-room."

"Ah. Him." *Damnation.*

"He's quite clever. I was surprised, the first time this friendly American sat down at the table next to me and engaged me in conversation. The second time, I was flattered. He's nice-looking, well mannered, and very good at getting a spinster lady to talk about her life. Ireland, my employers, the staff here, my work—as I say, his interest was flattering, and seemed quite sincere. A bit forward, perhaps, but then, one doesn't expect normal manners from an American. However, after a few days, it occurred to me that it was a most unlikely sort of flirtation. I shouldn't exactly think I'm his 'type,' socially or romantically, and there's not much about me that would suggest I'm a wealthy widow. I had to ask myself what he might be after. I didn't think he was looking to get his hands on my nature studies. The only thing about me that I thought might interest a handsome, silver-tongued fellow like him would be my employer. And when he let fall her name today, after I had taken some care in not giving it to him, I knew I was right."

Oh, Jake, I thought. *Beginner's mistake.*

"He's my uncle," I admitted.

She nodded. "I thought there was some resemblance about the eyes. Where are you and your uncle staying?"

I just looked at her. If she did intend to call the police, she might wish to give them both scoundrels rather than just the one young woman taking to her heels along the streets of Clevedon. I honestly had no idea what to make of this woman. I wanted to put her in front of Holmes, to see if he could figure her out.

Holmes and Jake both.

"We have a place outside of town," I lied.

"Which you don't want to tell me about. Look," she said, "I have some things I promised Lady Vicars I'd help her with." She gestured at the stack of waiting suit-cases. "She's off to Baden-Baden. Which always struck me as the most redundant name. I mean to say, does one not assume that there are Baths in Bath? But we should be finished by nine o'clock. What about if we meet at the bandstand after that? We can talk."

"About what?"

She looked down at her hands, frowning in thought. "There are things I know that could be useful to you. And there might be things you can do that would be useful to me."

"What are those?" I persisted, but she shook her head.

"I need to think them over, and make some decisions. Nine o'clock should do it."

In the end, I agreed to meet her that evening.

And if Holmes and Uncle Jake decided not to risk it, I thought, we could be long gone. Although I doubted those two would pass up the opportunity for a conversation with one of the more peculiar human beings I'd ever come across—which, after ten years with Sherlock Holmes, was saying a lot.

CHAPTER THIRTY-SEVEN

JAKE

Lady Vicars turned a page in her book. After a while, another. The neighbour's children came out to play in their back garden, some game involving sticks and balls and a whole lot of yelling. The threat of rain retreated. And the two of us stood like a couple of garden gnomes waiting for something to happen.

Anything.

(Well, maybe not *anything*.)

What I didn't expect was for Mary to come climbing out of the window—with Mrs Walsh stepping up to the window and watching her climb down. The woman then leaned out to look around the garden, as if expecting to see us. Fortunately, she didn't. She closed and locked the window, and went away into the house.

I didn't need to see Mr Holmes' face to know that he was as surprised as I was. His entire body had gone rigid.

Mary circled around the garden shed again, so as to keep out of view of the conservatory. We met her near the entrance to the churchyard and followed her through the ivy. A young woman and small boy, laying flowers at the base of a fresh tombstone, looked startled at our appearance, but we tipped our collective hats at them and walked briskly on.

Mary slowed as we turned onto the pavement leading down to the town, allowing us to come up beside her. She was still dressed as a boy and the set of her shoulders, her stride, the tip of her hat—they were all those of a young man (could've been Charlie, in his twenties). "Well," she said, "that was a curious experience. The Jewels were not in the safe. However, we may have an informant who knows something about them."

"Mrs Walsh caught you?" I asked. "Why didn't she raise a ruckus?"

"She seemed to want to talk. Although I'm not quite certain I followed everything she told me. She's certainly . . . an original."

"Eccentric as a bent bicycle wheel," I agreed.

"Why didn't you two whistle me a warning? I nearly had a heart attack when she spoke up behind me."

Holmes got in first. "She managed to outsmart your uncle."

"You can't expect a man on his own to follow a lady into a hair salon," I protested. "And anyway, you should've been watching the front of the house."

Mary broke in before things could escalate. "I think the woman has outsmarted us all. She proposes to meet us at the bandstand tonight. She says she has information, but there seems to also be something she wants."

"When you say 'us' . . . "

"You and me. She doesn't appear to know about Holmes."

"Small mercies," I muttered.

"Yes, it's always good to have someone on the outside who can post bail," she said, a bit pointedly.

"You think she intends to hand us over to the police?"

"It didn't sound like it, although she didn't deny it in so many words."

Holmes spoke up. "What do you imagine she wants?"

"Honestly, I haven't a clue. Not money—she seems less interested in clothes than I am, and her rooms are very basic, other than a couple of nice carpets. Her only obvious passion is natural history—she draws and paints, mostly plants and small animals. Beautiful work, thoroughly researched, but I don't even know if she sells them."

"A lady's companion with a watercolour hobby does not sound like much of a threat," Mr Holmes commented.

"Wait til she starts talking your ear off about the Amethyst Deceiver," I told them darkly.

They both looked at me. "Who is the Amethyst Deceiver?" Mary asked.

"Sounds like the Scarlet Pimpernel's brother, doesn't it? But it's a *what,* not a *who*—a kind of toadstool. No: Mrs Walsh would correct me. It's a mushroom, and edible, although it's almost identical to the Lilac something-or-other, and that one *is* poisonous and therefore is classified as a toadstool. However, just to complicate matters, if the Amethyst Deceiver happens to absorb arsenic from the soil it's growing in, it would become a poisonous mushroom, but not, strictly speaking, a toadstool. Shall I go on for twenty minutes or so?"

Holmes ignored my offer. "If the woman intended to lay a trap for us, she would have chosen a place such as the end of the pier. The bandstand is in an open area, difficult to create a drag-net around with a small town's limited police force."

"Shall we take another look at it before we go back to the hotel?" Mary suggested.

It was worth a detour. As we walked, she gave us the details of her adventure in Lady Vicars' house. Bedroom, dressing room, the surprisingly modern fittings and sensibility. Mrs Walsh's two rooms across the hall with her art-work and books. The built-in closets in Lady Vicars' dressing room wall, finding the safe, settling down to open it—and being discovered by the shoeless Mrs Walsh.

During the next bit, as she described their conversation, I had to break in. "You mean to tell me Mrs Walsh knew you were a woman?"

"Yes. I'd thought the disguise would stand up against more than a quick glance."

I shook my head. "I was just thinking how good your act was. Even I would have to take a closer look at your throat to be sure."

"Ah, that's something of a relief. I was afraid I was slipping. There aren't many who see through to the woman behind the clothes."

"You are not slipping," Holmes confirmed.

Mary gave a reluctant nod and went on with the peculiar conversation she'd had with Mrs Walsh: the woman's lack of concern over the break-in or the contents of the safe, her blunt questions, and her remarkable—and unexpected—astuteness.

At the end of her story, we continued to walk along, our footsteps occasionally meeting in rhythm. I was glad neither of them said anything about my mistake, although the politeness in Mary's voice spoke volumes. (Imagine, someone like me forgetting he hadn't been told a name. Time to retire, Jake old boy.)

After a minute, Mary said, "I suppose I should have taken a closer look at the papers I pulled out of the safe, but with the woman standing right there, it seemed a bit intrusive. I did spot the name of her bank, in Bristol, and the address of a London solicitor."

"I should prefer not to attempt breaking into the safe-deposit room of a bank," Mr Holmes said.

Mary gave him a glance. "If Lady Vicars did find the Crown Jewels in the Kilmorna safe, and if she did share her husband's determination to keep them hidden away, would she want to store them in such an obvious place as her bank? The police would only need a warrant to find them."

"What about the lawyer?" I asked.

"He would have a safe," Mary said, "but wouldn't the same

problem apply? More so, since an office is more vulnerable than a bank vault."

"You're stuck on thinking of Arthur Vicars' widow as a kindly old lady who wants only to preserve her husband's reputation. What if she's, in fact, as bad as"—(as bad as me, maybe?)—"Shackleton and Gorges. I wonder what kind of reputation that lawyer of hers has."

She pursed her lips. "You're suggesting she might have a dodgy solicitor who's hiding them for her—or even a partner in selling them?"

"Give me the name," Mr Holmes said to Mary, "I'll have Billy find out about him."

"Who's Billy?" I asked. (Friendly cop? One of his brother's spies?)

"A colleague," Holmes said, at the same instant that Mary said, "A friend."

"Well, I'm glad that's clear," I said. And, having reached the park alongside the town's rocky beach, "So, what do we think about the ambush possibilities of this bandstand?"

CHAPTER THIRTY-EIGHT

RUSSELL

We passed our hotel on the way down to the seaside park, as well as the long, spindly-looking pier and the seaside entertainments, some of them shuttered as the season drew to a close. The Welsh coastline on the other side of the Channel was a vague grey shape behind the lingering mist. The park retained a determined summer air, its bandstand still set with chairs, although nowhere near as many as there would be for a mid-summer's concert. The sun that had come out from under the clouds was cheerful, but had no warmth to it. I pulled my overcoat around me, and wondered if the woollen jumper in my room had dried out yet from the Irish rain.

The bandstand, naturally, was surrounded by open lawn, but nearby shops and cafés would offer concealment, and hinder all but the most fleet-footed constable. One trim little shop advertising tea and lemonade looked as if it had been open earlier in the day, but was closed now. Its shutters were loose-fitting enough to give Holmes a view from the inside. He glanced at the padlock as we strolled past, but it was nothing that would give him any problem.

"I imagine I'm the faster runner," I said to Jake, when we had circled the bandstand itself. "If the police show up, you head into the town—knock over whatever chairs or bins you come across to slow them down, while I lead the rest of them on a merry chase down the park."

"Sounds like you've had a lot of practice avoiding the police," he noted.

"I lead a diverse kind of life," I agreed.

"Make for the high ground," Holmes suggested. "Their shoes and the weight of their equipment gives them a handicap."

"Shall we pack up our things, in case we can't return to the hotel?"

"I can't imagine a police response to our break-in would be that extreme, even if the house does belong to the widow of a Knight Commander."

"Especially if it's Mrs Walsh who does the reporting," I added, trying to envision that particular conversation. Still, I thought, I should bring away anything important, just in case something went awry.

"So are we happy?" Jake asked. "We'll meet her here tonight?"

We were happy.

Holmes would let himself into the shop nearest the bandstand as soon as it was dark, to watch for any undue police activity. I would retain my boy's clothing, which Mrs Walsh would recognise and which would additionally offer me the best chance of outrunning pursuit. Jake announced that he would take advantage of the Turkish Hydropathic Bath-house he had seen in the town, and restore himself with a shave, a steam, and a nice pummel.

"Meet you at the entrance to the pier?" he suggested. "Around 8:40?"

"I'll be there," I said, and we went our separate ways.

I smelt Jake before I saw him, lounging against the gates to the pier in a cloud of sandalwood after-shave. I was grateful our plans were for the out-of-doors, or I might have needed to push him into the swimming baths as we went past.

Watering-places in October are not teeming with boisterous crowds. People were walking briskly along the front, most of them either pulling dogs or pushing rage-filled perambulators, but the evening was cooling down fast with a breeze off the water, and most of those we passed merely nodded and hurried on.

The bandstand was dark and uninhabited, the few chairs that had not been collected and stored away lurking in the gloom like man-traps. "Shall we take three of these and put them up near the shop?" I called to Jake, as if the thought had just struck me. "It would at least get us out of the wind."

"Good idea," he said, and if his voice was a touch emphatic for the purpose of a surreptitious meeting, his voice tended towards the loud anyway. With luck, it would not sound as if he was deliberately broadcasting our intentions.

We carried chairs up to the lee of the hut where Holmes was sheltering, then went back to the bandstand. Jake sat on the steps, but I continued up them and sank down onto the boards behind the relative shelter of the low perimeter wall, hugging my knees.

"Did you have a nice bath and massage?" I asked my uncle.

He took his time replying, so much so that I turned to see what had caught his attention. But his outline against the distant streetlamp was, if anything, distracted, as he gazed off in the direction of the water.

"It was . . . thought-provoking," he said at last.

"Really? I've always found bath-houses anything but."

"Not in this case."

"Was it because this one was, what did you call it—'hydropathic'? Did they have a compulsory lecture on Minerals and Your Health, or some such?"

"Oh, the baths themselves were perfect. Nice and clean, the steam piping hot, the massage mostly silent—well, other than the occasional grunt from the man pummelling me. Even the gent with the razor limited his chatter to strictly necessary questions. No, it was the other patrons. One in particular."

"Really?"

"Your husband."

"Oh? Oh."

"Yeah, surprised me, too."

"Is there . . ." I didn't know how to complete that sentence . . . *Anything wrong? Much damage to the building? Any hope that the two of you didn't snarl at each other?* I finally settled on, "Is there anything I should know?"

"Here and now? I don't think so. Though I will say, the man does seem quite fond of you. Oh, and by the way, as far as Mrs Walsh is concerned, my name is Richards."

CHAPTER THIRTY-NINE

JAKE

I was glad when we were interrupted by the approach of Mrs Walsh, saving me from further questions about my time in the baths. A funny thing, that odd bond that forms between men who sit together in a hot, steamy room. Distant, but intimate—especially since, for at least part of the time, her husband and I had been all on our lonesomes. If he hadn't been English, the situation might have deteriorated into a venturing of confidences. (Thank God it never got that far.) Still, just like an hour in the baths leaves a person's physical self all tingly and rejuvenated, so can time spent in sweaty companionship leave one with a lingering inner warmth as well.

In fact, we'd exchanged no more than a couple dozen sentences the entire time, most of them to do with the matter of the Monk's Tun changing hands, back when Mary was a kid. I wouldn't say that he and I were now friends. But at least some of his prickles had subsided. (I'm pretty sure: it was kind of hard to be certain with that man.)

I stood, brushing off my trousers as Mrs Walsh came up the path. Mary got off the floor and came to stand beside me.

"Hullo, you two," Mrs Walsh said. "I'm glad you didn't decide to leave town."

"Why would we do that?" I asked cheerfully. "I enjoy our talks far too much."

"Oh, Mr Richards, you are a rogue, are you not? And you, miss: you've been in my rooms and handled my work, but I don't believe you told me your name."

"Russell. Mary Russell."

"Kathleen Walsh," said Mrs Walsh.

"But you told me your name wasn't actually Walsh," Mary objected.

I looked up in surprise. "It isn't?"

The woman gave me one of those smiles that hide more than they show. "Here in Clevedon, I'm a Walsh."

After a moment, Mary thrust out her hand, and the two woman shook to seal the introduction.

When Mary had her hand again, she used it to pull up her collar. "That wind is getting chillier every minute. Jake and I moved some chairs over in the back of that little shop, to give us a bit more shelter."

Mrs Not-Walsh peered around as if this might be a trick, but Mary had been careful to put the chairs in a place where light fell from one of the streetlamps, so it wasn't like we were proposing to lead the woman into a dark alley. She gave a nod and marched across to the chairs, even pulling one closer up against the wall of the shop. Mr Holmes on the other side of the shutters would probably appreciate it. (Though I'll admit, at the moment, his hearing seemed better than mine.)

"I've had a chance to think," she said, before our backsides had landed on the other two chairs. "That's one advantage of living with Lady Vicars, a person has plenty of time to herself. Not like others I've lived with, natter-natter on all day and can't understand that it's hard to work and listen at the same time. Where do you live?" She was looking at Mary.

My niece thought about the question for a minute, her expression like Charlie's when you'd handed him a puzzle he suspected had a sting buried in it. She looked over at me, as if asking my advice.

I shrugged. I couldn't think of any reason not to answer the woman. (I mean, I'd have lied, but that's me.)

"Sussex," Mary said.

"The Weald, or the Downs?"

"It's sort of mixed."

"You have some remarkable orchids there—and bats. Yes, that's a thought."

"I'm sorry?"

"Sussex. The South Downs is built on chalk, so it has a completely distinctive nature, from plants to mammals. There are orchids growing on the Downs that—"

"Yes, I know." Mary was getting a little impatient with the Walsh method of conversation. "However, I don't see what orchids and bats have to do with what you can tell us."

"Tell you?"

"Your words were, 'There are things I know that could be useful to you.' If the only thing you know is that Sussex has some unusual wildlife, I'm going back to my warm rooms."

"Oh, no, of course not, don't be silly. I don't expect someone like you to be fascinated by the sundew and the spiked rampion. Although the sundew ought to be of general interest. Why, do you know that Darwin—"

"Proved that plants could be carnivorous by his work with the sundew, I know."

"Good heavens. Have you read the monograph? I understand it created quite a stir in 1875."

"Not all of it, no." Mary shot me a grim sort of look. "*Someone* brought a copy home one time. The thing is hundreds of pages long."

(I nearly spoke up to say I'd thought monographs were short, but I caught my tongue, rather than risk another Mrs Walsh lecture.)

"Perfectly fascinating," the lady was enthusing. "'Insectivorous Plants,' he called it, although he didn't limit his feeding experiments to insects, per se. As I recall, even cheese—"

"Mrs Walsh," Mary said in a very precise kind of a voice, "this is *not* useful to me."

"Not—? Hmm. I suppose it isn't. So, what was I . . . oh yes. The possible location of those Irish Jewels you were looking for."

I'm sure I imagined it, but I thought I heard a sound from inside the shop, as if Mr Holmes had straightened up sharply in his chair.

CHAPTER FORTY

Russell

I was going to strangle this maddening woman, I really was. Looking at her face, all wide-eyed innocence, one would have sworn that she had no idea of the effect her words had on Jake and me. She might have been asking if we had any wish to keep this scrap of note-paper she'd found behind the sofa cushions.

"The Irish Crown Jewels," I said. "Where might they be?"

"Well, they *might* be any number of places," she began.

"Let me restate that question," I interrupted. "Where do you believe they are?" The next question would have to be, *Why?*—but let her tackle one step at a time.

"Either Ireland, or London, or gone to Europe," she promptly replied. Fortunately for the lapels of her coat, she went on before I could reach out and shake her by them. "More specifically, a house in County Wicklow, a governmental office in Whitehall, or wherever it is diamond pieces are broken up and resold. Amsterdam, I believe?"

"Let's start with Ireland," I suggested, rather wishing that we might have done this in front of the hotel's large fireplace.

She made a sort of wiggling motion, either to indicate that she was feeling the chill or that she was settling down for a lengthy tale. I feared the latter.

"I met Lady Vicars—she wasn't Lady Vicars yet, of course, she was still Miss Gertrude Wright—in 1915. She was from York, but had come out to Ireland to stay with her sister, who was married to Sir Arthur's nephew, Pierce Mahony. Pierce Mahony was the son of Sir Arthur's Irish half-brother, who had inherited the Mahony estate, and he died—the son, that is, the father is still hale and hearty—climbing over a fence with a shotgun in his hand, which everyone agreed was a most peculiar sort of accident, for a man so accustomed to shooting. That was just days before the War was declared." Her face took on a look of puzzlement. "Where was I?"

"Nineteen fifteen."

"Oh yes. I applied for the position of companion to the widowed Mrs Mahony and Miss Wright—she didn't marry Sir Arthur until 1917—after my then-employers became terrified of the zeppelin threat and fled to Canada for the duration. The wife was kind enough to put out the word among friends that I was respectable and unemployed, and after some months of managing on their own, the two sisters had decided that a general companion would be helpful, someone who could keep the household staff in line. They hired me. I lived with them at Kilmurry House for a time—in Kerry, close enough to the sea that the storms would smell of it. A lively countryside, so different from England, all quite gratifying. Miss Wright married Sir Arthur and took over Kilmorna House—his half-brother, The O'Mahony, had given it to their sister, but she was living in Poland so she let Sir Arthur have it. I was going to stay at Kilmurry, but Mrs Mahony died very suddenly the day after her sister's wedding—ten years to the day after the Jewels were stolen, peculiarly enough—so I went to Kilmorna House instead." She paused to look off into the distance. "I did find it surprising, how much of a change one sees in areas that are only a few miles apart."

I had been working hard to keep hold of the central threads of this tangled narrative, but the startling non sequitur of a woman's sudden death followed by a meditation on the landscape nearly made me drop it entirely.

"So, er, you went to Kilmorna House with Lady Vicars. Were you there when Sir Arthur was murdered?"

"Oh yes. Poor thing—Lady Vicars, that is. Sir Arthur was a bit of a fool, and anyone in the kingdom could have told him he was flirting with danger. Fortunately, the IRA doesn't appear to hold women responsible for their husbands' sins, but still, having her house set afire and watching her husband bleed to death on the lawn, it's little wonder she couldn't leave Ireland quickly enough."

"With you."

"Who else did she have? The O'Mahony was very generous to her, but none of them were really family, so all she had were some distant relations in York. She'd been very close to her sister, and it was a shock to go from wedding to funeral like that—which if I believed in omens might have appeared to be some kind of message, but I don't. So it wasn't. Not to me, at any rate, although the villagers were—"

I broke into the threatened digression. "I understand that the police blew the door off the strong-room after the fire, is that right?"

"Looking for guns, which was ridiculous. I could have told them, if they'd asked."

"But they didn't find the safe?"

"No. It was very well hidden. Clever, the way that bracket bit just slid to the side."

Or once had, I thought, before three years of exposure to Irish weather. "Who emptied it for Lady Vicars? Or did she go in herself?"

"Good heavens, no. Lady Vicars, climbing around all that mess? She didn't even want to go to Kilmorna and oversee the salvage. Sir Arthur's valet and I went in."

"That's not what you told me," Jake objected.

She put on an expression that in a young woman would have been described as coquettish. "I didn't want you to think me unladylike."

Jake was, for once, speechless.

She laughed. "She gave me the combination, so it wasn't difficult, merely a matter of watching where one walked. I did try on the helmet from a suit of armour that someone had dragged out of the wreckage, thinking it might protect my skull if any stones came down, but it made it too difficult to see. The knights who wore them must have simply flailed away blindly."

"The safe," I said. "What was in it?"

"Oh, there was jewellery. Papers, too, all scorched from the heat. It took Lady Vicars months of applications and conversations with solicitors to get some of them replaced."

"Did you see the jewellery?"

"One or two pieces. She opened the leather boxes to check on them, but everything seemed fine."

"Boxes?" Jake asked sharply. "Was everything in cases?"

"No, only two boxes. The rest were in black velvet bags, the sort with drawstrings. Four or five of those—one was so fragile, it had a hole in the side. A ring fell out as I was putting it into the laundry bag I'd brought. A heavy man's ring, with a signet."

I caught Jake's eye, and saw the disappointment: there were no rings among the Irish Crown Jewels.

"How large were the bags?" I asked.

"Oh, let's see." She cupped her left hand as if judging it in her palm, then clenched it. "The smallest would have been a little larger than my fist, the biggest perhaps the size of two fists?" She brought up her other hand and studied what they looked like together. "Two large fists, perhaps."

The Star, the Badge, five collars—those massive jewelled and enamelled chains worn wide across the chest on ceremonial occasions. And Vicars' personal family necklace—or, no, Uncle Jake had taken that. "Did you think those were the Crown Jewels?"

"Not at the time, I was mostly concerned with getting away before the place fell on us, but afterwards? That weight, the feel of them, and her so secretive? I don't know what else they could have been."

"Have you any idea how they got there?"

She fixed me with a look. "Sir Arthur clearly took them at some point."

If they weren't in the safe here, I thought, where had Lady Vicars put them?

"What did Lady Vicars do with the things you rescued?"

"As I said, she opened the two boxes, then put them back in the laundry bag and knotted the strings, and had me carry it to the motor."

"She had gone with you, then? To Kilmorna House?"

"One of only three times that I know of, after the fire. She never went after that, so far as I am aware."

"I couldn't blame her. And after you'd got back to where you were living?"

"I took them to her dressing room, but the next time I went in, the bag was empty. Lying folded on the table."

"Where was this?"

"A house in Listowel. We stayed there for a bit, then moved back to Kilmurry House. I think she was hoping it might feel like home, but in the end, without her sister there, she just found it sad. The O'Mahony invited her to his home in Grange Con next—he'd been fond of Sir Arthur, fought to save his position at the castle, paid for solicitors in his legal battles. But when Lady Vicars decided to leave Ireland, he helped her find Fairview. And pay for it, too, I would guess."

Poor Lady Vicars indeed. Her sister's husband killed in a mysterious shooting, the sister dying before the wedding feast was packed away, her own husband murdered by revolutionaries a few years later. I couldn't blame the woman for seeking refuge in a sleepy English watering-place.

It was Jake who brought us back to the point this time. "Could she have left the Jewels in Ireland? At Kilmurry House, perhaps?"

"Oh God," I groaned—then discovered I'd said it aloud when the two of them turned to look at me. "Sorry, just, the thought of having to go back and splash through the mud."

"Why would one splash through mud?" she asked in surprise. "The house has a perfectly good drive."

I gave her a somewhat queasy smile, thinking of the requisite sea journey—two of them, unless I planned to relocate to Ireland for good. Which, in fact, I reflected, would not have been entirely awful. Fragrant air, the Russell estate, Viking villages and Ogham stones . . . But I said nothing.

Jake explained, "It was raining pretty hard most of the time we were there."

"It generally is," she said. "But yes, Kilmurry House is one possibility, although I'm not sure who is living there at present. The house now belongs to Pierce Mahony's brother, Dermot, but he tends to flit around a great deal. Still, they have a daughter, so unless they decided to return to the farm in Kenya, they may be there. However, I think it more likely that she turned the whole problem over to The O'Mahony. You might want to ask him."

"You said he lives at a place called 'Grange Con'?"

"That's where he lived then, in County Wicklow—he wanted nothing more to do with Kerry after his brother's death. Although he moved on from Grange Con to Mucklagh—or, come to think of it, this time of year it's more likely to be Coolballintaggart."

"Pardon?"

She pronounced it more slowly for my dull, non-Gaelic ears. "The O'Mahony is a keen horticulturalist, and has been creating gardens at his houses across County Wicklow. I suspect that's why he's kept them, since after all, how many houses does one man need for actually living in? His passion is gardens. He has a perverse affection for bagpipes, and keeps a piper on staff. Also dogs. Huge hairy creatures that a child could saddle and ride, although they're remarkably soppy—they try to climb into one's lap as if they were Pomeranians. He wears kilts."

After a brief vision of an Irish wolfhound in a kilt, I sorted out the pronouns and decided she'd meant the man.

I then had to back-track to remember what we'd been talking about. Jewels, and whether or not they were still in Ireland. She hadn't been a part of the discussion about why first Arthur Vicars, then Lady Vicars herself, might choose to keep the Jewels from coming to light. Perhaps I should ask Mrs Walsh for her thoughts.

"Why would she give the Jewels to The Mahony? Were they close?"

"The O'Mahony," she corrected me. "Not particularly, but he is her brother-in-law, and was one of the few who came to Sir Arthur's defence after the Jewels theft. Very strongly. He's also a man much in favour of Home Rule, and has been known to voice criticism of the King."

"Would you say that if he was given the Irish Jewels, he might not be in any hurry to send them back to London?"

She made a noise halfway between a laugh and a snort. "I think he'd be as likely to dress his hounds in the things."

I shook off this second picture—ten stone of shaggy dog draped with the St Patrick's Regalia—and asked, "Could one of us simply knock on his door and see if he has them?"

"Not without express permission from Lady Vicars," she said, sounding quite positive.

"And could we get that?"

"You remember I told you that I caught a guest from a garden party, rifling through her jewellery box?"

"I remember."

"When I ventured to her the possibility that he was looking for the Jewels, she collapsed in tears and took to her bed for a week. I do not believe Lady Vicars wishes the merest mention of the Irish Crown Jewels in her life."

I met Jake's eyes and ventured to make telepathic contact with the mind on the other side of the wall: breaking into three safes inside of a week seemed just the least bit excessive.

"Tell us about the governmental office in Whitehall," I said, thinking, *Please, is there some way to avoid another voyage over the Irish Sea?*

"I mentioned that because there are people in Ireland who believe it. I personally can't imagine any civil servant deliberately tucking them away in a filing cabinet somewhere—the scandal was too humiliating for the Crown. And it's difficult to imagine someone laying them in a corner for two decades by accident."

I did not agree with her, but I also did not think the Jewels were anywhere near Whitehall, simply because Mycroft did not. However, Mycroft Holmes was not a topic to be raised in front of Mrs Walsh.

There really was no way around it. The possibility of finding those damnable diamonds meant that, yes, another sea voyage loomed.

I sighed. "Mrs Walsh, what can you tell us about Coolballintaggart?"

CHAPTER FORTY-ONE

JAKE

It was getting pretty brass monkeys out there, and I was really looking forward to a nice strong drink in the nice snug hotel bar. Instead, I now got to sit and watch another verbal tennis match between two players who were well matched in both skill and determination, only this time Mrs Walsh was taking the place of Mr Holmes.

"I could tell you a fair amount about the house," she said. "I'd guess you are looking for another safe to break into?"

Mary tried to look outraged. "I don't intend to break into anything."

"It does seem to be a thing you're comfortable with doing. And why else would you want details of the house?"

"What if . . . what if we get there and he's not home?"

"Where else would he be?"

"Dublin?" Mary offered. "Cork? One of his dozens of houses?"

"You could wait for him to return."

"Mrs Walsh . . ." she started, but the older woman was already shaking her head.

"No, I can see you wouldn't want this to take any longer than necessary. Very well: I will give you what details I have about the house, but you have to promise me that you will neither damage anything nor hurt anyone. Nor take anything that isn't specifically related to those accursed Jewels."

"It's a deal," Mary said, sounding hugely relieved.

"Perhaps the simplest thing would be to do you a drawing of the interior, a floor-plan and description of the rooms."

"That would be excellent," Mary said, shifting around to push a hand into her pocket, which came out with a sheet of paper and a short pencil. She held both out to the woman.

Who made no move towards taking them. Instead, she pursed her mouth a little and said, "This is where we address the reciprocal side of the offer I made."

"The things that *we* could do for *you*," Mary said.

"Precisely. I need a house."

I think Mary and I both blinked at this. "What kind of house?" I asked. (That better be some damned solid information.)

"The kind doesn't matter as much as where it is. Sussex will do nicely."

"You want us to purchase a house for you in Sussex?" Mary asked.

"Good heavens, no. Why would I want to own a house, there or anywhere? Gardeners, maids, repairmen, never a minute to yourself—all the disadvantages of working for Lady Vicars and none of the freedoms? No, simply the use of a house, or even a quiet and self-contained portion of one would do nicely. For a year or so. And not too far from open countryside."

By this time, old Jake Russell had spent a lot of hours listening to the dizzy bat's monologues about orchids and toadstools—long enough to hazard a guess as to what she might be after. "Are you looking for a new part of England to explore?"

She beamed at me. "Precisely. And soon would be good. I can give notice to Lady Vicars before she and her friend set off for the redundant Baden-Baden. That's in two days—just enough time to pack up my things."

"But . . ." Mary said. "How . . ." If she'd been a less self-confident sort of person, I'd have said she was sputtering. (She really was sputtering.) "I don't have a house to give you. And certainly not in two days."

"Well, er," I said, a sort of clearing-my-throat noise. "Actually . . ."

Mary's glare pinned me to the wall of the hut—probably punched a hole through her husband on the other side of it as well. "I'm not having a stranger move into my house when we're not even there."

"Your house, no," I agreed. "But what about your *other* house?"

Handing over the key to where she and Mr Holmes lived—a house that was no doubt chockablock with all kinds of secrets and private things—was definitely not on the books. But I'd spent the night in Mary's farmhouse a few miles away, the place my brother had bought and where she'd lived before marrying, and I'd found it about as anonymous as one could ask. It even had a farm manager on the premises, to keep an eye on things.

She wasn't about to admit I was right (though I was), not with Mrs Walsh sitting right there. But eventually, after a very long sort of minute, she did go so far as to withdraw her skewering gaze and say, "I will consider it."

"Grand!" Mrs Walsh's reaction was more suited to an unqualified agreement than a consideration. (Though if anyone could turn this woman down, it was Mary Russell.)

"*If*," Mary said firmly, "I am satisfied with the information you give us about The O'Mahony's house in Ireland."

"I'll draw up some sketches tonight," Mrs Walsh promised. "I'll warn you, we only spent a few days there, and I was more taken up with the hills around it than the nooks and crannies of the house itself. But I have a good memory, and I can probably fill in some of the blank spaces. Would you like to come to the house tomorrow afternoon, while Lady Vicars has her nap? You needn't climb up the water-pipe this time, come around to the kitchen door."

"Good," I said, with a generous dose of enthusiasm. (Huzzah—the ladies pulling together!) "We'll meet up tomorrow, then, and trade a floor-plan for a key."

"I don't know that my sketches will amount to a floor-plan," Mrs Walsh said.

"I don't have a key with me," Mary added.

"Problems I'm sure we can solve," I said in a hearty voice. "Now, my good ladies, can we all toddle off before our toes"—(or other parts)—"freeze off?"

We watched Mrs Walsh make her way through the park and towards the town, waiting until she was out of sight before rapping on the hut wall to tell Mr Holmes the coast was clear. He stepped out of the back, refastened the padlock, and off we went on Mrs Walsh's trail.

"You heard all that?" Mary asked him.

"Every word."

"You agree the Jewels are unlikely to be in London?"

"They could not be," he said, with no give in his voice. "If my brother believes the Jewels are missing, they are missing. They are certainly not in any Whitehall office."

I thought it was possible he was wrong (I was pretty sure even Sherlock Holmes could be wrong) and that some governmental worker was, in fact, capable of stashing the things away in a private safe and keeping his mouth shut about it, but I couldn't see any point in arguing with him, not straight off.

"All right, it's back to Ireland we go."

Mary made a noise suspiciously like a whimper. I was willing to ignore it, but Mr Holmes (to my surprise) relented and gave her an alternative.

"You take Mrs Walsh down to Sussex and get her settled into

your house," he suggested. "You could also have a chat with Billy, to see if he can find out anything dubious about Lady Vicars' solicitor. Your uncle and I will go to Ireland for a preliminary reconnaissance of The O'Mahony situation. You can send us the drawings at whichever Post Office is closest to Coolballintaggart."

(Travel to Ireland, in the company of Sherlock Holmes? Oh, that didn't sound at all fun.)

"I don't think that's a great idea," she said, a bit darkly. (It really wasn't.)

"Do not worry, Russell," her husband said. "I promise not to let your uncle get eaten by the Hounds of the Mahonys."

CHAPTER FORTY-TWO

RUSSELL

As we walked through the quiet streets, I noted how my uncle's accent had shifted again. For Mrs Walsh, he had donned a quick American accent that evoked New York. For Holmes, it was vaguely mid-Atlantic. Back in Sussex, he had sounded like my father, with the distinctive vowels and missing R's of Boston—the accent I remembered Jake having when I was a child.

Now I had to wonder if he had retrieved that from the past and put it on for me, by way of reassurance.

"What do we know about The O'Mahony?" I asked them. "Apart from the fact that his mother remarried and gave him some English half-siblings, including Arthur Vicars."

Holmes, naturally, had an answer. "'The O'Mahony of Kerry,' he styles himself. Regards himself as a 'chieftain.' Irish born, Rugby and Magdalen College, elected to Parliament, supported Home Rule. Parnellite. Inherited as an infant when an uncle died, later managed to claim a fortune out of another inheritance in Czarist Russia, used some of it to build orphanages in . . . Bulgaria, I believe. Converted to Greek Orthodoxy for a while. Works for Home Rule. Given a CBE for his War work, sent it back in protest. I met him once, briefly, at the Queen's funeral. Hmm. Not sure anything else has come my way in the past decade or so."

It was always something of a relief to find the limits to what Holmes could dig out of his capacious memory. "Gardens, dogs, and bagpipes, apparently," I said. "It sounds as if he's distributed the various houses to relatives, though there's no telling if they're loans or if the deeds were actually signed over. Meanwhile, he divides his time between some of the smaller ones."

"Coolballintaggart," Holmes said, not even hesitating over the pronunciation.

"Yes, although we need to ask Mrs Walsh about the other house, too, where he stays the rest of the year. Mucklagh?" Wherever that might be. "I should also ask you to keep in mind what she said about the dogs."

"Wolfhounds, by the sound of it."

"Yes. Large pack animals bred to run down wolves, or indeed, anything they're pointed at. Such as intruders."

"But amiable until roused," he said, unconcerned.

"Please, I'd prefer that neither of you get eaten," I said.

"We need not assume they will immediately go for the throats of mere visitors."

"You intend to approach The O'Mahony openly?"

"Why not? I can always converse with him about bees."

"Bees?" Jake asked.

As we talked, we had neared the main road into and out of town. The streetlights here were more numerous, and we could hear voices—three homeward-bound pub-goers by the sound of it. A taxi had gone past in the direction of the sea-front, and as we neared the pavement now, head-lamps flashed across the buildings as another motor went in the opposite direction, heading out of town.

"Yes, bees," I said. "Actual honeybees. You didn't see Holmes' hives? No, I suppose you didn't go out into the— Uncle Jake?"

He was suddenly not beside me. I looked around, and found

him stopped dead, staring up the road. But when I snapped my head around, the pub-goers had just vanished down a side-lane, and the only thing that moved were the motorcar's retreating tail-lamps.

"What is it?" I demanded. "What did you see?"

"I . . . sorry—nothing. Just peculiar. All this talk about the Jewels," he said, in a voice that had almost no accent at all. Then he laughed, and started walking again. "It's bringing back my deep, dark, distant past. Fellow driving that car. Half-second of street-light, made me think it was Frank."

He looked at us, and shook his head in bemusement. "Frank Shackleton. Ridiculous, right?"

But this time, it was Holmes and I who stood frozen on the pavement, staring after the fading red spots.

CHAPTER FORTY-THREE

JAKE

I didn't think the driver was Frank, not really. (It couldn't have been.) Not for more than a brief instant, anyway, when the light flashed across his face. A pale oval with a manly moustache, might have been any of ten million Englishmen, right? Dublin and the Jewels were riding my brain and making me see diamonds in every corner. I ought to give up this crazy quest—

Except now these two idiot companions of mine took the bits in their teeth and hauled me away.

It was, actually, a revelation to watch the two of them move into action (despite my protests). It was as if they'd rehearsed darting across the road and heading up towards the hills. They exchanged not a word of debate, merely deciding as one that they needed to go to Fairview and make sure . . .

Make sure of what? Well, that it hadn't been Frank Shackleton, up to no good. At an hour when Lady Vicars was by herself in the house.

I trailed along behind, figuring what they were doing if not exactly why. They took the quickest way, along the front of Fairview, not through the churchyard at the back. As we drew near, Mary scooped up a handful of small pebbles from a neighbour's gravelled drive.

Holmes stopped me near the gates, letting Mary trot forward into the garden. Down below the corner windows, where lights from behind thin curtains gave shape to another of those monstrous rhododendrons, she stood and began tossing the stones against the glass, one at a time, with considerable accuracy. (She'd always had a great throwing arm.) After half a dozen small, sharp taps, the curtains drew back and Mrs Walsh looked out. Mary stepped into the shaft of light and gestured at the woman.

Mrs Walsh unlatched the window and leaned out. "Did you forget something, Miss Russell?" (At least, I thought that was what she said—I had to strain to hear her.)

"Was there any sign of an intruder, when you got home?"

"No. What makes you think—"

"Would you mind going and checking all the rooms, just to be sure?"

The woman stood for a moment, then disappeared, leaving the window open.

We could follow her progress through the house as each room's curtains went bright: one upstairs window, then the next, followed by the long panes on either side of the front door, then changing direction along the downstairs until she had reached the kitchen, at the ground floor's far corner and the only room without curtains. We could see her moving around, checking the back door and looking into the pantry. The light went off, followed by the others in reverse order. Had she crept into Lady Vicars' room to look under the bed? This was ridiculous. Frank Shackleton (It wasn't him, damn it.) was no thug. Con artist and second-rate forger, yes, but outright burglary was not his style. The only threat he represented to women was to their chequebooks.

No crashes, bangs, or screams had erupted during the entire process. Eventually, Mrs Walsh reappeared, leaning out of her window to say, "All is fine. Lady Vicars is asleep, but I shall ask her in the morning if any person came to the door."

"If . . ." Mary thought for a moment, then made up her mind. "If there was, please telephone me? I'm staying at the Cliffsedge Hotel."

"Whom do you imagine this would be?"

"Someone interested in the same matter we have been discussing. But—don't let him in just to show him you have nothing to hide."

"I don't. Have anything to hide."

"I know that. Another person might not believe it."

"Very well. I shall see you tomorrow, Miss Russell." And so saying, she closed the window and drew the curtains.

Mary crossed over the front of the house to join us, where her husband demanded, "Did you think her the sort of woman who would open her door to an intruder?"

"She let me open the safe because she didn't think there was anything of value inside. It didn't occur to her that a person who commits trespass and would-be burglary might find failure the first step to escalation."

I had to set them both right on something. "Frank Shackleton would not do physical violence to a woman. I can't even imagine him delivering an open threat."

"Merely rob them blind," Mary growled.

"The people Frank stole from could generally afford it."

The two of them stood looking at me with the sort of gaze that's called "pointed" because it sticks. And yes, saying that about Frank was as good as admitting it about myself, but we would deal with that later. I pushed past them and walked away, and listened to their footsteps behind me all the way to the hotel.

. . .

It took a while to fall asleep, down there in my travelling-salesman's room.

But it took no time at all to wake up at the racket of a fist pounding against the door.

CHAPTER FORTY-FOUR

RUSSELL

The telephone awakened me, jangling from the desk in the suite's adjoining room. I stumbled out of bed, hitting my shoulder against the door-frame and my toe against a stray chair-leg before my hand found the receiver and lifted it to my ear.

"Raugh," I said, then coughed and said more clearly, "Russell here."

"Miss Russell, this is the hotel desk. We have what claims to be a very urgent telephone call for you from a Mrs—"

"Put her through." While he was doing that, I fumbled around for the switch on the lamp, finally discovering it where switches generally are. The room took on substance—albeit out of focus, my spectacles being on the table beside the bed.

"Miss Russell?"

"What is it, Mrs Walsh?"

"I'm afraid we've shot someone."

I sat down with a *thump*. "Have you rung for a doctor?" I tried to think where the nearest hospital would be. Bristol?

"Oh, he isn't here. He ran off. And I don't think she could have hit anything important. The bullet went into the plaster, and there's only a few drops of blood on the floor."

"Vicars'" she keeps in her night-stand?"

"Yes. She's quite thrilled with herself. I've made her a cup of tea, though I think she'd have been better off with a tisane, they say tea keeps one awake. The caffeine, you know?"

"Mrs Walsh, tell me what happened."

"The gun going off was the first thing I knew. I'd only been asleep an hour or two—I had been working late on your sketches, downstairs in the kitchen where it was warm, before I retired to bed—and suddenly *Bang!* And then the crash of her door bouncing against the wall and someone running down the hallway and stairs, then the front door banging off of *its* wall. By that time I had my dressing gown on and I went to see if she was all right. I took my stout walking-stick with me, but the fellow was long gone. Fortunately I had the sense to call Lady Vicars' name before I got to her room, because she was sitting up in bed with that gun of hers, waving it around. It's unexpectedly heavy—have you ever used one?"

"I have. But she didn't shoot you, did she?"

"No, and I took it from her and put it back into the drawer, and then helped her get dressed and sat her in front of the fire. I went to make her a cup of tea, found the front door open, and closed it—locked it, too, in case you're worried—but that wasn't how he'd got in. The little window in the kitchen door had been smashed. Or less smashed than taken out. At any rate, the glass was broken and there were some pieces on the floor and on the step outside. I've swept it up."

Of course she had. "Try not to disturb anything else," I asked. "It makes it difficult for the police to see what happened."

"Oh—you think the police will come? That's exciting. So is this considered evidence?"

"It would have been. Did Lady Vicars see him?"

"Not very well, since the room was pretty dark. He was bald, she said. He had a cloth cap that fell off when she shot him, and his head was shiny in the light from the hallway."

"Bald. Any facial hair that she could see?"

"She thought he had a beard, or more like a scruffy kind of stubble."

It might have been possible, for a woman in bed to catch a glimpse of an intruder's profile as he turned into the hallway. And, I thought, I'd seen no sign of her needing glasses. "How much blood was there?"

"Just, as I say, drops—although come to think of it, there was a smear on the front doorknob, as well. As if . . . hmm. I think Lady Vicars must have hit him in the left shoulder."

"But you said there was not a large amount of blood?"

"A kind of splash about shoulder height on the wall, then a sort of dribble in the hallway—I wiped it up, along with cleaning the doorknob, though I must remember to tell the cleaner to deal with the carpet."

So much for finger-prints. I had to agree that the wound sounded minor enough for the blood to be held back by a hand's pressure.

"I'm surprised you didn't hear him break in," I said. The kitchen was directly underneath her rooms.

"I think I might have if I'd been awake. But it was after midnight when I finished, perhaps 12:30, and I then read for half an hour or so before turning off my lights."

What time was it, anyway? I found the decorative little clock that the hotel had provided among the other desk-top knick-knacks: 3:50. If she'd turned off her reading light at 1:00, by 1:30 a watcher might have decided that the house was asleep at last. *Good Lord,* I thought. *Could he have been hiding right behind me while I stood talking to Mrs Walsh through her window?* Those rhododendrons would conceal a rhinoceros, much less one burglar with enough experience to use some sound-muffling technique for breaking a window.

If the man had waited for the house to quiet and entered through the kitchen, where had he gone next?

"Did you notice anything disturbed?" I asked. "Other than the window."

The receiver crackled in my ear for a moment as she thought. "The door to the conservatory was open. I generally shut it all the way, since it sucks heat out of the house. And the sitting room door, that was the reverse—nearly closed, though Lady Vicars and I always leave it open."

Which meant he'd explored the downstairs before climbing to the first floor. "What alerted Lady Vicars to his presence?" I asked.

"I suppose that little squeak her door always makes. We've had two workmen try to fix it, but each time it comes back. I think it must be the hinges, not the door-frame."

"What time was this, that she woke?"

"What time is it now? Almost four," she answered herself, having consulted a nearby clock. "It would have been a little before half-three."

Perhaps he hadn't been hiding in the garden until the lights went off, then. Or he had been, but waited a long time before risking the noise. Or else he had taken the time to do a very thorough search of the house before getting to Lady Vicars' room. Including, perhaps, Mrs Walsh's rooms?

My heart skipped a beat. "You said you were working in the kitchen. Did you take the drawings with you when you went upstairs?"

Again the line crackled, this time for longer. "Oh dear," her voice said at last.

"Mrs Walsh, would you—" But the earpiece thumped down against a table and she was gone. I decided that I might as well be warm and sighted, so I went to fetch a robe and my spectacles, coming back to hear her voice squeaking out of the earpiece. I snatched it up.

"—gone, I'd been working on them and they were mostly finished, other than one section I thought I might want to correct in the morning. I even had the rooms labelled, ready to go."

"Sorry, Mrs Walsh, I had to step away from the telephone for a moment, could you repeat that for me?"

"The sketches I was doing for you, of Coolballintaggart and Mucklagh—and one of Grange Con, just in case. I left them on the table in the kitchen and they're gone. All of them."

Two minutes later, my knuckles were rapping on Holmes' door. Five minutes after that, his fist was rousing Uncle Jake.

CHAPTER FORTY-FIVE

RUSSELL

None of us were willing to assume that the invasion of Lady Vicars' home was unrelated to the man Jake had seen driving out of the town. Surely Jake's impression had been correct, and the driver had, in fact, been Frank Shackleton?

Except that word "surely": it always carried with it a note of doubt.

I was the one to bring up the uncomfortable possibility.

"Are we absolutely certain?" I asked the two men when they appeared, overcoats across arms and bags in hand, at my hotel-room door. I was packed to go as well, as matters had clearly changed. We spoke quietly, so as not to rouse the occupants of nearby rooms. "Could it not have been, as Jake said, his mind dwelling on the matter, and seeing someone who looked like Frank Shackleton? The man who broke into the Vicars house doesn't sound at all like him: baldish, cloth cap, possibly a beard."

"Sounds like a generic hired thug," Holmes remarked.

"Or Dickie Gorges, in need of a shave," said Jake.

"Or a local thug who thought he might see what Lady Vicars had to steal."

"You suggest *coincidence,* Russell?" Holmes' expression was on the edge of outright scorn.

"They do happen," I said—not for the first time in our acquaintance. "But we need to decide if it justifies racing off to Ireland in the hopes of reaching Coolballintaggart before him. Or them. When do the first trains leave Bristol heading to Fishguard? If we get to Ireland and find the trail cold, we'll have lost days of time." *To say nothing of wasting too many more hours at sea,* I thought, and tried not to let the idea show on my face.

"You're right," he said, but before I could express any astonishment, he went on. "But we needn't change plans. Your uncle and I will make for Ireland immediately. You go to Lady Vicars' house and see what needs doing. Try to avoid calling in the police, it will merely make for delay. One of us will need to lay hands on a map of the area, so that when Mrs Walsh has reproduced the drawings, you can post them to the nearest village, whichever that might—"

He broke off as Jake's hand came out of his knapsack with a map: COUNTY WICKLOW, it said—on the eastern side of Ireland, below Dublin. Jake took it to the room's desk and snapped it out flat.

We bent over the map. At some point, he'd added a large X at various spots. He now set his finger against one with the annotation *Coolb.* "It looks like maybe four miles from a village named 'Aughrim,' which does have a train station. Don't you think that means there'd be some kind of a Post Office?"

"It does," Holmes agreed. "Russell, send the sketches poste restante to Aughrim, using the name 'Jacob Holmes.' We will retrieve them, once we're certain that Shackleton's men aren't already at the house."

"What if you just did without the drawings?"

"You think we should perhaps knock on The O'Mahony's front door and ask for the Jewels?"

"Do you prefer to sneak through the house with some illicit floor-plans and wait for the dogs to notice?"

"Russell, we haven't time to discuss this, not if your uncle and I are going to catch the 5:52 for Fishguard. And you promised Mrs Walsh shelter in Sussex."

Jake consulted his pocket watch and shook his head. "We won't make it to Bristol before six, not unless you can commandeer a racing-car at the hotel door. Maybe we should make for Holyhead instead—it's farther from Bristol, but the crossing itself is shorter, and Aughrim looks to be about halfway between Dublin and Rosslare."

"We need a *Bradshaw's*," Holmes complained. "The desk should have one. Russell, kindly take care Lady Vicars doesn't shoot you. I'll cable you in Sussex when I have news."

And they left me, alone and upset and unable to argue with their logic, even if it was male. Either Holmes or I had to stay with Jake—there was no trusting him on his own. And unless we wanted to risk breaking into a house blind, someone needed to wait for a new set of drawings from Mrs Walsh, who had never met Holmes.

I looked down at what I was wearing and decided that, considering the sensibilities of the elderly Lady Vicars, I should wear a skirt this morning, rather than yesterday's trousers.

CHAPTER FORTY-SIX

RUSSELL

One thing I could deal with, left behind or no, was bringing Billy into the matter. In fact, I thought as I finished folding my one spare shirt into the valise, considering the time of day, I might have better luck finding an operating telephone exchange than an open telegraph office.

The hotel was modern enough to have a row of three comfortable telephone booths. I closed myself into one, and set about finding an Exchange operator who was both awake and able to handle the connexion to a private telephone in London.

"Yes," I told her, keeping my voice friendly, "I do know what time it is. However, the person I'm telephoning to will answer. Just let it ring a few times."

Fortunately, he picked up the receiver before I had to argue with her, and as soon as he heard my name, he reassured her that it was fine.

We both waited for the sound of her leaving the line, and then he said, "Mary? What's happened?"

Billy Mudd had come into Holmes' life at the same time Mrs Hudson had. As a child, he had been the head of Holmes' Baker

Street Irregulars, those street urchins whose eyes and fingers were in every corner of London. He now had his own firm of private investigations—again with eyes all over.

"We need some information," I told him. Which also served to tell him that we were fine, and that I was working with Holmes on something.

"I have a pencil," he said.

"There's a solicitor in London, I need to know how honest he is." I recited the name and address. "One of his clients is an old woman who appears completely upright and law-abiding, but is on the edges of a matter of stolen gemstones."

"And you're thinking he might be storing or fencing them for her."

"That sort of thing. I also need to know the whereabouts of two men—or rather, I need fairly urgently to know if they've suddenly left home. Although you'll have to find their homes first."

I gave him what Jake had told me about Francis Shackleton and Richard Gorges—Shackleton's change of surname to Mellor, his employment in the City, both men's general neighbourhoods. He laughed when he heard Shackleton's name—"Oh, is that rascal up to something new?"—and grunted at that of "Gorges."

"You want to telephone to me this afternoon, I'll give you what I have?" he asked.

"I . . ." Somehow, in the minutes since sitting down in the little booth, my mind had taken itself on a new turn. I absolutely did not want to spend the day escorting Mrs Walsh to Sussex, or waiting to pass on information gathered by others. No: if I had to tie myself to a ship's mast and sail to Dublin, I would rather be there than here. "I'm not sure of my plans, but let's say if you haven't heard from me by three o'clock, put together a telegram and send it to me at . . . let's see. How about the Royal Marine Hotel in Dublin—or Dunleary, I guess."

"You're off to Ireland?"

"For my sins," I said darkly.

He laughed again, wished me luck, and rang off.

When I reached Fairview, it was not yet dawn. On the front door, I found a note:

> Come round to the kitchen, I'm working there.

Mrs Walsh had fastened dish-towels up to the kitchen windows, so all I could see was that the lights were on. The small window in the kitchen door itself was roughly patched with brown paper and slats from a broken-up crate. I tapped lightly on the wood and heard a chair scrape against tile. Footsteps, then the door came open, to warmth and the odour of coffee.

"Miss Russell," she said. "I'm sorry to have disturbed your sleep. I suppose it could have waited til morning, but we were a bit alarmed."

"I'm very glad you didn't wait," I told her. "Is Lady Vicars all right?"

"I gave her a soporific. Well, she thought it was a cup of warm milk with nutmeg, but she went out like a light."

I cursed under my breath at the further delay this was going to mean. I didn't see how I could in all conscience leave this house until its residents were out of the way.

My eye caught on an unlikely addition to the cooking utensils on the counter. I picked it up. "Is this the cap the man left behind?"

"It is."

I looked at it closely under the strongest light I could find, but without a magnifying glass it told me little: not brand new, not old enough to have collected much of a history, with a few short hairs inside the brim. I looked around, and found a high spot above a cupboard where it would lie unnoticed until needed. Then I asked, "Where did you put the broken window-glass?"

"It's in the bin there." She gestured to the pail in the corner. I pulled it into the light and lifted the top. As I'd expected, the burglar had coated a cloth with rubbery glue, pressed it to the window, and used it to keep the larger shards of glass from falling noisily to the tile floor. Professional.

"Have you telephoned to the police?"

"No, I wanted Lady Vicars to get some sleep first."

"Good idea. However, I think you and she should both leave here today."

"I agree. I'll telephone to her friend after breakfast and let her know we're coming a day early. I'll have to go with her."

"Can you get yourself ready to leave Clevedon, as well?"

"For Sussex? It won't take me long to pack up my things, and I can send for them later. I'll have to talk to the others," she added, thinking aloud. "Debs—she's the maid—will be happy to help me pack. And I'll ask the gardener to repair the window."

On my walk up the hill from the hotel, I'd had time to think about my conversation with Billy, and decided that it had been the right decision: I could not take Holmes' proffered alternative and leave Ireland to the two men. "I'll give you instructions on where to go, and a letter to my farm manager. He's a very dependable person, you needn't be in the least concerned."

"Where are you going?"

"I'm meeting up with my uncle."

"In Coolballintaggart?"

I sighed. "So it would seem."

"Help yourself if you'd like coffee, or toast—bread is in that cupboard, butter on the sideboard. I'll finish with the sketches—although I realised that I didn't know Mucklagh very well, so that one is mostly the outside. Oh, and there are some maps I thought might be useful."

I knew that parts of Ireland had become all but deserted after the famine, but how many houses did this one family possess? More than they could actually inhabit, clearly. I poured myself a cup of coffee from the pot on the back of the stove, and picked up the maps.

They were quite magnificent—heavily used, mud-stained, and marked-up, but they showed every building and fence-line.

"I want them back," she said.

"I would, too," I agreed.

The coffee was delicious, the bread fresh, the mixed-peel marmalade home-made and pleasingly bitter, and it all helped stifle my impatience while she finished the three drawings to her satisfaction. She didn't seem to mind talking while she worked—no surprise there—so I questioned her about the night before, hoping for more details. Her repetitions served to confirm her previous story, and the only new thing she remembered was the sound of a motorcar starting up, shortly after the man had run out of the front door.

She finished the last drawing, frowning in dissatisfaction. "That's the best I can do with Mucklagh. We were only there for a few hours one day while Lady Vicars picked up some flower cuttings. Grange Con and Coolballintaggart I'm more certain about."

She pushed them across the table; I wiped my hands on the napkin she'd given me and picked them up. Neatly labelled, sketched maps with estimated distances, precise floor-plans of the three houses, with perfect angles, placement of doors and windows, and broken lines where her memory went vague.

Everything a burglar could ask for.

"Did I warn you about the dogs?"

"Large and hairy, you said. Wolfhounds?"

"Yes. Amusing, since Lady Vicars at the time had a pack of Yorkshire terriers that barely came up to the hounds' ankles. They're amiable dogs, but I wouldn't recommend you run when you see them. Running seems to trigger their hunting instinct. More coffee?"

She didn't sound very worried about it. However, I had to hope the hunting instincts of the Irish wolfhound were one of those odd facts of life that Holmes had tucked away in his brain.

If not, I might arrive to find parts of the two men strewn across half of Wicklow.

CHAPTER FORTY-SEVEN

JAKE

I'll admit, I wasn't looking forward to spending hours and hours in the company of this man. I'll even say I was dreading it, because with Mary out of the way, there was no reason for things not to become . . . blunt.

The hotel dug up a car for us, with a driver who looked like he'd been turned out of bed for the purpose, yawning and unshaven. We piled in, and when Mr Holmes promised the man an extra shilling for every five minutes he cut off the journey, away we went with a squeal.

My companion had one of those old-fashioned bags with him called a "Gladstone," which he'd dropped at his feet. He now bent over and undid the fastenings, coming out with a torch and one of those massive *Bradshaw's* time-tables, which he had acquired (stolen) from the hotel. The torch he handed to me; the tome he unfolded on his knees.

"Holyhead is better," I told him.

He did not reply, and I could see that he was trying to compare the possibilities of the northern passage with that of the south. The car was bouncing enough that reading the tiny print must have been a job. So I leaned forward to ask the local resident for advice.

"We're looking to get to Ireland as soon as possible. From Bristol, would you say we'd have better luck going through Fishguard, or Holyhead?"

It was quickly apparent that the man had no idea, although he was very willing to share various tales about desperate dashes for the station. It did serve to keep him awake, and also to delay any blunt discussions between me and my travelling companion.

I didn't bother to listen, and I don't think Mr Holmes even heard, as he flipped over the pages and ran a finger down the columns under the bouncing light. But if he wasn't interested in my advice, why should I interfere with his going blind?

(In my opinion, even after jamming a lot of train companies together over the previous few years, Britain still had too many ways to get from here to there. It shouldn't require a 1200-page book and a magnifying glass to figure things out. Still, it was a comfort to know that Frank—if it was Frank—and Gorges—if he was the man with the bullet hole in his shoulder—were faced with the same problems.)

(Which reminded me of something.) I leaned over to ask, very quietly, "Do you by any chance have a gun in that bag of yours?"

He gave me a quick glance out of the corner of his eye. "Do you anticipate that we shall require one?"

"Well, if it is Frank we're dealing with, I'd say no, not unless he's become a lot more desperate over the past ten years. But the man Lady Vicars described obviously wasn't him. Whether it's Dickie Gorges or someone else Frank's wrangled into helping him, hired toughs are never the most stable individuals."

I then realised what I'd just told him. (Oh, shit. Shit shit shit.) To cover my mistake, I reached down for the map. (Because okay yes, I knew what Frank looked like now, and I'd lied to both of them to say I hadn't seen him. Can you blame me?)

"'Obviously'?"

But I had the expression back on now, and as I sat up with the map, I turned it to him. "Well, yeah. The driver of the car had a moustache, not a beard. And when I knew Frank, eighteen years ago, he had really great hair. I can't imagine him going bald. Or wearing a cloth cap, for that matter."

He turned on me one of his patented grey-eye glares, but all he saw was innocence. (Suspicious in itself, sure, but nothing he could work with.) "It sounds as if you've decided it was Richard Gorges."

I shrugged. "In August, Gorges had some hair left and was more or less clean-shaven, though both those things can change. And he looked old, after ten years in prison, but he's younger than I am, plenty fit enough to run down a set of stairs. Still, I have to say, my impression was that he'd had the gumption knocked out of him. I don't think he'd have broken into that house under his own steam."

"But if someone talked him into it?"

"Frank Shackleton, you mean. Well, if Frank managed to talk himself back into Dickie's life, maybe? But it would take some talking."

"I see." After what seemed like a very long minute (hour) he went back to the tiny print of the *Bradshaw's*.

"Well," I said, "that was sure a nice chat. Wake me when you've decided where we're going." I propped the torch up under his collar, stretched out my legs, and tipped my hat over my eyes.

I woke as the car slowed, and found we'd made it to the Bristol station. Mr Holmes shoved money at the driver and jumped out. I hastened to do so on my side.

"Figured it out?" I asked.

"I believe we are in time to make the Fishguard train." But in case I imagined that he was letting me contribute to the decision, he then delivered his logic. "The mail packet from Fishguard reaches Ireland slightly later than the one out of Holyhead gets to

Dunleary, but the times are offset by the train north from Rosslare, which reaches Aughrim an hour and five minutes before the train south out of Dublin."

"You're putting a lot of confidence in your *Bradshaw's*," I noted mildly.

That grey eye tried to drill another hole in me. "Have you reason to believe the time-tables will be wrong?"

(Aren't they usually, when one is in a desperate rush?) Since there was no controlling the weather or the Irish train system, I shook my head. "Fishguard it is. And I hope to hell the dining car has their coffee on."

CHAPTER FORTY-EIGHT

SHERLOCK HOLMES

The dining car proved well supplied with coffee. And Jacob Russell succeeded in talking the cook into providing him with a generous pile of crisp, American-style bacon to go with his American-style eggs and American-style hot toast.

Holmes told the attendant that he would make do with English food.

They had been unable to get seats in a private compartment, and the dining car was popular enough to make the kind of conversation he required from Jacob Russell difficult, particularly considering the American's poor hearing. When they had finished their breakfast, Holmes made the firm suggestion that they move to the smoking car. As he'd anticipated, that time of the morning the occupants were married men more interested in their newspapers than in the company of their wives, and the open windows made for a convenient background noise.

However, Jake Russell seemed determined either to avoid conversation or to finish up his lost night's sleep. He settled his shoulders into the wooden panelling, then again stretched out his legs and tipped his hat over his nose.

Russell would have recognised the expression on Holmes' face as one of amusement, although to the rest of the world it might have been interpreted as mild dyspepsia. He lit a cigarette, then stretched out an arm for the deck of cards abandoned on a nearby table. The sound of his shuffling was particularly crisp, the tap of the deck on the table rang down the length of the car. His companion gave out a nearly realistic snore.

The cards required a most thorough shuffle, followed each time by a rap to neaten them up. When he was satisfied, he turned the deck face-up, fanned them out in a semicircle, and picked out the two black jacks and the queen of hearts. In a deft gesture, he collected the remaining forty-nine cards and laid them aside. The three survivors he flexed against the palm of his right hand, then dealt them out, faces down.

Each of the three cards had taken on a slight arch from his vigorous shuffling process. The long fingers skated them back and forth on the surface, mixing them around in a gesture both precise and hypnotic.

An attendant appeared at the far end of the car. He made his way down, picking up an abandoned paper or glass here, exchanging a word with a passenger there. As he came up to the corner table, Holmes' hand swept up the three cards, flipped them over, and spread them out on the worn wooden surface: jack, queen, jack.

The man stopped, looking very like a headmaster about to address a boy concerning a piece of pending mischief. He glanced at the card-player's apparently sleeping accomplice—Three-Card Monte most often used a shill, whose job was to convince the audience that winning was possible—then gave Holmes a smile that had teeth behind it.

"Playing a nice game of cards, are we, sir?"

"Only for the experience it might impart," Holmes said, "not for coin."

His hands flicked the cards face-down, then gathered them up:

left, right, left. His left hand then spat out one of the cards it held, then the right, left again, and he began to mix the cards—left right, right left. After six or eight rounds, he raised his hands, inviting the attendant to choose. The man found the queen. He found it the second time as well, but the third attempt turned up the jack of spades instead. Holmes plucked up that card, lifted the next card and showed the attendant the jack of clubs, and then the next—another jack of spades. He then laid them back down and did the same routine, only this time, the three cards exposed were all the queen of hearts.

The attendant chuckled, patted Holmes on the shoulder, and went on.

Jake was watching from under the brim of his hat. "You got good hands," he said.

"They've had practice," Holmes said, then neatened the cards and slid the deck across the table.

Jake looked at the innocent rectangle, then sat upright, took off his hat, and did a shuffle of his own before splaying them out, backs up, and extracting the same three cards—no hesitation.

It made for more of a challenge, playing against a man who knew what he was doing. Normally, surrounded by gullible marks and a shill to lead them, the key to Three-Card Monte was to show the face of the lower card, then actually toss down the card that was hidden behind it, keeping up the distracting patter all the while. The untrained eye let itself be convinced that the displayed card was the one that the hand laid down.

But playing against a person with equal skills, well, that was a game of the mind, not the hands. The differences in how the fingers moved when delivering from the top or from the bottom were so faint as to be imperceptible. Jake frowned at his opponent's moving hands the whole time. Holmes did not.

They traded off whenever one dealer lost. At first, their turns were roughly equal, but after a while, Holmes' began to stretch out. Not a lot, but enough to be noticeable.

Finally, Jake slumped back in his chair with a chuckle. "You're good, all right. And what I can't get over is how you're not even looking at my hands. How do you do that?"

"Practice," Holmes said again. In fact, he'd been watching Jake's eyes for the tell, not the tiny motion of muscles in the man's fingers—but he saw no reason to give away his methods.

Jake shuffled, fanned out the cards, shuffled. "I taught that game to Mary, when she was, oh, maybe ten. Her hands weren't very good, but boy, was she determined to learn."

"Was that before or after you taught her the card-toss that won you a pub?"

"The summer before. I wanted her and her brother to understand that there was trickery in the world. That just because a man was encouraging you to watch the queen didn't mean that the queen was ever in action." He extracted three cards—this time, the two red jacks and the king of clubs—and laid the rest of the deck to one side, starting the game. "Levi was too young to get it, but Mary caught on fast. All on her own, too. I gave her one hint, that there was deceit involved, then started the routine and the patter. She sat there with her nose about six inches away from my hands. I'll admit I slowed things down a little bit, but it didn't take long before she sat up and told me to start over. So, I showed them the queen and began tossing the cards, and when I came to a halt, she found it. Four times in a row, even when I did it full speed. She was proud as Punch when she told me, 'Just because you say it's the queen doesn't mean it is.'"

The uncle looked more than a little proud himself, Holmes noticed. "I imagine you didn't try mixing in the occasional bottom-card-toss."

Jake grinned. "Oh, c'mon, she was ten years old, I wasn't looking to steal her pocket-money. I was only trying to teach the kids a lesson."

"That even a trusted family member can be a deceiver."

The grin faded a bit, the cards went round and round, the hands slowed, then stopped. "It's a lesson worth learning, wouldn't you say?" He reached out and turned each card over.

Jack of hearts. Jack of diamonds. Jack . . . of diamonds.

Holmes was too controlled to allow his face to look startled, but he did pause, and one eyebrow did twitch in a stifled attempt to rise. After a moment, he picked up the neatly stacked deck and turned it over: the card facing him was the king of clubs.

His features relaxed into a smile of appreciation. "Nicely done."

Jake gave a chuckle. "Never too old to learn a lesson, I say."

"Or indeed, to teach one. Tell me, Mr Russell, why did you disappear from Mary's life for so long?"

Jake nodded, to acknowledge that payment was due. "I didn't think she needed me around just then, especially not considering the . . . circumstances of my life when the car accident happened. I was, shall we say, inextricably tied up when I first got word of it, and by the time I was free again, she'd gone off to Boston. I figured her grandparents' house was the best place for her, considering her age—but then she disappeared entirely. I shot off a bunch of cables to friends all over, and got on a boat going north, but by the time I hit the US of A, she'd turned up in Sussex. I wired to a friend in London to check on her, and he said she seemed fine. A little later I heard she'd met you, and I figured that was my sign to keep clear."

Holmes took out his cigarette case, his motions deliberate, his thoughts elsewhere. When he had the tobacco going, he rubbed off its burning end into the tray, watching the fall of ash with great attention. "It was not an accident."

"What wasn't an accident?"

"The motorcar crash that killed your brother and his wife and son."

"What do you mean? Charlie's car went off a cliff. They died, she survived. And blamed herself for it."

"True, but it was not an accident. The brakes were interfered with."

"Jesus. You're sure? Who . . . ?"

"An old friend of your brother's by name of Robert Greenfield."

"*Bobby Greenfield?* I knew him. He helped Charlie and me fix up a cabin in the woods. Bit of a troublemaker—and that's me saying it—but he was young."

"He'd stolen something during the earthquake. Your brother found out, Greenfield didn't want to take the chance of being exposed. We only discovered it last year."

"Christ. What the hell did he steal that he thought was worth their lives?"

"It hardly matters, does it?"

"I suppose not. Where is he now?"

"Prison."

"They didn't hang him?"

"They might have, but Russell intervened."

"Why the hell would she do that?"

"There are parts of the Hebrew Bible to which she does not subscribe. 'An eye for an eye' is one of those."

"I'd have torn the bastard's head off."

"It was a temptation," Holmes admitted.

Jake's hands had absently begun to lay out a game of Patience. Holmes wondered if the man was aware that he was using a deck with two Jacks of diamonds (and Holmes had to admit, he hadn't even noticed Jake lift an entire deck as they came through the smoking car). The lack of focus in his blue eyes suggested that he neither noticed, nor cared.

"I loved my big brother," the younger man said at last. "He stood up for me, even sometimes when he shouldn't have. And his wife was the greatest person in the world. Judith always treated me like a trusted friend, even though she must have known I could be pretty crooked. I loved my nephew, Levi, who was a weird kid with a brain like a clock. He'd have done great things for the world. And . . ." He reeled his gaze in from the far distance to meet Holmes' eyes. "I love my niece. I let her down when she needed me, and the decisions I made after that might not have been the right ones. But I won't do it again. Not with anything that matters."

Oh, Jacob, Holmes thought sadly. *You just had to add that caveat at the end, didn't you?*

CHAPTER FORTY-NINE

JAKE

As Mr Holmes and I sat in that shabby train smoking car, a game of solitaire unfolding on the table between us, I waited for the tension to drift out the windows. I'd opened my heart to the man (a little—no need to frighten the horses) in hopes of reassuring him that I wasn't out to rob my niece blind. That I might actually be of some use to the girl.

Should I tell him that Mary had offered me a chunk of her inheritance? Or would that seem like protesting too much? She might have told him already, since my refusal would be a fairly major point to consider, when it came to motives, and what I was actually after.

(That assumed she was taking my side here. Which . . . maybe?)

And what about telling him what I was really after here? He might understand. Might even think, well, since I was doing it for Mary . . . I just couldn't read him well enough to be sure, and I could feel that things were getting so close, could I take that risk?

Hell, why not just stretch out on the seat like someone in Dr Freud's offices and spill my guts about everything? Tell him how, sure, I'd been to Cator Road to see Frank Shackleton, but I'd run out of nerve, and ended up following him at a distance like some lovesick adolescent, lurking in a doorway as he let himself in, watching the lights go on, seeing that clever, handsome, icy, unscrupulous man walk through his house and close the curtains on me. Tell Mr Holmes how seeing Frank two months ago, even with all those years weighing him down, hit me every bit as hard as the first time I'd laid eyes on him in that gilded salon in London, the summer of 1906. *Coup de foudre,* the French call it: lightning bolt. *Coup de folie,* more like it—madness striking.

No, I decided. Mary's husband didn't need to know any of that, any more than he needed to know what old JR was looking for. And I didn't need to tell him that his young wife had offered her uncle money. If he did know about her offer, my not saying anything might make me look more trustworthy than if I shoved her offer in his face. Anyway, I could always use it later if I needed to.

It made me a little happier to feel that I wouldn't have to spend the next few days cheek-to-jowl with a man bristling with suspicion (and for all I knew, watching for an excuse to slap me behind bars). Husbands tend to be wary enough around their wives' male relatives, even without my history.

But wouldn't you know, it was like he heard that last thought, and it turned out he wasn't quite so de-fused as I'd imagined. "Mr Russell, how much have you revealed to your niece about your activities?"

The air blowing from the window turned a tiny bit arctic. "Activities?"

"Of the criminal variety."

"Mary knows I'm a crook. She's known that since she was a kid."

"But the details?"

(I definitely hope not.) "The last few days have been a bit hectic."

"I take it that means she is not aware of certain episodes involving a Los Angeles Post Office, or a Philadelphia businessman whose safe was emptied one summer's night, or the failure of a quantity of bullion to reach its destination in Vancouver, Canada?"

"How the hell— No, you're taking stabs in the dark. There's nothing to tic mc to any of those."

"Three paintings from a Boston museum. A rather nice gold cross that had been pulled out of a ship-wreck off the coast of the Carolinas. A weekend's takings from a casino in northern Italy, and another such from a race-track in Sydney. The rather botched attempt last April at breaking into a private safe in Bordeaux, which despite literally blowing up in your faces, nonetheless permitted all of your partners to escape. I will note that it was one of your few near-failures, as well as one of the few times you worked with men you seemed not to know well, two facts which I imagine were not unrelated. Shall I go on?"

"How can you possibly know those things?"

"Mr Russell, it is my business to know what other people do not. You have been, shall we say, a hobby of mine since before I ever met your niece. When I returned home from Europe in the spring of 1912, I was told an amusing tale of how a clever American had duped a nearby publican out of his establishment. What puzzled me was the fact that the American had apparently then sold the business for considerably less than one might have expected, and left the area. This interested me, Mr Russell. Over the next few months, I conducted interviews with several of those involved, which led me to the somewhat troubling conclusion that the two children the man had with him that night were not, in fact, entirely innocent bystanders."

"Oh, but they—"

"When I met Russell three years later, I soon realised that she had been one of those children, and added a number of points to my watching brief. Then, when she told me her side of the story at last, one winter's night a year or two ago . . . well, as I said, I make it my business to know.

"For some years now, I have listened for certain sorts of crime.

Cleverly planned. Very lucrative. Quiet, neither showy nor violent. And often with a short, charming, blond-headed man somewhere in the background—a new bank customer, a volunteer docent at the museum, a uniformed postal inspector whose name failed to appear on any employee roster."

I watched the telegraph wires rise and fall, rise and fall, and wondered if jumping off a moving train would leave a person able to run.

Instead of leaping to my feet and making a break for it, I picked up the cards again and began to shuffle, using the motion to let me think. The hands were healing, I thought. Not when I had to hold still for delicate work, but they were pretty good when I could keep them moving. The hearing was a different matter, and from what the doctors told me, I might be stuck with it.

Which was one reason why I was trying to finish up the pieces of unfinished business while I still could. Old men should be able to retire when they wanted to, and not work until they were introduced to a cell. (Or a bullet.)

"My father and I used to aggravate each other," I said to Mr Holmes. "No, don't worry, I'm not about to get all Freud on you, just that there's another part of the pattern you may not have noticed. My brother, Charlie, was Dad's blue-eyed boy—his right hand in the business, always knew how to make the old man laugh, and how to disagree without provoking him. I, on the other hand, got bored with paperwork, and kissing his boots really rubbed me the wrong way. The first time I deliberately set out to steal something that wasn't mine, it belonged to my father. Just money. And I didn't even intend to keep it, just take it and then show him what I'd done and how. You'd think he might be grateful to learn about a hole in his system, right?

"Wrong. He got mad and I got madder. That was the first time he kicked me out. I told him that in that case, I'd keep the money and count it as part of my inheritance.

"Turns out, a young man tends to underestimate how much

things cost. After two or three years, I could see that before long I was going to have to make a decision: either crawl home like the Prodigal and hope he chose the fatted calf over handing me a broom to sweep the floors in one of the factories, or I could find my own way forward. It was Charlie who helped me decide—though he never knew, or he'd have kicked me out, too.

"I was living in San Francisco, helping Charlie out. This was before Mary was born—he and Judith had just got engaged, I think, and Charlie was having a beef with Wells Fargo, who'd lost a shipment and were refusing to pay him back. It was going to be a blow to the old finances. Now, like I said, I'm not a natural when it comes to running a business, but this was hurting my brother, and I'd been working around him long enough to be up on how things were done. And one day I was fretting over it, asking myself how the hell something could have just disappeared on the train between San Francisco and Salt Lake City, and suddenly I spotted it. I could see how they'd done it, right there in front of me. I was going to tell Charlie, as soon as he got home from the office, but when I thought about it, I knew it wouldn't help get the stuff back. I decided that I could either tell him, or I could do something with the idea.

"So I took off for a couple weeks, said I was going to Los Angeles, and I came back with enough of Wells Fargo's cash to cover what he'd lost. Plus some for me, of course—I'm not an idiot. I told him I'd been in a card game, and made him take the money. A wedding present. Anyway, that's how it began."

"Are you claiming you are a modern-day Robin Hood, Mr Russell?"

"Be nice to think so, wouldn't it? There have been a few times when I've done a job from the goodness of my heart, but no, it's not usually that simple." (Not even the Philly job.) "However, believe it or not, I do have rules. I don't hurt people—you said that yourself. I sometimes carry a gun, but it's never loaded. Twice, I've had to hit someone hard enough to knock them down, but the last time for that was twelve years ago. And frankly, the people I steal from not only can afford to lose it, they pretty much deserve to be fleeced. Like that Los Angeles postmaster—he had a couple of pretty nasty side-businesses, and I'm glad he lost most of them when they found out. That gold bullion was paying for a shipment of opium, so you can be sure there was plenty more where it came from. And those safe-deposit boxes? I mostly took from the big ones with ladies' necklaces and the odd gold bar, not from the ones with house mortgage papers and a few twenty-dollar notes."

"Noble of you."

"I like to be able to live with myself."

"Do you mind telling me, then, how laying your hands upon the Irish Crown Jewels will help you to do that?"

"Far as I'm concerned, that little collection might as well be a bank note blowing along the street. Who does it even belong to? George IV gave the diamonds to his mistress, who had the good manners to return them when he died, but no one wanted the new Queen wearing a concubine's rejects, so they were taken apart and given to Ireland. The current King doesn't really own them. The Irish might claim them, but which flavour of Irish? If they were sold and put to use building roads or schools or something, I might have some sympathy, but you think the Irish government would do that? Nah. I always think it's ironic that we talk about gold and diamonds as being 'pure' when they're about the dirtiest things on earth. Shiny baubles that drag a vicious trail behind them. I've seen how diamonds are mined. If anyone said that the poor bastards who dug them out of the hillsides in Brazil owned the things, I'd make no argument."

"A Socialist thief," Holmes mused.

"A thief is all about the redistribution of wealth," I pointed out—and then laughed. "I know, it sounds ridiculous. And to tell you the truth, between the English King and the Irish Republicans, I don't honestly care which of them ends up with the Jewels. Just so it isn't Frank Shackleton or Dickie Gorges."

That last sentence made him look up with those penetrating grey eyes of his. And this time, I let him see my bitterness, my sense of betrayal, and my determination to keep them from their prize. He didn't entirely believe me. (With reason, granted.) The man had been around long enough to know—theoretically, at least—that it might be possible to deceive even the great Sherlock Holmes.

However, belief and trust are two very different matters. And I could see, in the lowering of his shoulders and the relaxation in his jaw, that in some small way, in the corner of his heart if not the workings of his brain, he was beginning to trust me.

Funny thing was, I felt the same way towards him. I almost gave him the last, small truth at the centre of it all—I drew a breath in and could feel the words pressing on my tongue.

But no: This was something from me, for Mary. Or at least, for Mary to decide. A small token of my regret, over all the times I had failed her.

So instead, I tipped my head and gave Mary's husband my most blatantly amiable smile, a smile that didn't even pretend it was anything but that of a shark.

"Mr Holmes, could I interest you in a game of poker?"

CHAPTER FIFTY

Russell

Having finally succeeded in shoving Lady Vicars and Mrs Walsh onto their train and catching one of my own, I went in pursuit of husband and uncle. I shall not inflict on the reader a description of my watery voyage from Wales to Dublin, other than to say that the journey felt like forever.

Without Jake's hand on my elbow when I reached Dunleary, it was even odds as to whether I would end up in the Royal Marine or in the greasy water between the docks, but fortunately the flow of passengers was thick enough to carry me with it as far as the street, and the thought of a cup of tea took me the remainder of the way. Also any news from Billy, of course, but mostly the tea.

I did stop at the desk first, where I collected a telegram. I laid it unread beside my plate while a kindly maternal waitress brought me tea and, without my asking, a rack of dull, dry, English toast, a combination that began to restore my brain to its land-based status. When I had finished my second cup and half the toast, I surreptitiously used the edge of the linen table-cloth to clear my salt-rimed spectacles, and opened Billy's telegram.

FRANCIS QUOTE MELLOR SICK FROM WORK AND AWAY FROM HOME SINCE WEDNESDAY STOP GORGES GONE ALSO WEDNESDAY STOP SOLICITOR NEXT BUT RUMOUR SAYS SOLID

"Ah, sure, them telegrams," said a voice at my side. "They can be desperate bad news. Still, from the looks of you it doesn't seem like the news was too terrible bad."

I smiled up at the waitress, enjoying her broad accent. "No, it mostly confirms what I'd expected."

"Well, pet, glad I am the Lord's not inflictin' on you new troubles. What about a bit more toast? Surely that's gone cold."

"No, thank you," I said, fishing out my coin-purse. "But it has restored me nicely."

"Yer lookin' less peaky."

"I imagine you see a fair number of green-gilled passengers staggering off the boat."

"Enough to be knowin' what the doctor ordered," she said.

"I don't suppose you have equal skills when it comes to recommending trains?"

"Where you hopin' to go, darlin'?"

"A place called 'Coolballintaggart,'" I said, "down past—"

"Wicklow, to be sure—Aughrim's your station. Not the one off in County Galway, of course."

"Of course," I said, making a note to take care that I didn't hare off to the other side of the country.

"Today's Sunday, not all the trains'll be runnin'. Best way is to wait a bit for the evenin' train, sets out from Dunleary coupla minutes before six. There's a nice hotel in Woodenbridge, get the Shillelagh train in the morning."

My heart sank. "There's no way of getting there tonight?"

"Oh, if it's in a hurry y'are, you moit try poppin' up to Dublin itself, and if there is a Sunday train to Shillelagh—a person never knows, not truly, but I tink there's one sets off a shade after six.

You still won't reach Aughrim til half-eight or so, but you could take a nice room at the Lawless."

The recommendation of an establishment called "Lawless" made me check what I was wearing: decent skirt, of a reassuringly conservative length, with footwear that might have been questionable, but could hardly be thought anarchic. I gave her a ladylike smile. "Perhaps I can find someone willing to take me out to Coolballintaggart, directly."

She shook her head in doubt. "It's only four, five miles, but you'll not find many taxis in Aughrim on a Sunday."

Oh, to be in a pagan land.

"A man willing to hang a lantern from his dog-cart will do me."

"I don't know what you'd be looking fer in Coolballintaggart," she said, seeming ever more doubtful as to my sanity.

"A man named O'Mahony has a house there—"

Her eyebrows rose. "You're off to see The O'Mahony?"

"I'm going to try."

"Ah, sure, that's a whole different matter. You finish up now, darlin', I'll be roit back."

Three minutes later she was, with a young man in a uniform of some kind with a brimmed cap. "Diss'll be young Danny, to take you to the roit train—get on now and p'raps you'll make it."

He tugged at the hat-brim, and said, "If I can take your bag, ma'am, I'll meet you out front in two minutes." The accent had once been local but had taken on a thick layer of New York. The attitude and the tip of his hat were pure Yank.

My helpful waitress was all but pulling me to my feet. Since matters seemed to be out of my control, I dumped a handful of coins on the table, hoping there was enough to express my gratitude. Two minutes even gave me time to visit the Ladies, and the motor pulled up just as I hurried out of the hotel entrance.

A shiny American Pierce-Arrow touring car was about the last thing I expected.

"Is this yours?" I asked, my voice rather climbing in astonishment.

"At the moment it is," he said.

I pulled my eyes away from the gleaming paint. "Did you steal it?"

"Do I look like a car thief?"

When I did not reply, he tipped his head and gave me a grin that Uncle Jake would be proud of. "Nah, I'm joshin' you. My boss bought it just before we got on the boat from New York. I need to break it in for a day or two before we set off. A quick jaunt into the city is just the trick."

I gave a mental shrug, since I had witnesses to my innocence in the matter, and stepped forward, only to be interrupted by a call from behind me.

"Madam! Sorry, madam, this just arrived, I'm glad we caught you! *Two* Sunday telegrams—it must be important." He held out the day's second flimsy envelope, hoping that I would tell him what was so urgent as to justify another Sunday surcharge. Instead, I found a coin to fill his palm and turned away to rip it open.

GORGES ARRIVED HOME WITH INJURED SHOULDER YOUR WORK QUESTION MARK

I smiled, relieved that Jake's "drunken thug" was out of the picture and amused by Billy's assumption that I was to blame, and allowed my Yankee chauffeur to usher me into the back of his borrowed American motor with the left-hand drive.

"Quick" was indeed the word, and a true experience when one was looking out the wrong side of the windscreen.

We skidded, just a bit, when Danny swerved to a halt in front of the Dublin station. He leapt out, snatched my bag, and accompanied me inside, talking all the while—as indeed, he had talked from the moment he put the motor into gear. "Plenty of time, nearly three minutes, try to get a seat on the side of the water, it's pretty at least til the sun goes down. And when you get to Aughrim, make for the Lawless, you'll see it not long after you leave the station, but before you get there, on the right side of the road there's a pub, doesn't have a name on the outside but go in there—looks a bit rough, but the snug's nice, be fine for a lady like you, just knock if the door isn't open. Once you're in, tell them Sara—your waitress back there in the restaurant—said you're to speak to Matty Donovan—he's a sort of a cousin of hers who works in the pub and he might—*might*—be able to help you out. Though make sure you check how long anyone you hire to take you into the countryside has been sitting at the bar. If Matty's not there, go back and see if the Lawless can help you. Here we go, I won't stop and get a platform ticket since that'll only slow you down, but a strapping girl like you can carry a bag, safe travels, now," and with that, he whipped off his hat in a salute and saw me on my way.

CHAPTER FIFTY-ONE

RUSSELL

I can't say I paid a great deal of attention to the scenery out of the carriage window, being too busy chewing my finger-nails and urging the train wheels forward. I was the first passenger off the train when we reached Woodenbridge, where I was ridiculously grateful to find that a) there was indeed a Sunday train to Shillelagh, b) it had not yet left, and c) it did, in fact, intend to leave. It was only four or five miles to Aughrim, but adding on the same distance to Coolballintaggart, my ankle would not be pleased.

How far had Holmes and Jake got in their similar journey? Were they ahead of me, or still making their way up from the southern mail-boat port? Knowing the two of them, they were sitting in front of The O'Mahony's turf fire with glasses in their hands and the diamonds sparkling across their laps.

I checked the station clock, which assured me that I had seven minutes before the doors would shut. I had promised to send my two missing partners a wire with Billy's information . . . but I'd be in Aughrim before any cable, and there was nothing they urgently needed to know. Instead, I used the time to ask if the bearded station master had seen two men, one tall and grey-haired, the other shorter and with yellow hair, both clean-shaven, with . . . after a moment's thought, I offered that they were American but occasionally sounded English. That would cover the bases.

The station master shook his head, the ticket seller looked blank, and the cleaning woman trundling her cart out of the back room was effusive in her apologies, but no, they hadn't been seen. Was I sairtain the two had got off the train? Because if they'd stayed on, well, there was no way to know, though if Dermot over there was to get on the telephone machine and ask up further on if . . .

By the time I extracted myself from the talkative cleaner and her silent colleague, there were signs of departure. I gave the station master a smile as I went past, and he tipped his hat, then said something that took me a moment to interpret out of his accent.

"Pardon?" I tried.

"I said, if it was a man with a moosetache you were lookin' for, I coulda gi'en you one a them."

"A moustache."

"Right. English, that one was—here, better hop on," he suggested as a shout came from up the train.

He drew out his shiny whistle and firmly herded me on board, but I balked in the doorway, turning to ask, "What time was that? That the Englishman with the moustache was here?"

"Oh, hours ago. On you go, ma'am."

"How many hours?" I demanded, fending off the conductor in desperation.

"Hours," he repeated, and drowned out my continued questions with his shrill whistle.

"How many?" I shouted as the train gave a jerk.

"At least three or—oh, no, I'm a liar," he said. "It was the Wexford train, couldn't be more than . . ."

I nearly leapt off the train to pull it out of him, and to demand if the moustached Englishman had anyone with him, but the conductor had my arm in a panicked grip and drew me inside. However, I had seen the station master's mouth move. He'd ended his sentence with the words, *an hour: Couldn't be more than an hour.* Even with the accent and through the beard, I could replay the motions of his jaws and lips. It couldn't be anything else, right?

I only took a seat because the conductor was so unhappy at the idea of a woman standing. Perhaps if I lingered near the door on my feet, it required all the gentlemen on the train to rise, as well? So I sat, although the distance was so minor, we barely got up to speed before we were slowing. And again, I was the first out onto the platform.

I was expecting a tiny rural stop like the one in Kilmorna, where an outsider's every action would attract a group of fascinated urchins. Instead, there was a trim station with an actual private motorcar waiting for a passenger. Unfortunately, no taxi rank, and the station itself was not open at this hour on a Sunday, meaning no attendant to question about arriving Englishmen, either solitary with a moustache or clean-shaven and accompanied by an American.

As I walked up the station's access road into the town, even in the dark, I could see that Aughrim was a considerably larger settlement than I had pictured, with a broad central road and large, prosperous stone buildings. It was clearly a market town—a cattle market, by the smell in the air—and up ahead, the Lawless hotel looked absolutely respectable.

However, I made instead for the rough-looking public house across the way, where I might find Sara's friend Matty Donovan, who might or might not be able to help me. The snug was aptly named, a small room with a low-burning turf fire—a place for the wealthy, the snooty, or the female to take a quiet glass of what-have-you. This one was, to my surprise, actually occupied, with the rural Irish equivalent of the flapper: three girls who looked no older than seventeen, with short hair beneath new-looking cloche hats, each wearing inexpertly applied lipstick. Below the neck, modernity gradually gave way to Ireland, with warm cardigans around their shoulders, then tweed skirts that fell below the knees, followed by slightly grubby lisle stockings. By the girls' feet, their country had reasserted itself, since all three wore brogues sturdy enough to deal with rocky fields and streets the cows had been down.

One of them had been bravely attempting a cigarette, although her hand snatched it out of her mouth and crushed it into the pristine ash-tray the moment I came in the door.

"Good evening, ladies," I said.

They giggled. The one with the cigarette blushed furiously.

"I was told to ask for Matty Donovan," I said, working off my gloves to give the impression that I intended to settle in for a time.

The trio giggled again, more loudly than the first time. Fortunately, the one nearest the back of the snug then turned on her bench to rap on a wooden hatch. I could hear voices from the other side, and after a minute, she slapped the wood three times with the flat of her hand.

This time, she was heard. The hatch came open, a man's voice already speaking. "—you, Moira, I didn't think yer mother would—ah, sorry," he said, spotting me in with the girls. "I didn't hear ye come in. Is there something I can be getting for you, my dear?"

Yet more giggles—and seeing the handsome face and muscular shoulders framed by the hatch, I could guess why.

"A kind waitress at the Royal Marine in Dublin suggested that I speak with a Matty Donovan, when I got to Aughrim."

"You're speaking at him. What can I—girls, isn't it time you were getting home? I don't want your father coming after you again, Bridie."

I started to tell him that wasn't necessary, but they were already rising, and their glasses were all empty. I wished them a good night, but Matty called after them, "And Dierdre, let your clothes air out on the way home or your mam'll smell them ciggies."

More laughter, then the door shut and I was granted a really quite attractive smile from the young man behind the bar.

"I need to get out to Coolballintaggart tonight," I told him. "Sara said you might be able to help. It's urgent."

"Friends with our Sara, are you?" He was polite enough not to look dubious.

I laughed. "I don't even know her last name, only that she works in the Royal Marine, she's very good at prescribing toast for a seasick patient, and that she wanted to help me get to The O'Mahony as soon as I could."

He straightened, and showed me the difference between his professional smile and his real one. "That'd be Phillips—Sara Phillips. So it's the madman you're wanting, is it?"

"I have heard he's a touch eccentric," I admitted. Multiple gardens, self-proclaimed titles, bagpipes, kilts, large hounds . . .

"Nobody around here'd argue with you there," he said.

"Well, I need to get out there. Tonight."

"It's already late, and he's an old man."

"If I can't find someone to take me, I'll have to walk."

He studied me through the hatch window, taking in my firm determination. He gave me a nod. "It'll be ten minutes or so, here—" He stepped back and I could see him doing something at the bar. In a minute he reappeared, placing a glass on the hatch. "It'll be cold, get that inside you." And the hatch went down.

The glass steamed, even in the warm room. A scrap of fresh lemon floated in it, with some dark objects that might have been bits of tree bark. I retrieved it, gingerly held it under my nose, and took a small sip. Then a larger one. By the time Matty Donovan stuck his head in at the door, I was very well insulated against any arctic blast Ireland could throw at me.

Which was just as well, since my jest about dog-carts with a lantern hanging on top was precisely what stood waiting.

It was an up-scale one, with actual bench seating rather than having to sit on the flat bed with one's legs dangling above the ground, inches from the donkey's tail end. Unfortunately, the added height made the perch feel precarious, as if leaning back too vigorously might cause the donkey to lift into the air. Mr Donovan helped me up, wrapped me in a blanket that I suspected he'd taken from the back of a horse in a nearby field, and dropped onto the bench beside me. He took up the reins and slapped the donkey into motion.

"Er," I said, taking care to not let my teeth rattle together too sharply with the jerks of the cart, "aren't you going to light the lantern?"

"Ah, no, sure and the moon's plenty bright."

I looked up at the sky, and noticed for the first time that the usual Irish clouds had parted, giving way to a vast sweep of crisp stars and a moon perhaps five days from full. My night vision was bad enough that the creature before us still seemed to be trotting merrily into stygian blackness, but it did not seem to bother him. I told myself that man and beast knew the road, that donkeys were smart enough not to fling themselves off a cliff, and that I could always get out and walk if my nerves failed.

The hot toddy I had drunk perhaps explained why I merely pulled the rough blanket around my shoulders, trusting my soul to the Celtic gods. And we were still in the town itself—lights from some of the buildings along the road showed life within. It would be fine. And it was only four or five miles, the donkey's brisk trot would get us there in half an hour.

I was unable to avoid pressing against the man, but his shoulder was at least warm. He began to hum, a pleasant baritone noise that blended with the quick rhythm of hooves. My thoughts wandered up the road ahead of us. Would I find Holmes and Jake there before the fire, the Jewels safely rescued? Would Francis Shackleton be in a nearby room, hands and feet bound, awaiting the morning and a summoning of the police? How far ahead of me was Shackleton, anyway? If it was Frank Shackleton, of course. The station master had said *an hour.* Or had he? Damn men and their obscuring beards, anyway.

"Mr Donovan, do you—"

"Oh, Matty is fine, for a friend of me cousin's who's willin' to ride out alone into the night with me."

Hmm, I thought. Was this such a good idea? "Matty, then. What time would the previous train have come through Aughrim?"

"That would've been the half-five, though I'm afraid the trains here aren't always quite to time," he admitted. "I heard it come in some three hours ago." And as if my question had been a permission, his low rumbling hum turned into song. "'In eighteen hundred'n forty-one, my dungaree breeches I put on, those dungaree breeches I put on, to work upon the railway, the railway . . .'"

Three hours would still put the train's arrival in daylight. Would an Englishman set out then and there for the road to The O'Mahony's house? Knowing that eyes would be upon him? Or would he wait and—

"Stop!" I grabbed my driver's arm. The song broke off as he hauled back on the reins.

"What's wrong?" he asked, looking over his shoulder at the road behind us. "Did ya hear—"

"The Lawless," I said, thinking aloud. "If an outsider arrived in town—an Englishman, who had money and needed a quiet place to sit for a bit—what hotel would they go to?"

"There's not that many hotels in all of Aughrim," he said. "Though there's three boarding houses, and plenty of farms to put someone up."

I cursed my head, and the powerful drink I had so carelessly downed. "I need to go back to the Lawless."

"But we're near halfway to—"

"I'm sorry, I have to see if someone is there. You can leave me off there if you like, I don't want to take up your entire evening."

He was too polite to shake his head, but I could feel just a touch of male exasperation in his posture as he negotiated with the donkey to reverse course on a road that was too narrow to do so with ease. In the end, he jumped down and took the donkey's halter strap, pushing the cart and pulling the animal into the awkward turn.

When he had retaken his seat and slapped the beast into motion, I apologised again.

"Not a problem," he assured me, and I vowed to find a way to give him a large gratuity before the business was over.

On the forecourt in front of the Lawless, he brought the cart to a halt behind a well-travelled motorcar. I untangled the horse blanket and availed myself of his offered hand to climb down from the teetering cart. "Honestly," I told him, "if you hand me my valise from under the seat, I can make my own way from here. You should be getting home."

"Nah, it's a beautiful evening and if I wasn't here, I'd just be doin' the washin' up. This way I get some sweet night air with a handsome young lady and my brother has to clean."

"Well, thank him for me, and I shouldn't be more than a few minutes."

The hotel was still open—not the restaurant, but a few late customers had settled into the saloon bar for nightcaps. I did not hesitate, but braved the disapproving glances to walk up and ask the man behind the shiny bar if I could talk to someone about their guests.

"They've mostly gone home," he said as he polished a glass. "Are ye lookin' for someone?"

"An Englishman, who may have either taken a room or simply come here for a time earlier this evening. He may or may not have had a moustache, and may or may not have had an American friend with him." I listened to what I was saying, and had to laugh—a description that embraced either the single Shackleton or the pair of Holmes and Jake Russell made for an absurd sort of question. "This is a man who . . . left something on the train, and as I was coming through Woodenbridge, the station master asked if anyone heading to Aughrim would be willing to take it to him. And the station master's memory was not entirely certain." A ridiculous tale, but the best I could come up with at the drop of my slightly tipsy hat.

He finished shining the glass, reached for the next. "No Americans today, not that I noticed, but there was an English fella here for a time. Tall, moustache. Friendly gent, easy to talk to, interested in everything. Not every man thinks to buy the publican a drink."

That sounded like Francis Shackleton, professional charmer.

"When was he here?"

"Came in on the train, I think. Wasn't interested in dinner, but he had a coupla drinks and left."

"What time was that?"

He set down the glass, picked up another. "Oh, not long. Hour ago, maybe? We got busy and when I looked around, he was gone."

"That isn't his motorcar out in front?"

"No, both those drivers are still here." He nodded at the table of three in the corner.

"Both? There's only one car there."

His hands stopped moving. "There's two."

"Not when I came in."

He set down both glass and cloth and marched to the door. I followed, and stood behind him as he stared at the empty place behind the motorcar with the mud up its rims. Matty, lying across the cart's bench with his feet propped up and a cigarette in his hand, stopped singing and craned his head around to watch with interest. I noticed that he'd lit the small hanging lantern at the end of the pole over the donkey's head. The publican stared at the drive, then whirled and broke into a trot, back through the doors and around the end of the long bar. I followed.

He patted around, then dropped to his heels to search the floor. When he rose, he cast an agonised glance at the corner table.

"What's happened?" I asked.

"Old McGinty loves his motor, but when he's too much drink

taken, he tends to drive into things. So he always leaves his key with me, and if at the end of the night I think he's had one too many, I have someone take him home. The key's not here."

"Did you tell your English visitor that story?"

The publican stared at me, then at the telephone.

I had no idea where the nearest police station might be, but it was time for me to leave.

I eased myself out of the door, scrambled up into the donkey-cart, and told my driver rather urgently to go.

CHAPTER FIFTY-TWO

SHERLOCK HOLMES

Holmes assured himself that there was no cause for apprehension. He had no actual evidence that Francis Shackleton or Richard Gorges were even interested in the Jewels, much less that either man had rushed to Ireland before them.

No cause for apprehension, he reflected, other than a break-in, a shooting, a major unsolved crime, one delay in Fishguard and another on the north-bound train out of Rosslare, a wife and partner uncertain in her own mind, a brother up to his usual meddling, and a temporary partner who was absolutely not to be trusted.

Holmes was smiling as he lit his pipe.

Jacob Russell noticed. "If you're finding something worth laughing about, I wish you'd let me in on it."

"I was merely comparing the level of calamities on this outing with others in my experience."

"Well, nobody's died yet. And the train is still moving forward."

"I admire your optimism, Mr Russell."

"And that child's vomit has mostly come out of my trouser-leg."

"It scarcely smells at all."

"We might get to Aughrim before they roll up the sidewalks. Oh, sorry, you'd call them 'pavements.'"

"I spent enough time in America to become more or less bilingual."

"When was that?"

Holmes poked at the burning tobacco, trying to rearrange its draw. "My longest sojourn in the States was just before the War, investigating a German spy ring. That was the year before I met Russell, who saw through my purported retirement because of the uneven tan on my skin. I'd worn a goatee in Chicago."

Jake studied the face across from him. "Can't imagine you in a fussy little beard."

"I shaved it off the first minute I could."

"I bet. But at least we haven't dragged Mary into our calamities. You think she's set off for Sussex yet?"

Holmes did not reply. He wanted to believe that Russell was taking Mrs Walsh off to her temporary home on the other side of England. Somehow, that image failed to become firm in his mind.

Jake glanced at his watch, then squinted up at the descending sun. "I wonder if we should rethink our plans. I'm not sure we want to delay too many hours, once we get there."

Holmes frowned irritably at his pipe, which was proving as recalcitrant as everything else had been that day. It seemed a very long time ago that he and Jacob had worked out a plan for approaching Coolballintaggart. The variables under consideration had been many: Where The O'Mahony's loyalties lay, for example, to family and to country. The chances of the man actually having the Irish Crown Jewels. Whether his Irish convictions would make him suspect the motives of an Englishman and an American. And, of course, the possible complications in confronting a pack of large and aggressive hounds.

Curiously, Jake Russell had made the radical proposition of

honesty: knock on the man's door, tell him the story, see what his involvement with the Jewels was and what he intended to do with them.

And, he'd added with a sly smile, *he might give us a clue as to where he's got them, so we could return and help ourselves.*

Holmes had to acknowledge certain benefits to the proposal. On the other hand, they needed to know whether or not Shackleton and his bald-headed companion were there before them. And that raised another question: Were they armed?

Given the original time of arrival, Holmes had insisted on surveillance first, and Jake had reluctantly agreed: they would locate some kind of restaurant or tea-house in Aughrim, and near to dusk, when the local residents were settling down to their evening tea, they would make their way to Coolballintaggart, by car, cart, or shoe-leather. There they would silently take up positions to watch over the house, and wait.

If no one appeared by morning, they would brush the leaves from their trousers and openly make their own approach to The O'Mahony's door.

This, Jacob had made clear, was not his idea of a pleasant night. Holmes suggested that he remain in Aughrim until matters were settled. This, Jacob decided, was even less acceptable.

However, all of that was before the seven hours of delay on their journey. Holmes now had to agree that a reconsideration was in order.

Food and drink in Aughrim was no longer on the schedule.

Any news from Russell would need to wait until the Post Office opened in the morning.

And walking the five miles to Coolballintaggart felt like too slow an option.

However, when the train finally pulled into Aughrim, there appeared to be little in the way of taxicabs, horse carriages, or even bicycles on offer at the station.

As they stood, looking at the lack of transport, Jake cleared his throat. "So, I meant to tell you. About those dogs Mrs Walsh said we might come across."

"The O'Mahony's wolfhounds."

"Right. Well, while we were waiting for the train in Rosslare, I went for a poke around the station's cleaning closet. I sort of helped myself to a bottle of cleaning fluid."

Holmes turned his head, eyebrows arched in surprise. "Ammonia. To repel dogs."

Jake shrugged. "Thought it might come in handy."

After a minute, the detective turned back to the road. "Working with you, Mr Russell, is proving something of a revelation."

The train had left, the last disembarking passengers had disappeared into the hinterland of Aughrim, leaving the two men alone on the silent street.

"So," Jake said into the stillness. "Would you rather steal a car, or a couple of horses?"

CHAPTER FIFTY-THREE

RUSSELL

My spine was thoroughly exercised by the five miles of rural road we rattled over, and I'd heard a sampling of Irish songs that began with the railway, wandered through politics, then shied away from a fairly blatant anti-British ditty before settling down to a number of songs about lovers visiting at night. This last might have caused me to feel a bit apprehensive of our increasingly lonely journey—down the road, onto a lesser road, then taking to a rough and half-overgrown track—if Mr Donovan hadn't been so completely oblivious of my presence. Man and donkey seemed happy to keep trotting and singing until we reached the Atlantic, but in fact, before long he eased back on the reins and walked the tireless creature to the near-invisible side of the track.

"Well, pet, here's the drive," he said. "Gate'll be locked or I'd take you in, but it's easy enough to slip along the side."

At the edges of the lantern's illumination, I could make out the uncertain proportions of a gate. Again I used his calloused hand to climb down, and accepted my valise.

"How far up is the house?"

"No distance at all, less than a half-mile. You'll see lights once you get to the top o' the little rise." A vague motion indicated that he was pointing at a high spot in the all-but-invisible driveway.

He sucked at his teeth in the way that told the donkey to back up. This time there seemed to be enough room behind the cart, and he did not have to climb down.

"If you walk brisk-like, you'll not freeze, and I'm all but certain The O'Mahony's at home this week. He'll have a fire going." The cart had finished the tight circle, bringing it back on the road to town, so he wished me a pleasant evening and slapped the reins. Trotting resumed, rattling commenced, and as he drew away, I heard his voice call back to me, "Oh, and when the dogs come a'roarin' out, just stand yourself still, they're all pussies, really."

And as his dot of light faded among the hedges, I heard his voice, full-throated now, belting out, "'In the year of our Lord eighteen and six, we sailed from Cork with a cargo of bricks, our ship she was a wonderful craft, and they called her the *Irish Rover . . .*'"

Bemused, I turned to hunt for his promised way around the gates, idly wondering if the song choice had dropped randomly into the man's mind, or if he had been making a subtle link to the ship's name.

Somehow, I found it hard to imagine a wolfhound named Rover.

CHAPTER FIFTY-FOUR

JAKE

When we got up to the main road, at least we saw signs that Aughrim was not a complete ghost town. (Only a Catholic town on the sabbath.) Curtains had warm lights behind them. A child was screeching somewhere. A gramophone scratched and warbled. What looked like a public house invited attention up at one side, and a little further along and on the other side of the road, half a dozen men were standing out in front of an actual hotel, arguing and waving their arms.

Mr Holmes watched the commotion for a minute, then fished the map out of his pocket and turned in the other direction. "I hope your shoes are comfortable. I suspect the only motorcars in Aughrim are to the north of here."

It did look like most of the town itself was on the other side of a bridge. I buttoned up my coat (at least it wasn't raining) and went after him.

The moon was not yet full, but it was high in the sky and gave a hard enough light that, once our eyes had adjusted, we didn't have any problems following the road. During the first mile or so, we saw one car, half a dozen donkeys, and a horse—any of which we might have borrowed, had they not been smack up against houses with lamps burning and life inside. A crossroads appeared. We took the left fork, and shortly after that spotted a motorcycle. We were tempted, but a closer examination showed that one of the tyres was completely flat and generations of spiders had built webs on the motor. We kept walking.

The next turn indicated by the map was to the smallest road yet, but as we drew near the possible joining, we could hear something approaching. We moved to the side and stood up against a barn of some kind, and after a minute, a cart with an inadequate little lamp came trotting along.

The driver was singing at the top of his lungs. "'For a sailor it's always a bother in life, nights and days of trouble and strife, but for love of a maid, he is never afraid, he's a salt of the *Irish Rover . . .*'"

Inexorably, on he came. In the house across the way, someone pulled back the curtain to see what was happening. I didn't need to keep my voice down when I said to Mr Holmes, "That fellow sounds well sloshed. Shall we help ourselves to his cart?"

"He's not slurring the words, and he's keeping perfect rhythm with the hoofbeats. We are more than halfway there. It might be more trouble than it's worth."

As the cart trotted through the beam of light from the drawn-back curtain, I was glad for the decision: the man looked both large and upright.

"'—nine times around, the old dog was drowned, I'm the last of the *Irish Rover . . .*'"

We watched the bobbing lantern fade away.

"Curious version of the song," Mr Holmes commented.

"Isn't that the Coolballintaggart road that he came from?" I asked.

He didn't answer, just set off again, those long legs of his moving fast enough that I had to occasionally break into a trot to keep up.

This road was little more than a farm track, hedges pushing up at both sides and a grass line down the middle. When we were far enough along it that a light would not be noticed from the farmhouse, Mr Holmes turned his torch on the ground, walking slowly now so as to compare the dryer areas with the low, boggy bits.

The tracks of the donkey-cart were clear, the two wheels—going in, coming out—and two sets of hoof-prints, again in both directions. And then Holmes grunted, and I went to look.

"That's a car," I said.

"Fresh tracks."

Though he searched, there was only one set. And the criss-cross of the cart's tracks showed that the car had gone along this road before the singing man.

There was nothing to say that it hadn't been a car coming out of the farms. But we both knew that, if any other vehicle had been going along this narrow lane tonight, the chances of it meaning trouble had just gone up. (As in, sky-high.)

It's hard to measure distance when things get urgent, and I kept getting into a panic thinking that we'd gone past it. (Mr Holmes was feeling it, too—not so icy as he appeared, that man.) It was also harder to make out the side-roads here, with greenery and trees blocking the moonlight, and after a few minutes, he started switching on his torch every time there was a change in the night around us. Time and again we would search, and find only a wide spot, left for farm carts to squeak past each other, or the side of a derelict shed, or a weed-grown lane far too rustic for a dedicated gardener and self-proclaimed clan chieftain.

At last we found a promising shape in the night: a wide iron gate set into stone—and yes, hoof-marks and scuffs from the two wheels of a labouriously turning cart immediately in front. The gate itself was locked, but the gaps on either side were generous enough.

I started to push my way through the one on the left, then realised that Mr Holmes had stayed behind.

He was playing the torch closely over the area before the gates. Here were the hooves of the donkey, obediently digging in to pull the heavy wooden cart in a full circle. And there were the places where the wooden wheels, dragging around, had rucked up the dirt of the road.

What was Mr—oh.

The tyre-marks did not turn in at the gate.

"That's good, isn't it?" I asked. "That the car went on down the road, I mean? It must belong to the next farmer along."

"The depth of the tyre-prints and the distance between the wheels point to a substantial vehicle," he said absently. "And the new tread on all four tyres argues against a farmer's lorry." He shone the light further up the lane, where the hedges grew even more ragged and the track's surface seemed to deteriorate rapidly.

I had to admit, any car going up there was going to be more scrape than paint.

The torch-light beam began to bounce around as he strode away into the wilds.

"Where are you—" I started to say, until his beam rested for a moment on a freshly broken branch.

Thirty feet up the road, the light reflected off of glass: the back window of a car, abandoned to the hedges.

Thorns grabbed at his overcoat as he pushed his way up to the front end. He paused there for a moment, then fought his way back. "Not yet cold," he said, walking past me towards the gates.

"Any idea how long it's been there?" Like him, I kept my voice very low.

"Assuming he drove from the town, perhaps an hour."

(A lot could happen in an hour. Too much.)

Mr Holmes squeezed through the gates, I followed on his heels—but before we could straighten our garments, the gunshots began.

CHAPTER FIFTY-FIVE

RUSSELL

The surface underfoot improved distinctly inside the gates, with a faint crunch of recently maintained gravel under my boots. The vegetation closed in overhead, further blocking the moonlight. I waited, listening to the night sounds and letting my retinas adjust to the absence of a lantern. There was no breeze at all. An owl, off in the distance. The startling shriek of a vixen, even further away. Then up close, a rustling sound. I tensed . . . but tiny grunts and scuffles declared it only a hedgehog. By then, the gravel had proved itself pale enough to catch the moonlight, offering me guidance into the dark.

There was, as Donovan had said, a rise. When I was at the top, I could indeed catch glimpses of artificial light ahead. I kept to the beaten-down tracks in the drive where motorcar tyres had pressed the stones into the soil, and I was dressed mostly in soft, frictionless fabric. Even with no breeze to stir the leaves, my passing made less of an impression on the night than the hedgehog.

I could see the outline of the building now. Not as large as I'd have thought, for the home of a self-declared clan chieftain. Perhaps he preferred to spend his attentions on his beloved horticulture, rather than stones and timber.

Someone was still awake. The odour of peat smoke might linger, but yellow light spilling through carelessly pulled curtains in a corner room suggested that more than one lamp was being used. According to Mrs Walsh's drawings, currently a squashed lump in my pocket, the housekeeper and groundsman had a separate cottage, out of sight but nearby.

I needed to see what lay inside the room before I committed myself to the knocker or bell. There seemed to be a garden path along the front of the building—the shaft of light showed a slice of shrubs and paving stone, close enough to give a view through the curtain's gap. I set down my valise, to free both hands for feeling my way along the bushes, and took a small step forward.

A branch cracked—so close that for an instant, I thought it was my boot that caused it.

The muffled curse that followed said otherwise.

I froze. So did he. A single *he,* or multiple? There was no whispered exchange, so perhaps one . . .

After a minute, I heard movement—clothing, but not soft enough for silence. It sounded like a waterproof, made from gabardine or waxed cotton. *Slick. Slick.* His feet returned to the paving stone path, betrayed by the *click* of hard-soled city shoes.

Then I could see him—or an outline of him, a dark figure moving across the organic shapes of The O'Mahony's garden. He, too, was making for the gap in the curtains.

He had no idea I was there. If he came out of the garden this way, I could tackle him the moment he stepped onto the drive. I stood motionless, and could see him now—a tall figure in a hat and long coat. He crept closer to the window, slowly, even though no one inside the room could possibly see him without placing themselves in view. Perhaps he feared that the dogs would catch his scent? He was close now to the windows, his right arm coming up as if under an impulse to pull the curtains aside—but then I saw what he held, and everything changed.

Something metallic flared in the shaft of light—a military pistol, at the end of an outstretched arm. And with that, I was out of time. No moments left to search for a large stone or even pull the throwing knife from my boot, no time for anything more than an urgent warning and to fling myself out of harm's way.

"Don't shoot him!" I shouted at the top of my lungs as I dove into the dark bushes beside the path.

And Irish hell broke loose.

CHAPTER FIFTY-SIX

JAKE

Mr Holmes took off like a sprinter at the starting line. I pounded along in his wake, tempted to dump my heavy rucksack but unwilling to take the time to dig out the ammonia bottle. Why hadn't I thought to stick it in a pocket before we'd left town?

Shots and shouting and damn this endless driveway (Jake, you need to practice running)—and then more shouts—*a woman?* It sounded like—oh, for Christ sake, could that be *Mary*? How the hell would she have—

CHAPTER FIFTY-SEVEN

SHERLOCK HOLMES

The gunshots ceased, but Holmes had been counting and could only hope the weapon was empty, because the shouting now rose up, a man—English—and now another man, this one Irish—and then the voices were drowned out by the dogs, barking and then snarling, deep and savage noises.

But above all the tumult, like a flash of lightning on a moonless night, a voice.

Russell.

He ran faster, pulling his own revolver from his pocket.

CHAPTER FIFTY-EIGHT

Russell

I huddled down as small as I could get, bullets whizzing over my back, alarmingly close—a person can actually hear them rip the air. When, that is, the next shot hasn't drowned out the sound. Six shots, and I stayed cowering on the ground. Was that the weapon's entire cartridge, or was it an eight-shot? Was my delay giving him the chance to reload? Could I tell the difference between a .38 and a .455 Webley by the sound of the thing? Of course I couldn't, but why was I here with my face pressed onto the ground? I should be making a move before the man could reload and—

And then the timbre of hell shifted and voices rose all around me, baying voices and the scrabble of clawed feet, accompanied by a brighter light—a lamp, a man's voice shouting—Irish: the old man?—and then the dogs were on me.

And past me, other than one that paused to snuffle at the back of my neck—the very exposed back of my neck—before leaping past to join the rest of the pack in their snarls.

"Don't run!" I shouted from my bushes. "They'll chase you down if you run, just curl up." And why the hell did I care if the creatures ate him? They weren't eating me, so maybe I should . . . But no, I was on my knees now, screaming as loud as my voice would go, "Stay still! Don't run! Put your gun down and cover your head!" Not that the dogs would care about a revolver in his hand, but if there were shots left in it, I didn't want to be hit by a stray round.

Now the lamp was here and the Irish voice was bellowing commands in some foreign tongue. The owner of the voice lifted the lantern as he came up to me—beard, kilt, accent, authority, shotgun: had to be The O'Mahony himself. He stared down for a moment, then continued down the stones of the path to rescue his hounds from their prey.

I climbed to my feet and went after him, somewhat tentatively, but the chaos seemed to be subsiding. Three huge dogs—only three, though there had to be close to four hundredweight of canine, tongues hanging and tails whipping. One of them was standing triumphantly on the back of the gabardine coat. The man's hands, I could see, were empty.

"Gi'down, Granua lass," the old man chided. "Stop playin' with the man."

Granua climbed off the back, less with an air of canine obedience than as if she agreed that it was time to let him up. She walked over to inspect me, found nothing to disapprove of, and turned around to watch her master, nearly sending me flying as she bumped into me on the narrow path.

"All right, let's have a look at ye," said the master of the hounds. I could see the back of his would-be murderer in the lamplight—his actual back in one spot, where half a dozen layers of clothing had been torn down to the skin. Astonishingly, that skin was not a welter of blood.

And when he half-rolled to the side, both skin and garments were nearly intact.

The man got to his feet warily, although the dogs showed no further sign of aggression. A man of about fifty years, slim, handsome, with a trim moustache. One of the dogs had retrieved a fallen hat, and was mouthing its prize sloppily.

"Drop it, lad," the old man said, and after a few more mastications, the command penetrated to the jaws and the hat fell to the ground. Gingerly, the victim bent and picked it up, transferring the once-shapely felt onto his head.

"I was—" he started to say, and then chaos struck again. All three dogs whirled, stared in my direction, and leapt—but before I could do more than shriek, they were past me, baying and scrabbling.

Whoever was approaching was not shooting at us, so again I raised my voice. "Don't move! Just stand still, they won't eat you!" Probably.

I could see nothing—though who else could it be but Holmes, here in the distant reaches of Ireland? I turned to ask the man with the lantern to call off his hounds when I saw that he had already taken a step towards the drive—and that the man in the coat was seizing the opportunity to flee.

I went past the old man only slightly less rapidly than his dogs had, and hit the gunman's ravaged back in a tackle. We both ended up in some fortunately non-thorny bush, where I decided the simplest thing was to follow the dog's example and sit on him while I waited for reinforcement. I also spotted his pistol, resting on a branch, and transferred it to a pocket.

The second round of shouting died down, three men's voices exchanged preliminary questions and answers, and eventually the lantern began to bobble back in my direction, followed by the dogs. The man beneath me, meanwhile, had either given up the fight or had the breath knocked out of him.

Holmes was the first to emerge from the gloom. He stared at me, seated firmly on a man's back, then saw the front of my coat.

"You're bleeding!" he exclaimed.

I looked down at my front, and my hands. "It's not mine. The dogs—"

But to my surprise, he yanked me to my feet, and flung his arms around me. Then, more reassuringly, he stood back and seized both my shoulders to berate me.

"What the *hell* are you doing here? Last I heard, you were setting off to Sussex with the Walsh woman, and then I hear your screams and gunshots—which, granted, is hardly a rare occurrence, but for pity's sake, Russell, I'm an old man who . . ."

His voice ran down, less from emotion than distraction. Jake had appeared while Holmes was building up his steam, merely giving me a nod of greeting as he pushed past us. Holmes was now looking at him. I turned my head, and when my husband's hands loosened their grip, turned the rest of me, as well.

Jake was on his heels before the now-seated figure. His hand went out to pluck at the garments, so as to judge the injuries beneath them.

The man stared up at my uncle, his battered face lifting in what looked near to a smile. "I have to say, you're about the last person I'd have expected to see here."

Jake's hand let go of the suit's ruined lapels, and paused, as if it yearned to reach out and touch the scraped cheek. But instead, he continued the motion of withdrawal, rising to his feet to stand looking down at the man on the ground.

"Hullo, Frank."

CHAPTER FIFTY-NINE

RUSSELL

The self-proclaimed chieftain of the O'Mahony clan looked every bit the part. Seventy-five years old with white hair to his shoulders and a beard halfway down his chest; his back was straight, his shoulders wide, and his eyes as sharp as a young man's. He wore a military kilt of a dark saffron colour, whose fabric showed a close acquaintance with brambles and whose lower hem indicated that the old man could still kneel amongst the garden beds.

At this time of night, he also wore bedroom slippers, which I thought understandable.

When we'd been ushered into the house, we were interrupted by the arrival of the servants, a couple in their sixties similarly half-dressed. They were all for starting up the motor and fetching the "polis," but their master gave an irritable gesture and sent them back to their quarters. Eventually.

While the old man was dealing with that, I emptied my over-laden pockets, checking the revolver—it was out of bullets—before handing it to Holmes, then looking at the lump of much-folded and compacted paper that remained. Mrs Walsh's floor-plans, I realised, and after a moment, handed them over as well.

"Saved me from queueing at the Post Office," I told him.

Bemused, he accepted them and followed me into the house.

The lighted room with the gap in the curtains proved to be a library, dark wood bookshelves, dark wood panelling, dark wood furniture, most of which needed a dust or a deep clean. There we stood: the chieftain of the O'Mahony tribe and his four unexpected guests: one would-be assailant, two unexplained men, and a young woman. Plus three hairy dogs, two of which had instantly flung themselves down in front of the wide fireplace. The third was the female he had called "Granua," who had remained beside her owner, head down, eyeing me from beneath eyebrows as bushy as the old man's. The creature's shoulders came near to her owner's hip—and The O'Mahony was not a small man. She looked at me. I looked at her. The dog wasn't showing her teeth, I told myself. On the other hand, she didn't need to, no more than her owner needed to brandish a shotgun to assert his authority.

And indeed, The O'Mahony had leaned the shotgun in the corner as he came into the room.

"Who wants to go first?" he said.

I tore myself away from the dog's dark, watchful gaze and met the man's similar one. "Perhaps I should. Good evening . . ." Oh, heavens, how did one address an Irish chieftain? ". . . sir. My name is Mary Russell; this is my husband, Sherlock Holmes, and my uncle, Jacob Russell. And this, I believe, is Francis Shackleton, whom you may know."

The old man's gaze went to the man in the ripped clothing. "Arthur's friend? I thought you looked familiar. What the devil brings you to my door at this hour? No good, that's for certain. But . . ." The other name had struck a bell, too. "Sherlock Holmes? The detecting fellow?"

Holmes tipped his head in acknowledgment.

The bushy eyebrows came back to me. "'Husband'?"

I gave him a similar wry expression.

He studied us all, shook his head, and walked over to the fire, sitting down in a decrepit leather chair, which required stepping over half a dozen canine extremities. The female sat down beside him, her massive head resting on his knee. As he fondled her soft and foolish-looking ears, her brown eyes closed in pleasure. "Sit down, all of you. And you . . ." He looked over at Jake. "Get everyone something to drink. Cabinet's in the corner. I'll have the Jameson."

Jake looked around at us. Holmes said, "Jameson's fine," and I shrugged to agree. He didn't consult Frank Shackleton, but he did come back with a glass for the man, as well, then settled into a chair halfway between Shackleton's assigned divan at the window and the rest of us, seated before the fire.

The O'Mahony took a swallow and said in a resigned voice, "This'll be about the Jewels, I expect, if Shackleton is involved."

"I'm afraid so," I agreed. "It's a convoluted story, as you might imagine, but essentially, Mr Shackleton here discovered that the woman who works for your sister-in-law, Lady Vicars, thought you might know where they are."

"The mad Walsh woman?"

"Er, that's her."

"Why would she think that?"

"They have to be somewhere, and people seem to have looked everywhere else."

"Might as well take a shovel and start working your way south from Dublin Castle," the man said.

Holmes stepped in. "Are you saying, sir, that you do not have them?"

"Why would I want those things? An English King's baubles given to his wh—his mistress? And when his Queen widow wanted nothing to do with them, they were tidied up and used to bring Ireland to heel. Shows how far down Ireland stood in the Crown's affections. I grew up in England. School, university. I know what their opinion is of this land, and how willing they are to overlook our actual treasures—our craftsmen's hands, our poets' tongues, the perfect fit of our people and their creatures." The dog opened one eye, and he tugged at her ears. "And they send their stolen, reworked refuse over to show us that Ireland is the equal of England and Scotland? Ha. I wouldn't burn the St Patrick's Regalia to heat my house."

I was watching Frank Shackleton, and as the old man delivered his tirade, I saw the haunted look of a convict come over him, his body slowly crumpling into his ragged clothing. His face took on ten years, and swallowing a large gulp of whiskey didn't put the colour back into it.

The four of us looked at him, waiting for him to speak.

He did, eventually. "I'm sorry. I was . . . I'm a fool, a dangerous idiot. Take me in, I won't fight you. I deserve to be locked away for the rest of my days."

He had a pleasant voice, a mix of Ireland and England, light and well educated. It went with his appearance, which, despite its present battering, was both naturally handsome and carefully maintained: moustache and hair showed just enough grey to suit a man of fifty, and his body was fit and slim. Before the dogs had attended to his clothing, he might have been described as dapper. The sort of man who would, indeed, be appalled to find himself in his present situation, abjectly humiliated and knowing that the only fault was his.

But this was a man who had charmed and defrauded dozens of people over the years. Was he showing us his honest face, or merely a pitiful mask?

I couldn't tell.

Before anyone else in his audience could feel sympathy stir, I spoke up. "Mr Shackleton, I imagine it was Richard Gorges who sent you in this direction, am I right?"

"It was," he said, with a kind of wary surprise.

"How?"

"Well, Dickie and I, we're old friends, but he's—"

"We know all about Richard Gorges, Mr Shackleton. He was involved in the theft of the Jewels, he shot a London policeman in 1915, and he just got out of Broadmoor in the spring."

The man's eyes went to Jake, but didn't appear to find much sympathy there, so returned to me. "That's right. I went to see the poor fellow after he got out of prison. That was June, I think it was. He wouldn't talk to me—wouldn't even let me in the door, some excuse about his parole licence. I think he just didn't want to see me. He looked pretty dreadful. I made him take my card, told him to telephone if he changed his mind."

"And he did?"

"Not until last week. He said that J—" He broke off, shot a quick glance at Jake and then The O'Mahony, clearly trying to remember if the old man had been standing close enough to hear Jake's greeting. He decided to study his glass. "He said that a mutual friend from the Dublin days happened to show up, and over the course of several conversations—a period of weeks, you understand, just casual chat—they naturally talked about the Jewels. Dickie ended up telling him everything he knew, the idiot. It was only afterwards, when . . . our friend had disappeared again with some convenient excuse about travelling for work, that Dickie got to thinking about the conversations. He's not the brightest, but eventually even he had to wonder if maybe it wasn't just a coincidence that they'd spent all those hours jawing about old times.

"So, he finally dug out my card and gave me a ring. I went to see him, we talked for a while, and he told me all about it. He was wondering if maybe our friend was up to something, and one of us might want to check on the matter."

"Did he know where to go?"

"Not exactly. But Lady Vicars is in the *Landed Gentry* so her address wasn't hard to find. I went home to pack up a change of shirts and off we went."

"You talked him into going with you to Clevedon so he could help you break into Lady Vicars' house."

"What?" The O'Mahony sat up sharply; all three dogs raised their heads at the alarm in his voice. "You broke into Fairview?"

I hastened to reassure him. "Lady Vicars is fine, sir. It was a minor excitement, didn't even make her delay a trip to Europe with a friend." It wasn't entirely a lie—a woman whose house and husband had fallen to an armed mob might well regard a simple bedroom intruder as minor.

He subsided, but his glare had sharpened, and it took some time for the dogs' eyes to drift shut again.

"I didn't break into the house," Shackleton said. "It was Gorges." As if that made any difference.

I continued. "You had picked up a motorcar somewhere, either hired or stolen in Bristol." He tipped his head, not committing to which method he'd used. "You motored out to Clevedon, where you dropped Gorges at the house after dark, then you left the immediate area for a time, so as not to attract attention. Is that right?"

"Did he tell you that?"

"Mr Shackleton, we *saw* you."

"What, in Clevedon?"

"Yes."

His eyes went to Jake again, and lingered.

My uncle did not look up.

I went on. "Gorges broke in, found some . . ." Hmm: I wouldn't want anyone to think that we'd been preparing to break into The O'Mahony's home ourselves. ". . . some notes and sketches of The O'Mahony's houses in Coolballintaggart and Mucklagh, and stole them. Gorges was then injured getting away. He went back to London—he's all right, by the way, since you didn't ask. I heard from Billy," I said in an aside to Holmes, then turned back to Shackleton—"while you came here to Ireland. Did you go to the Mucklagh house first?"

"That drawing was on the top," he admitted.

Sheer luck, that Mrs Walsh's problems recalling that house reduced his head start.

The O'Mahony leaned forward in his chair; three pair of dark canine eyes opened to fix on the prisoner. "I hope to God you didn't shoot anyone *there*?"

"No, I . . . two women came in while I was inside, but they only worked in the kitchen for an hour or so, then left. I'd parked my motorcar in the woods and walked in, so they didn't see it."

"You then took a train to Aughrim," I continued, "where you stole a motorcar—another motorcar—which you found in front of the Lawless Hotel, and came here."

"I don't know how you learned all that, but yes, that's the long and the short of it," Shackleton agreed. "A foolish venture, as I said. And I can only say that I'm very sorry—"

But I had to cut it off there. As his shock at being caught, savaged, and informed of his failure had begun to fade, his automatic response to the world had begun to reassert itself: wry smile, tousled hair, self-deprecation. Manipulation par excellence.

"No," I said sharply. "Mr Shackleton, tonight you tried to kill Mr—The O'Mahony. There are judges who would hang you for that."

His head jerked up. "I didn't! I wasn't trying to kill him—only the dog. I thought there was just the one," he added, as if that explained anything.

"You were going to shoot my *Granua*?" The O'Mahony demanded, more outraged by that idea than at any of the previous list of offences.

"I'm sorry, I really am, I thought—perhaps if you were undefended, I could get you to tell me where they were. The Jewels, I mean. Stupid, I was desperate and didn't think it over and . . . I'm sorry."

"If I had them, I'd have thrown them at you to get you off the place," the old man growled.

Holmes decided that it was time to talk business. "Do you have somewhere we could leave him locked up for a bit?" he asked. "He's left that stolen motorcar just up the lane from your gates. I'll walk down and bring it up here, then take him to the police in Aughrim. You can go in and make a statement in the morning. Or," he added, "they'd no doubt send someone here to take it."

But to the consternation of at least two people in the room, the old man was vigorously shaking his head. "No. I want nothing to do with the matter."

"But this man tried to—"

"The world is full of idjits and gullibles. Every time some blood—some fool journalist writes another article about the 'Irish Crown Jewels mystery,' I get people tramping over my garden and troubling the dogs. From all over, too—had some Americans here last year, seemed to think I should invite them in for tea. Pah! It took my shotgun to convince them I was serious about their leaving. If word gets round that a friend of my poor brother thought the Jewels were here, I'll have madmen climbing in my windows at night."

Holmes and I looked at each other, then at the other two men. Shackleton was wide-eyed, as if he'd just heard the click of a gaol door unlocking. Jake, however . . . I couldn't tell. He had his face carefully schooled to show nothing at all.

In the end, I left the decision to Holmes.

After a time, he got to his feet and went over to our captive, pulling up a stool so their faces were on the same level.

"Mr Shackleton. Were it up to me, you would be on your way to prison. Either that, or to the bottom of a dry well. You need to be very clear on this: you have one chance to walk away from this entire matter. You know who I am. You know what it means when I say that I will make it my business to watch you. You are not good enough to evade me. If I am given the faintest indication that you are venturing away from what is colloquially known as the straight-and-narrow, I will descend on you with all my considerable weight. Is this clear?" The man did not look dapper now.

He swallowed, and nodded. "Very well. You will stand up and go down the drive and retrieve that motorcar from the lane. You will take it back to Aughrim and wait at the station for the next train out. North or south, it matters not, so long as there is a mail-boat at your destination, and a train across England to your home.

"Do you understand me?"

Shackleton's face, his posture, made it clear that he did.

"I do not know if you have found gainful employment in recent years, or if you are still playing at fraud. I actually don't care. But when it comes to matters Irish, you are finished."

Holmes rose and moved away from the prisoner. Shackleton got to his feet, looked at The O'Mahony, looked at the dogs, and sidled away with the disbelief of a man who had escaped the gallows.

His single hesitation was when he came up to Jake's chair. There he paused. "You could . . . come see me. Sometime."

Jake did not look up. "No, I don't think I could."

The man's shoulders dropped, and he moved towards the door.

"Wait," Holmes said.

Shackleton's entire body went rigid, but if he was tempted to make a break for it, he did not. Holmes went over to the armchair where we'd tossed our outer garments and retrieved his overcoat, going through the pockets to transfer various belongings to his suit. He held it out. "You'll attract attention in those clothes. Keep this on until you get home."

Shackleton accepted it without thanks, picked up his gnawed hat, and left.

The front door closed. Holmes went to the windows and opened one of them, standing near it to listen. Footsteps went by. A few minutes later, a motor started up near the base of the drive, followed by some terrific screechings as it met stone walls while reversing in the dark. Turning around at the gate required a lot of backing and filling, but eventually, the sounds of the stolen motorcar faded, and silence fell.

One of the dogs gave a gusty sigh.

Holmes latched the window and resumed his seat. I took another sip from my glass, wondering if we might beg a resting place for the night on these comfortable chairs. Jake fetched the bottle and refilled the glasses. And when he had sat down in the empty chair before the fire, The O'Mahony fixed us with a patriarchal glare and asked, "Who the deuces are you all? And why shouldn't I have my man toss you out on your ears?"

CHAPTER SIXTY

JAKE

Who the deuces we were took some explaining. I mean, the man obviously knew who Sherlock Holmes was (who doesn't?) but there was Mary to explain, and me. He had no reason to trust any of us an inch.

He did warm up a little when Mary dropped the fact that she and I were related to the Russells of County Waterford, even though I didn't think there were many of us around anymore. (His warming was no doubt helped by the whiskey.) And he could definitely sympathise with Mr Holmes' resentments, that Scotland Yard, Buckingham Palace, and even the detective's great-and-mighty brother had set aside the investigation he'd done after the theft. (Holmes might have played down his feelings about the guilt of Arthur Vicars, just a little.) And he seemed to have a soft place for Mrs Walsh, laughing aloud when he heard how the woman had finagled herself into Mary's life and farmhouse.

None of us mentioned the Jewels.

And somehow, the topic of my friendship with Frank Shackleton failed to come up.

I mostly kept my mouth shut and watched him.

An hour later and well into the next bottle, the old man stood up (rock steady on his feet, too) and said, "I imagine you three could use something to eat. I'll bring it here. If you want to wash your hands, it's at the end of the hallway."

He left, the three dogs heaving themselves to their feet to amble along after him. Mary followed, Mr Holmes took out his pipe, I arranged some squares of turf on the fire.

The old man and Mary came back at the same time, the dogs trailing along behind. He was carrying a large silver tray (tarnished—I don't think he had a lot of servants) with a linen dish-cloth over the top. I fetched a small table from the corner. He grunted his thanks and lifted the cloth off a heap of what looked like rectangular Cornish pasties and smelt like heaven. (I couldn't remember when we'd last eaten.)

"The cook doesn't come in Sundays, she always leaves me enough for a whole family."

The three dogs had sat in an attentive row, their flopping ears as near to upright as they could get. The O'Mahony nodded at their manners, took a pie, and broke it in two, tossing one half to each of the males. The next pie went mostly to the female. The animals waited, in case there was more coming, then finished licking their chops and settled down on the hearth rug again.

I tried not to gulp my pie as fast as the dogs had.

The female had stretched out across Mary's boots. When her own pie was gone, Mary worked her feet out from under the thing's weight and, after a moment's hesitation, lowered them onto the massive rib cage. The creature gave a single flap of that absurdly long tail, apparently happy to be used as a hassock.

The old man studied the scene for a bit, and then launched off on a review of breeding practices and blood lines for the Irish wolf-dog, which was apparently in danger of dying out. (Having rid Ireland of wolves, I'd guess, and not being useful for much else besides eating.)

It was now very late, or perhaps early. Mary's jaws had been fighting yawns for a while, and even Mr Holmes was starting to droop. I hoped to God our host didn't plan on turning us out entirely, but a house this size wasn't likely to have a vast number of guest bedrooms, and anyway, he'd sent the servants back to their beds.

Maybe we could just curl up on the carpet with the hounds.

Warmth, drink, and a full belly finally conspired to squeeze an actual yawn from my niece. "Sorry," she said, "it's been a long—"

"Sir, would you mind if we—" Holmes began at the same instant.

I just watched, as I'd been watching since Frank left.

"She's named after the wife, or some say daughter, of Finn McCool," The O'Mahony said, unexpectedly. "Granua, that is. You know the story?"

Mary looked around, then gave him an answer. "I know Finn McCool. Mythical Irish hero, may have been an actual figure during the Iron Age. Led warriors, fought monsters, repelled Ireland's enemies."

The old man nodded, then said, "She likes you."

He was looking at Mary, but it seemed to cover all three of us. It also seemed to be some kind of declaration, as if the beast's acceptance had cast a vote on something.

The other two heard it, too, and stopped talking.

The old man lifted his glass, emptied it, set it down again, and said, "So, I imagine the three of you would like to see the Jewels."

CHAPTER SIXTY-ONE

SHERLOCK HOLMES

Eighteen years after he'd been dragged into the Irish Jewels case, Holmes would have believed the Regalia were anywhere.

Anywhere, perhaps, but on a dusty bookshelf in a rural Irish house where any visitor, servant, or American treasure-hunter might have found them.

The O'Mahony pulled down a few volumes, dropping them onto a desk littered with papers and books, then stretched an arm into the gap.

The shelf was deeper than it appeared. Out his hand came with an old linen laundry bag. A heavy linen laundry bag, the size of a large throw-pillow.

"Would you—" he started to say, but Jake Russell had already shot to his feet to clear the scraps and cloth from the table before the fire, leaving the silver tray.

Everyone but the dogs had got to their feet—in disbelief? in reverence? merely the better to see?—while The O'Mahony tugged open the bag's ties and upended the whole thing over the tray.

Each of the smaller bags and packages inside hit the metal with a hard thump. One came open, spitting to the carpet an object the size of a small pea that glittered fiercely as it flew through the firelight.

Jake snatched it up before it had stopped rolling, and placed it in his palm, holding it out for his two companions to see: a diamond, faceted and perfect.

"Good God," Russell said.

"Quite . . ." Holmes began, but could not seem to find an adjective.

"Well," Jacob Russell said. "There's a thing."

And gingerly placed it beside the heavy golden chain resting on its velvet wrap.

CHAPTER SIXTY-TWO

RUSSELL

The O'Mahony had certainly dropped a bombshell into the evening.

Even more extraordinary, he then declared that we would talk about it in the morning, that we were welcome to sleep on the furniture, that there would be tea at seven.

I'd thought Jake would leap over and rip the laden tray from the man's hands. He might have, had the dogs not already got to their feet, moved by some unknown signal that bed was near.

Instead, we stood and watched an old man in a kilt and bed-slippers walk out of the room carrying a King's ransom in gemstones and precious metal.

Either stunned or stupefied by exhaustion and whiskey, the three of us all seemed to accept that there was not much to be done but, as he'd said, sleep. After a time we found ourselves wrapped in travelling-rugs, me on the leather sofa against the wall, Holmes on two chairs pushed together with an ottoman, and Jake arranged over some pillows on the carpet.

I did not imagine any of us could sleep after the shock of that glittering diamond in the firelight. But in fact, I was only occasionally aware of the men snoring, and the curtains were bright by the time voices woke me.

I found The O'Mahony in the breakfast room—the dining room, period, to judge by the formality of the wallpaper and paintings, even though it was on the eastern side of the house. He was sitting with a newspaper at one end of the long table, where three other places had been laid for us.

He glanced up through his eyebrows. "Tea's there, coffee's coming. My housekeeper is having a grand time giving me the rough side of her tongue for not warning her we had guests."

"Tea and a slice of toast would be marvellous," I assured him, wondering where the hell the Jewels were. Had he regretted his action as the result of our plying him with drink? Was he going to pretend we had hallucinated last night? I prayed it was only because the servants were in earshot.

"Oh, you'll get more than tea, she's crashing and steaming a storm up there."

He seemed almost pleased at the turmoil we'd inflicted on his cook. "Er, thank you?" I said, and helped myself to a cup.

Holmes and Jake came in shortly after, and a massive breakfast descended two minutes after that. Following a brief non-verbal consultation, we obediently addressed ourselves to food, saying not a word about diamonds or gold or nocturnal revelations.

It was in the library afterwards that the Jewels returned, the old man having taken care to latch the door behind him.

He carried the tray over to the desk beneath the window, where the morning sun streamed through glass that could have done with a wash.

He laid the tray down, unwrapped one piece from its cloth, and stepped back.

Diamonds that shimmer under candle- or lamplight are spectacular under sunlight. Dots of colour splashed up and over the walls and ceiling, as effervescent as a room filled with champagne.

"Wow." I think it was I who said it, but it could have been any of us. Even the dog looked impressed.

Holmes reached out first to claim the eight-pointed star, hundreds of gems radiating out from a three-leafed shamrock made of emeralds, a ruby cross behind it, and a blue enamel circle with Latin words: *QUIS SEPARABIT*—Who will separate us?—and the date MDCCLXXXIII.

"Seventeen eighty-three?" I asked.

"The founding of the Order of St Patrick," The O'Mahony provided.

"Ah." I did not comment on the irony of the motto—when it came to the Jewels themselves, yes, but more so to the recent change in Irish government. I held out my hand.

Holmes laid the Star on my palm, and I nearly dropped it, having been misled by the sparkle into thinking the object was built from light, rather than a mass of silver and gemstones. I cupped it in both hands and tipped it away from the direct sunlight, that I might see the details more clearly. "I think this is where that loose diamond came from," I said.

"There's another missing as well," he pointed out. I found it, a second, a small gap near the centre.

The silver was in need of polishing. I handed it carefully to Jake, who treated it with considerably less awe. "Yes, that's the one," he said, and returned it to its velvet square to begin turning back the corners of the other wrappings. A ceremonial "collar" or necklace made of heavy gold links interspersed with symbols of whichever order it is connected to, in this case, Irish harps and Tudor Roses. The thing gave a hard thump when Jake set it on the table. Three collars soon lay amidst the velvet scraps, but the next folded back to reveal a second solid piece.

"The Badge," Holmes said. This, too, was a brilliant expanse of diamonds decorated with emeralds, rubies, and enamel, but it was oval, and had a harp with a crown—more diamonds—at the top. The gems in this bit of the Regalia seemed to have survived unscathed.

The last two packets Jake unfolded held collars as well—more harps and roses, enamel and gemstones. I found myself longing for a mere pearl by way of contrast. Although the fourth one Jake uncovered was marginally simpler—the gold links less massive, the workmanship less ornate, with emeralds rather than diamonds and fewer gems set into the three equally spaced enamel roses. I was not surprised when Jake pushed this one to the side and spread out the final one for us to admire.

When I blinked, I found that the sharp gleam from the table had left spots in my eyes. "I feel I should be wearing sun-glasses," I remarked.

"One is indeed meant to take notice of the wearer," Holmes said. He had picked up the linen sack and was cautiously turning it inside-out.

Jake held the last, most ornate collar up to the window. "If I had one of these, I'd be tempted to wear it to breakfast every morning."

"You'd start the day with neck strain if you did," I told him.

Holmes made a sound of minor triumph and plucked a sparkling object from the bottom corner of the bag, laying it onto a free patch of velvet: a diamond of perhaps a quarter carat, which looked as if it would fit the larger gap in the Star. Our host got up and went over to a desk, coming back with an envelope into which his gnarled fingers carefully placed the two stray stones. He folded the envelope twice, ran his work-hardened thumb-nail across the folds, and tucked the resulting packet under the edge of the Star.

The four of us sat, looking down at a table of stunning, cold, beautiful, inhuman perfection. Millions—billions?—of years ago, the earth's turmoil trapped bits of carbon deep underground, where it lay, being heated and compressed until a stray volcano threw it up near the surface. The hardest thing in the world, dull crystalline lumps until human beings discovered that a precise tap would cause the crystal to sheer away, leaving a gleaming facet. And now, all over the world, slaves dug them up, thieves stole them away, women displayed them on their bodies, and men used them to assert their power and rank.

"How meaningless gems become," I mused, "when there are so many of them in one place."

"Like longing for a simple plate of stew after being wined and dined by royalty," The O'Mahony surprised me by saying.

"Lady Vicars gave these to you, didn't she?" I asked.

"She did. After she'd made her decision to leave Ireland. Do you know how she came to have them? You do seem to know a great deal."

"Sir Arthur found them in a drawer in his secretaire when he moved out of Dublin," I said.

The bushy eyebrows went up. "Who told you?"

I carefully did not look at Jake. "Richard Gorges gave us the story, too. It's quite a tale."

"Absurd. I didn't believe it when my sister-in-law first told me. But then, it did make a kind of sense. Arthur was so embarrassed by his foolishness that he preferred to keep them a secret rather than ask me for help. I was angry at first—I thought it might have made a difference, the day the Kerry mob shot him, but when I'd thought about it, I had to agree that it wouldn't have changed matters at all.

"But Gertrude didn't want to be burdened with them, and I am the head of the family, so it was either throw them into a river, or take over her problem."

It was Holmes who brought these family-based reflections to a halt, setting down the Badge he'd been examining. "Sir, what do you intend to do with these?"

The O'Mahony turned his grizzled face on the collection. "These belong to the people of Ireland," he said flatly. "They were given by William IV to Ireland—a statement, with no ambiguity, that our St Patrick was an Order equal to England's Bath and Scotland's Thistle. Before we were partitioned, four years ago, one might have argued that the Jewels belonged to the King. Now my Ireland is independent, and we no longer bow to England, although to the English, the controls remain. So if you ask what I would do with them, sir, it is this: I would do nothing, as yet. Not until Ireland stands free and united, and her people can decide how they wish to use them."

"I hope you don't plan to leave them tucked behind the books on your shelf," Holmes told him. "Not unless you'd like one of your servants to come across it, or a builder hired to do some repairs."

All four of us looked at the empty shelf with the hole behind it, and I had to agree: sooner or later, an enthusiastic housemaid was going to dust and polish her way into a fortune.

"You think I should place them somewhere slightly more permanent?" The O'Mahony nodded. "You may be right. Although having them fall into a builder's hands would be oddly appropriate—there is a tradition in this part of the world of farmers digging up Viking hoards."

Jake's fingers slipped on the collar he'd been holding, which gave a startlingly loud *clunk* as it fell to the table. "Sorry," he said, rubbing first at the enamel rose that had hit down, then at the dent in the polished wood.

As if to rectify matters, he spread out the velvet shroud and began wrapping the collar back into it.

"Does such a place come to mind?" Holmes asked.

"Yes, in fact, a suitable place would be—"

Holmes cut him off sharply. "I think . . . it would be better to keep the number of people who know to a minimum."

He did not look in Jake's direction, although The O'Mahony did, seeing only an innocent, pleasant-faced man taking care to preserve someone else's treasure. He also looked at me, no doubt wondering about a marriage with such openly declared mistrust.

"If you say so. But someone should know in addition to me. Unless we want this hoard to disappear for centuries, as well."

"I can assist, if you will trust me. You two," he said, again not directly confronting Jake with his gaze. "If you want to finish wrapping those up, we'll see if we can find a safe home for them."

"I'll get my boots," The O'Mahony said, and strode out of the room.

"You will, I hope, pardon me for saying this, Mr Russell, but—Russell, keep an eye on your uncle's clever fingers."

"Holmes!"

"No, Mary, he's right," Jake said. "If these things disappear again, I don't want to be on the top of your husband's list of suspects."

He calmly laid the first snug velvet packet into one corner of the linen bag and picked up another square. I shot Holmes a dark look and sat down next to Jake, preparing to watch his hands.

Holmes left the door to the library wide open.

Jake straightened the second collar and began folding the soft fabric around it. There was, as I'd noticed before, no shaking of his hands when he was using them, only when motion was paused.

"Do you think . . ." I began, then stopped. Did I really want to sound like some eager undergraduate recently introduced to Freudian psychoanalysis? No. On the other hand, my observation was not entirely without merit. "Jake, have you had an actual doctor tell you that the shake in your hands is due to injury?"

"Hmm," he replied, sounding preoccupied.

I couldn't tell if he hadn't heard me, or if he was distracted by the collar, flashing in the sun.

Or perhaps it was the hearing loss. I raised my voice a little. "Sometimes, the body manifests the mind's concerns. Such as the trauma of being near to an explosion. It clearly affected your ears, though it doesn't seem to have left scars on your arms. I have to wonder if some part of you has decided that your days of safe-cracking and card-sharping are over? Because if you had a physical reason to retire, it would be more of a justific—"

He leapt to his feet. I thought he was reacting, albeit violently, to my meddling amateur psychoanalysis, but then realised that he was digging furiously in one of his pockets. I noticed, too, that his abrupt rise had immediately followed the sound of the lodge door shutting and The O'Mahony's voice cutting off.

He sat down again, shoved the collar he'd been wrapping to one side, and pulled over the second-to-last that had come to light, the one I'd thought somewhat less ornate than the others. He flipped it around so that the pendant was away from him and picked up the decorative element at the far end of the loop, one of the roses that would sit over the spine when it was worn. "Ha!" he crowed, and brought out the thing he'd pulled from his pocket.

A small pair of jeweller's pliers.

"Jake, stop—what are you doing!" I reached out to grab the pliers, but he batted me away.

"We don't have much time," he said. "Look."

"Jake, you can't—"

"Will you *look* at the damned thing?" he demanded, and held the reversed Tudor Rose under my nose. "Look!"

I looked, although having never examined a ceremonial collar before, I had no way of knowing what I was seeing. The roses on the chain's two sides were considerably flatter than the one at the back—but perhaps the thickness was to help the person wearing it make sure it was lying correctly? "What am I seeing?"

He snatched it back and began to work the pliers. This time, I was curious enough to let him.

"The old man was right. England slaps a bunch of gems together and sees them as treasure, but sometimes, that's only a form of currency. I mean, cash is great, no argument from me, but one thing I've learned in a life like mine: there's other things that count, too. Sometimes even more."

The rose's gold links separated easily. In less than a minute, the lump came free from the back of the rose. He discarded the collar itself on the table, and held the object directly in the beam of sunlight.

"And this," he said in a voice I'd never heard from him before, "*this* is one of the true Crown Jewels of Ireland."

Pride and deep satisfaction and a clear indication that this was the only thing in the heap of gemstones that mattered. Reverently, he placed it in my palm.

It was not, in fact, something designed merely to thicken a Tudor Rose. Instead, I was looking at a very old, rather worn, absolutely exquisite little Celtic brooch, missing its pin. It was small, a circle no more than an inch and a half across, with an open centre where its missing pin would have threaded through the fabric of a garment. The lower portion was wider and more ornately worked than the rest of the circle. Minuscule arabesques of gold and silver filigree were set with bits of amber and enamel-work, some of which were missing.

I took the thing with a wordless sound of wonder, wishing for a magnifying glass. "What is this? How did you know it was there?"

"I wish to *hell* I'd known about it when we stole the damned things in the first place," he snarled, picking up the pliers to rejoin the collar's links. "It would have saved me a whole lot of headache. That, my girl, is the Russell brooch. The piece that Maria Russell dug out of the Irish earth in 1720, only to have it taken away by her family to win an English favour."

I looked sharply over at the side of his face. "I thought you said it was in a museum somewhere."

"No, that's what *you* said. I told you it was turned over to the government. What I did not say—what I only found out the year *after* I helped Frank steal all this—was that the Irish government had given it to the Crown, who stuck it in a drawer somewhere until George IV died and the Palace thought it might be better to quietly clear away the jewellery his mistress had worn, stripping them down to make the new Order of St Patrick Regalia. They must have come across this at the same time and thought—Ireland, fine, let's give them back this, as well. The jewellers decided to hide it at the back—either because it was an old, battered thing that would stand out against the fresh work, or someone there saw its beauty and worried that it would make the rest of the collar look like a piece of gaudy modern rubbish. Personally, I'd like to think they had an Irishman on their staff who decided that concealing it behind the rose made it an invisible but symbolic source of power. Take your choice."

My gaze, and my exploring fingers, had returned to the brooch. "When did you learn it was on the collar?"

He shook his head. "The following year. Wouldn't you know it?"

"That makes it 1908. The year you were disowned from the family."

"Yes. And Father was the one who told me. He adored the idea that a Russell family treasure was secretly there at all those important ceremonies taking place in the Old Country. And now, thanks to his own son's friends, the Irish Crown Jewels were gone, and the Russell brooch was no longer there in the centre of things."

One of the filigree panels, I had discovered, showed a long and sinuous sea-monster, biting its own tail. "Did he know you actually stole them?"

"God, no. If he had, he'd probably have taken down his shotgun rather than just throw me out on the street. But there was a magazine article making the rounds that summer about Frank Shackleton's involvement in the theft, and he knew I was friends with Frank, so it wasn't hard to put the two together. There," he said, sitting up from his work. "That should do it."

I checked, and had to agree: if one didn't know that the rose at the back of the collar used to have a lump on its reverse side, it would look as if nothing had happened.

He picked up one of the velvet squares and started wrapping the collar. "I'd put that away, if I were you," he said. "Before your husband and The O'Mahony come back."

I was startled. "Jake, I can't keep this, it's a national treasure!"

"It's a piece of old jewellery belonging to the Russell family," he said. "And you are the Russell family, most of it anyway. I think Maria herself would have wanted you to have it."

"Jake, I really couldn't—"

He slammed his fist down on the table, causing everything to jump, including me. "Mary, why the hell do you think I did all this? Because of the damned diamonds? I couldn't give a good goddamn about them—throw them in the fire if you want, they're worthless crap compared to the brooch." He caught himself, pulling the anger and humiliation back into its hidden corner, and took a steadying breath. "Look, I know I've spent my whole life being a selfish jerk. I let my brother down when I sailed away after the earthquake. I disappointed my father too many times to count, up to the day I took the Jewels from that safe. And then six years later when your mother and father and brother were all killed—*all* of them—did I show up and do my part? I did not. I let you down like I've let everyone else down, and I *know* this doesn't make up for any of it, but it's all I could think of to do right now. I'm making changes. It'll take some time. But this is . . . as much a promise as it is a piece of old jewellery."

For a moment, his eyes held mine, and I could see the tears. And then his face closed, and he looked down at the collar that had spilled from its wrap, embarrassed but unrepentant.

I stood, and laid my hand on his head, and kissed his hair. When I sat, he reached for the gold collar.

"Your mother used to do that," he said.

"I know. And I thank you for this. I don't agree that you let me down, but I forgive you, anyway. Although I'll have to think about keeping it. And I'm not going to hide it from Holmes."

"Of course you aren't. However, I wouldn't show it to The O'Mahony if I were you. It would simply complicate matters."

I found that I had curled my hand tight around the beguiling object. After a minute, in mimicry of Jake, I dug out a mostly clean handkerchief and wrapped it around the brooch, thrusting it deep in a pocket.

And none too soon: voices from the hall warned us of the men's return. Jake had finished with the collars and was wrapping the St Patrick's Badge. I reached for the glory that was the St Patrick's Star, pressed it against the envelope that held its mis-placed diamonds, and buried it back in its length of velvet.

CHAPTER SIXTY-THREE

RUSSELL

I half-expected The O'Mahony to unwrap the contents of the linen bag and check that we hadn't replaced the treasure with rocks, but he did not. Although the look he gave the neatly folded package suggested that he might, as soon as we were out the door.

He invited us to stay for luncheon, which sounded good to me but Holmes got his reply in first.

"Thank you, but we need to make our way back to Sussex as quickly as possible."

"Do we?" I asked.

He raised an eyebrow. "You have a house guest in need of attention."

I had all but forgotten Mrs Walsh. I stifled the sigh, and turned a bright smile onto our host. "It has been a pleasure, sir. I am sorry we did not have the time for a tour of your garden."

"Come back," he ordered. "Soon. The primula are particularly beautiful in April."

Oh lovely, I thought, *another boat ride.*

"And Granua might have her next litter by then."

I couldn't help hearing that as an offer, and wondered what my Sussex neighbours would make of ten stone of hound galloping merrily around their grazing sheep.

CHAPTER SIXTY-FOUR

RUSSELL

My Uncle Jake gave us the slip somewhere in the chaos of Victoria Station: one moment he was there, the next he came out from a cluster of people—only it was not Jake, but a man in a similar hat.

I was startled, and disappointed, but not completely surprised. We had spent much of the journey back from Ireland in conversation, and I now knew more about him, and about my father, than I had ever imagined I would, from their childhood summers by a lake in New Hampshire to their months building the holiday cabin south of San Francisco. He talked a lot about my mother as well, and how her respect—and her expectations—had changed him. Made him a better person, as he put it.

"She gave me one of her lectures on Hebrew," he told me. "I didn't usually talk to your parents about what I did, but one day we were up at the cabin—this was the early days, when they were first married—and I'd been crowing just a little about something clever I'd done. Not illegal, you understand. Well, not *very* illegal, and based on outsmarting a man who deserved to be taken down a peg or two. She smiled and agreed it was clever, but a little while later she starting telling me about this Hebrew saying on the evils of pride."

"'Pride goes before destruction, and an arrogant spirit before a fall.'"

"That's the one."

"Proverbs, chapter 16. I received that lecture more than once myself."

"You astonish me," he said, sounding not in the least astonished. "But you'll then remember what the point of it was."

"That arrogance is not the same as satisfaction. That a pride which acknowledges the contribution and accomplishments of others is a way to praise God."

"Sounds like Judith. Although, since she knew I was never much of one for Bibles and church-going, she played down the God talk and made it more about being a good person. And what's more, she made being a good person seem like something I should want to be. I mean, I had to laugh at her attempt to convert me to the path of righteousness, but that conversation just stuck with me. I think of her whenever I find myself imagining that I am vastly superior to the crowd. Well, that is to say, I *am* superior, no doubt about that, but I do hear her voice telling me to try not to take it for granted."

And he grinned, to let me know it was a joke.

I thought of that carefree expression as Holmes and I travelled in an otherwise empty compartment through the darkening countryside from London towards Eastbourne. I thought of my mother, who was no fool, and who had loved her disreputable brother-in-law enough to trust him with her children. And then I thought of how he had chosen to apologise. Why had his promise for the future sounded like an ending?

"Do you think Jake is all right?" I asked Holmes, my voice small.

"I think your uncle is quite capable of watching over himself," he said dryly.

"No, I mean—did he seem well to you? Something he said

about making amends, when you and The O'Mahony were off looking at a place to leave the Jewels. I didn't realise it at the time, but it sounded . . ." I had to take a steadying breath. "You don't think he's dying, do you?"

"Good heavens, no, I'd say he's one of the healthiest fifty-year-olds I've ever seen. Why on earth would you think he was unwell?"

For a moment, the relief made me light-headed. "Oh, I know, it's ridiculous. He just sounded . . ." No, I thought: his words had not been final. They had been . . . what? "Decisive. He told me that he felt guilty for having let me and the rest of the family down, but that he was making changes, which would take some time."

He snorted, at the implication that Jacob Russell was promising reform.

"I know," I said. "But he also told me what exactly he'd been after all along. And I know he's an accomplished liar, but I saw his face. He was telling me the truth."

I pulled the handkerchief out of my pocket. Holmes watched me undo the knot and fold back the linen. I picked up the brooch and handed it to him.

"This is what Jake wanted," I told him. "It was attached to the back of a rose on one of the collars. It's something my four-times-great-grandmother dug up on the grounds of the Russell estate in Ireland, in the early eighteenth century. Her family took it away from her and gave it to England. He called it a piece of 'true Irish treasure,' and wanted me to have it back."

Holmes' raised eyebrow betrayed some rapid reevaluation of my uncle's motives and goals. However: "You believe this was all he wanted?"

I laughed. "I think this was primarily what he wanted, but I wouldn't be surprised if he's already on a train back towards Ireland."

"No," he said. "He'll wait a few days, but I would wager that he will be back in Coolballintaggart before the grass has grown enough to conceal signs of digging." He laid the brooch back on the cloth and fished around for his tobacco, stretching up first to open the window.

"Was that what The O'Mahony intended? To bury them again?"

"So he said. At the base of a rather distinctive tree."

"Are you going to warn him? That Jake will be back?"

"No."

"Will you tell the police—or Mycroft?"

"Mycroft . . . I imagine Mycroft will be busy for a time, with a certain old woman in Nanterre."

"You're quite sure he didn't know about her?"

"He did not, and I told him nothing. Merely gave him the address and ordered him to bestir himself out of London."

I relished the thought of Mycroft's face when he looked down at the tiny old woman and realised who she was. I had to agree, it was a nice touch of comeuppance. "And what about Scotland Yard?"

"The entire matter is nothing to do with me," he said. "Once it might have been, but I finished with the case eighteen years ago, when my advice was not taken."

"You sound quite complacent. Doesn't it worry you that Jake might be getting his hands on the Irish Crown Jewels?"

"Why should it? If the alternatives are sticking them back underground, or returning them to the Crown as part of the royal dragon hoard, or giving them to the Irish Republicans as a lesson in the temptations of corruption, why not let Jacob Russell have them?"

I admit I stared at the man in the seat across from me. Holmes, letting go of a case? It was almost as if . . .

What agreements had he and Jake come to, in the hours they had been together? Or perhaps it was merely professional pride.

"Does this have anything to do with Mycroft?"

He struck a match and held it to the bowl of his pipe. "In what way?" he asked when the tobacco was burning.

"It does, doesn't it? He dragged you into the matter in the first place, then overrode your recommendations."

"As I said, I solved it once. It is not required that I do so a second time."

And perhaps a little revenge? I could understand that.

"Besides," I said, "you like Jake. Admit it."

He looked down at the tobacco, but I caught a brief glimpse of an expression I could not remember ever seeing there, although it often played over the face of one Jacob Russell. For an instant, he looked like a mischievous fourteen-year-old.

"Do I like your uncle?" Holmes mused. "Well, yes," he said. "I suppose I do."

CHAPTER SIXTY-FIVE

Russell

The next morning, we woke to a final element of this much-travelled problem of the Irish Crown Jewels.

I opened the door, and there was Patrick. There was his motor. And there was a familiar figure standing behind him on the gravel of the drive.

"Morning, Patrick," I said, then looking over his shoulder I added, "and Mrs Walsh."

"Sorry, Mary, I told her we needed to telephone and ask—"

But Mrs Walsh had already elbowed her way past him and into the portico. She was carrying a grubby cloth bag, which she deposited with unexpected gentleness on the bench built into the porch, then bent to undo the laces of a pair of very muddy boots, talking all the time.

"I wanted to get these while the day was young, I hoped yesterday's rain would have brought them out perfectly—and there they were, exactly where I expected to find them! So perfect—oh, drat this knot, Patrick, would you bring my knife? Oh, never mind, that's got it." One boot thumped after the other into the corner and she stood up in her stockinged feet, retrieving the mud-smeared bag that made me wonder for an instant if she had been digging up the Irish Jewels. But no, this one held something considerably lighter than silver and gemstones. "Look!" she exclaimed, tugging it open. "Aren't they glorious?"

I wasn't sure what I was looking at, other than a tangle of some attractively coloured substance. I moved my head to the side so Holmes could look over my shoulder.

"The Deceiver," he said.

"Amethyst Deceiver," she agreed. "*Laccaria amethystina* itself, the woods north of the village are just filled with them. Of course, they won't preserve that beautiful colour after they're cooked, but I'll set aside a few for the sketch-book. You must be that Holmes fellow," she said abruptly, and thrust out a hand, seizing Holmes' and shaking it vigorously. "Mr Mason told me to expect you, I look forward to many fine conversations."

And with that pronouncement, she stepped past us into the house, without so much as a by-your-leave.

Holmes raised an eyebrow at me. "Was there some part of this discussion that I missed?"

I turned to Patrick, who threw up his hands. "That woman has some very strong ideas," he said. "One of them was, she belonged here. Her things are in the boot."

"She's coming *here*? Oh, no, that wasn't at all what I agreed to."

I followed her into the house and found her in the kitchen, frying pan in one hand and butter dish in the other. "Mrs Walsh, what are you doing?"

"They're best when absolutely fresh. It doesn't smell as if you've had your breakfast yet. Do you want to put on some coffee, or do you stick with tea?" She picked up a cutting board, examined it, and opened drawers until she found the knives. Moving over to the work-table, she laid down board and knife, then upended the bag in a spill of magnificently purple fungus.

"Are those the mushrooms that are occasionally filled with arsenic?" I asked.

Holmes eyed them dubiously, Patrick looked appalled, but Mrs Walsh just made a *tsking* sound and set me straight. "That's only when there's arsenic in the ground, and here on chalk, with no industrial dump-sites for miles, we'll be fine."

I did not find it more than mildly reassuring that she used the word "we" rather than "you."

The three of us stood and watched her with the fascination given to any implacable piece of machinery. She quickly sorted the . . . mushrooms—yes, let's call them "mushrooms" . . . brushing away bits of soil and leaf. Three of the more perfect specimens she laid aside, the rest she de-stemmed and chopped into uniform pieces with the dexterity of a professional chef. She finished just as the odour of toasted butter had begun to come from the skillet, and scooped them into the pan, turning up the heat a fraction.

She waited until the enticing aroma of mushrooms had filled the air before she said, "I don't do the heavy cleaning, although I'll supervise. Lunch you're on your own, and if I plan to be out in the morning or evening I'll leave something prepared. We can figure on thirty hours a week, more or less, and we can talk about money in two weeks, when you've had a chance to see how I do."

We had watched, captivated, as her hands stirred, pinched herbs from the jars at the back, added salt, and stirred again. I don't know about the two men, but my own mouth was watering by the time she swept the pan from the heat, swirled the contents into a small serving bowl, set it with a sharp rap onto the work-table, and handed each of us a fork.

We had seen her taste the mix after adding a couple of herbs, then again after adjusting the salt. Holmes and I watched Patrick (who, mouth full, had closed his eyes in appreciation—and this was a man who ate from the kitchen of Tillie Whiteneck, the best cook in Sussex). We glanced at each other in wordless consultation, and reached out with our own implements.

Thirty seconds later, I swallowed and said, "You're hired." I then clashed forks with the two men over the remainder of the dish.

When it was empty—and we hadn't quite resorted to licking it out with our tongues—I reluctantly laid down my fork.

"Mrs—" I stopped, as something occurred to me. "You said your name wasn't actually 'Walsh.' What is it? What do we call you?"

She looked over at my farm manager. "What did you say the last housekeeper here was called?"

"Mrs Hudson? Oh, you needn't worry, she's moved to—"

"Yes, that'll do fine." She picked up the well-scraped bowl and forks and moved over to the sink.

"Sorry?" I asked.

"Hudson," she said over the sound of the water. "It's a good name, that'll be fine. You can call me 'Mrs Hudson.'"

The thought was ridiculous. Outrageous, even. But the woman was remarkably stubborn, and somehow, as the weeks went by, the name felt less uncomfortable on our tongues.

It appeared that we had a second Mrs Hudson in our lives.

One who would prove a very different and gloriously idiosyncratic kind of gem.

ENDNOTES

The Irish Crown Jewels disappeared from their locked safe in Dublin Castle in July 1907, under more or less the circumstances given in this story. To this day, they have never come to light. Nor has the report written by Scotland Yard Inspector John Kane. It is hardly surprising that numerous theories exist about the disappearance.

Two books that give alternate but detailed histories and proposed explanations are *The Stealing of the Irish Crown Jewels* by Myles Dungan and *Scandal and Betrayal* by John Cafferky and Kevin Hannafin.

There is little doubt that the failure to solve the theft was heavily influenced by the fear of revealing what were called "homosexual rings" in high levels of government. *The Gaelic American* article that drove a wedge between Jacob Russell and his father, published on July 4, 1908, began with the headline, ABOMINATIONS OF DUBLIN CASTLE EXPOSED. Many papers were sold on the promise of exposing how the "Gang of Aristocratic Degenerates Carried on Their Orgies in the Citadel of British

Rule" (overlooking the minor fact that the "orgies" overseen by Arthur Vicars were mostly sherry parties). One can only hope that the repercussions of being outed will continue to lose their power to destroy.

The author of historical novels is often confronted with the problem of real-life individuals who seem implausibly colourful. That is certainly the case with the characters in *Knave of Diamonds.*

The O'Mahony of Kerry—born Pierce Charles de Lacy Mahony—needed to have some of his more extraordinary exploits played down here, for fear of losing control of the story entirely. There is, one must note, no evidence whatsoever that The O'Mahony—horticulturalist, Nationalist, philanthropist to Bulgarian orphans, and proud owner of Granua, the last of the truebred Irish wolfhounds—was ever in possession of the Jewels. Please don't go digging up the old trees on the grounds of his estate in Wicklow. All you'll find there are foundation stones and monkey puzzle trees.

His half-brother, Arthur Vicars, would have gone down in history as a pale academic, were it not for his lamentable choice in friends, who ruined him in the most spectacular possible way.

Francis Shackleton, the heroic explorer's brother, was never charged in the case of the Irish Crown Jewels theft, although from the beginning even his friend Vicars accused him of being the person behind it. Shackleton died of an illness in 1941, three years before Richard Gorges met his end in a London Underground accident.

Inspector Kane died in 1915, but in this story, I have chosen to extend his life by a decade so that he could meet with Mr Sherlock Holmes. It seemed the least one could do for a Scotland Yard man whose work was so cruelly suppressed.

The spelling of names changes over the years. The Dublin ferry/ mail-boat terminus, known in the nineteenth century as Kingstown, in 1921 reverted to its former name of Dún Laoghaire, now often spelled Dún Laoire, and is often anglicised to Dunleary or Dun Leary. The first name of The O'Mahony was spelled either Pierce or Peirce, while his son, Pierce Gun, took his middle name from his mother's maiden surname, Gunn.

THANKS PAGE

The meandering months, even years, of producing a book could not possibly be traversed alone.

My family provides encouragement, support, and the kind of endless and often invisible labor that makes living under a roof and eating regular meals possible.

My agents continue to insist I'm a genius as they're wrangling their way through contracts and negotiations: I would have gone under without Alec Shane of Writers House and Mary Alice Kier and Anna Cottle of Cinelit.

My publishing house just rocks: editor Hilary Teeman, Allison Schuster (I'm going to miss you, Allison!), Elsa Richardson-Bach, Kim Hovey, Melissa Folds, Emma Tomasch, Caroline Weishuhn, Rachel Kind, Carlos Beltran, Kelly Chian, Saige Francis, Meghan O'Leary, Ali Wagner, Caroline Cunningham, Pam Alders, and Pam Feinstein, and a thousand others put this book before your eyes.

Thanks as always to The Dude at Recorded Books, Brian Sweany, and—though we miss Jenny Sterlin every day—my new Russell, Amy Scanlon. To Sue Trowbridge, who saves me, week in and week out, from drowning in web and newsletter matters. And to Sarah King, for knocking my Irish speech into shape, and Matt Burrough, a Friend of Russell whose book *Locksport* I can recommend for anyone embarking on a hobby of safe-cracking.

And I give a free admission that I would not have got far were it not for the "fans"—educated and enthusiastic readers who know me (and my characters) better than I do. My beta readers, Alice, Merrily, Karen, John, Erin, and Sabrina, help keep me on the right track. People like Breanna Grigsby prove amazingly generous with their time and expertise, along with my right-hand partner in all things Russell, the hard-working and multi-talented Zoë Quinton. And in no way last, the ladies and gents of "The Beekeeper's Apprentices" on Facebook let me start each day with a smile and a virtual hug, with people like the real Sara Phillips embracing all the fun.

Finally, one of the joys of 2024 was getting to do so many events celebrating the 30th anniversary of the first Russell & Holmes adventure, *The Beekeeper's Apprentice.* As I write this, the year is drawing towards its close, after four daylong mini-conferences, a dozen library talks, loads of art and writing projects and contests and giveaways and virtual events of all kinds.

The Russell & Holmes community is just great, in all ways.

ABOUT THE AUTHOR

LAURIE R. KING is the award-winning, bestselling author of nineteen previous Mary Russell/Sherlock Holmes mysteries, a series featuring SFPD cold-case Inspector Raquel Laing, the contemporary Kate Martinelli series, the historical Stuyvesant & Grey stories, and five acclaimed standalone novels. She lives in Northern California, where she is at work on her next Raquel Laing story.

laurierking.com
Facebook.com/LaurieRKing
Instagram: @laurierking
Bluesky: @maryrussell.bsky.social

ABOUT THE TYPE

This book was set in Caslon, a typeface first designed in 1722 by William Caslon (1692–1766). Its widespread use by most English printers in the early eighteenth century soon supplanted the Dutch typefaces that had formerly prevailed. The roman is considered a "workhorse" typeface due to its pleasant, open appearance, while the italic is exceedingly decorative.